ESMEC
Eastern Shore of Maryland
Educational Consortium

IN APPRECIATION

This book is dedicated to
Dr. Memo Diriker
Executive Director, BEACON
Salisbury University

Commemorating his presentation at the annual Summer Conference of the
Eastern Shore of Maryland Educational Consortium on June 19, 2017.

The Inquisitor's Tale

Or, The Three Magical Children and Their Holy Dog

The Inquisitor's Tale

Or, The Three Magical Children
and Their Holy Dog

Adam Gidwitz

ILLUMINATED BY
Hatem Aly

DUTTON CHILDREN'S BOOKS

DUTTON CHILDREN'S BOOKS
PENGUIN YOUNG READERS GROUP

An imprint of Penguin Random House LLC
375 Hudson Street
New York, NY 10014

CIP is available

Printed in the United States of America

9780525426165

7 9 10 8

Edited by Julie Strauss-Gabel

Design by Kristin Smith
Text set in Elysium

To all those who labor in obscurity
to bring dark ages to light
—A.G.

To my parents, who unceasingly agreed
there is always enough room for doodles
—H.A.

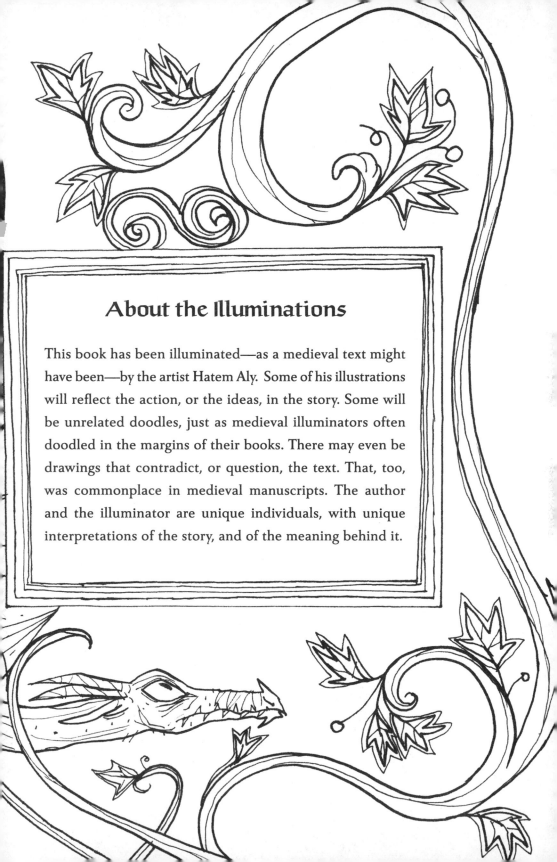

About the Illuminations

This book has been illuminated—as a medieval text might have been—by the artist Hatem Aly. Some of his illustrations will reflect the action, or the ideas, in the story. Some will be unrelated doodles, just as medieval illuminators often doodled in the margins of their books. There may even be drawings that contradict, or question, the text. That, too, was commonplace in medieval manuscripts. The author and the illuminator are unique individuals, with unique interpretations of the story, and of the meaning behind it.

Glory be to God for dappled things . . .
All things counter, original, spare, strange.
—G. M. Hopkins, "Pied Beauty"

You shall love your crooked neighbour
With your crooked heart.
—W. H. Auden, "As I Walked Out One Evening"

The king is ready for war.

Louis of France is not yet thirty, and already he is the greatest king in Europe. He loves his subjects. He loves God. And his armies have never been defeated.

This war, though, is different.

He is not fighting another army.

He is not fighting another king.

He is fighting three children.

And their dog.

A week ago, Louis hadn't heard of these three children. No one had. But now they are the most famous children in France. And the most wanted.

How did this happen?

That's what I'm wondering.

It's why I'm at the Holy Cross-Roads Inn, a day's walk

north of Paris. It's early March, in the year of our Lord 1242. Outside, the sky is dark and getting darker. The wind is throwing the branches of an oak against the walls of the inn. The shutters are closed tight, to keep the dark out.

It's the perfect night for a story.

The inn is packed. Butchers and brewers, peasants and priests, knights and nobodies. Everyone's here to see the king march by. Who knows? Maybe we'll see the children, too. And that dog of theirs. I would really like to see that dog.

I'm sitting on a wobbly stool at a rough, wooden table. It's sticky with spilled ale. We're packed in, shoulder to shoulder.

"So!" I say, rubbing my hands together. "Does anyone know anything about these kids? The wanted ones? With the dog?"

The table practically erupts.

They're all trying to tell me at once.

Beside me is a woman with thick arms, brown hair, and brown teeth. Her name is Marie, and she's a brewster, a beer maker. I ask her where she's from. She tells me she's from the town of Saint-Geneviève.

"That's where the girl is from!" I say. "Did you know her? Before she became famous?"

"Know her?" Marie says, indignant. "I practically raised her! Well, I didn't *raise* her, but I know her real well."

She smiles with her brown teeth at me. I smile back.

"Okay," I say. "Let's hear about her, then."

And so Marie tells us all about the most famous girl in France.

The one the king has declared war on.

CHAPTER 1

The Brewster's Tale

Jeanne's story starts when she was a baby.

Her mother and father were regular peasants. Spent all day in the fields, just like most of the folks in our town. But there was one thing that made them special. They had this dog. A beautiful dog. A white greyhound, with a copper blaze down its nose. They called her Gwenforte—which is a ridiculous name for a dog, if you ask me. But they never did ask me, so that's what they called her.

They loved Gwenforte. And they trusted her.

And so one day they went off to the fields to work, and they left baby Jeanne with Gwenforte.

"What?" I interrupt. "They used a *dog* as a babysitter?"

"Well . . . Yes. I suppose they did."

"Is that normal? For peasants? To use dogs as babysitters?"

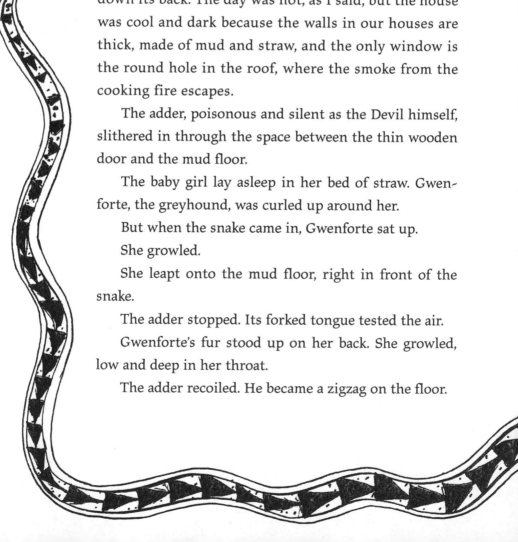

"No. I suppose it ain't. But she was a real good dog."

"Oh. That explains it."

You gotta understand: Gwenforte loved that little girl so much, and was so protective of her, that nobody worried about it.

But maybe we should have.

For as Jeanne's folks were out in the fields, working in the hot sun, a snake slithered into their house. It was an adder, with beady eyes and black triangles down its back. The day was hot, as I said, but the house was cool and dark because the walls in our houses are thick, made of mud and straw, and the only window is the round hole in the roof, where the smoke from the cooking fire escapes.

The adder, poisonous and silent as the Devil himself, slithered in through the space between the thin wooden door and the mud floor.

The baby girl lay asleep in her bed of straw. Gwenforte, the greyhound, was curled up around her.

But when the snake came in, Gwenforte sat up.

She growled.

She leapt onto the mud floor, right in front of the snake.

The adder stopped. Its forked tongue tested the air.

Gwenforte's fur stood up on her back. She growled, low and deep in her throat.

The adder recoiled. He became a zigzag on the floor.

Gwenforte growled again.

The adder struck.

Adders, as you may know, are very fast.

But so are greyhounds.

Gwenforte shimmied out of the way just in time and snapped her jaws shut on the back of the adder's neck. Then she began to shake the snake. She danced around the one-room house, shaking and shaking that snake, until the hay of the beds was scattered and the stone circle of the fire was ruined and the adder's back was broken. Finally she tossed its carcass into a corner.

Jeanne's parents were coming home from the fields just then. They were sweaty and tired. They had been up since long before sunrise. Their eyelids were heavy, and their arms and backs ached.

They pushed open the door of their little house. As the yellow light of summer streamed into the darkness, they saw the straw of the beds scattered all over the floor. They saw the fire circle, ruined. They saw Gwenforte, standing in the center of the dark room, panting, her tail wagging, her head high with pride—completely covered in blood.

What they did not see was their baby girl.

Well, they got panicked. They figured the worst. So they took that dog outside. And they killed her.

———

"Wait!" I cry. "But the dog—the dog isn't dead! It's alive!"

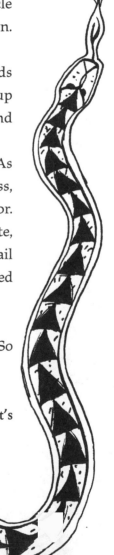

"It *was* dead," says Marie. "Now it's alive."

I open my mouth and no sound comes out.

———————

They come back into that house and try to put their lives back together. They were crying, a-course, because they loved that dog, and they loved their little girl even more. But we peasants know that life ain't gonna stop for our tears. So they clean up. They put the embers back in the fire pit, they pick up the straw from the beds. And that's when they see her. Baby Jeanne. Lying asleep in the hay. And in a corner, the dead snake.

Well, they picked up their daughter and held her tight and cried for joy. And after a little bit of that, they looked at each other, mother and father, and realized the horrible mistake they had made.

So they took the body of Gwenforte, and they buried her out in a beautiful grove in the forest, a short walk from the village. They dug up purple crocuses and planted them all around her grave. As the years went by, we started to venerate that dog proper, like the saint she is. Every time a new baby was born, they'd always go out to the Holy Grove, and pray to Saint Gwenforte, the Holy Greyhound, to keep that baby safe.

Well, years passed, and baby Jeanne grew and grew. She was a happy little thing. She liked to run down the long dirt road of the village, stopping into the dark doorways, waving to the people who lived inside each house. She came

and saw me and helped me stir the hops in my old oak barrel. She visited Peter the priest, who lived with his wife, Ygraine—even though he's not supposed to have a wife, on account of him being a priest. She would stop by and see Marc son of Marc, who had a little boy named Marc, too. She didn't visit with Charles the bailiff, though—who's my brother-in-law—because in addition to being our officer of the peace, he's also about as kind as an old stick.

But of all the peasants in our town—and there were more than that, but I don't want to bore you with long lists of people who don't come into the story—Jeanne's favorite was Old Theresa.

Old Theresa was a strange one. She collected frogs from the streams in the forest and put their blood in jars, to give to people when they were sick. She stared at the stars at night and told us our futures by how they moved. She was, I think it's fair to say, a witch. But she was a nice old witch, and she was always kind to little Jeanne.

And then, one day, it turned out little Jeanne was just as strange as Theresa.

I was there the first time it happened. She couldn't have been more than three years old. She was chasing Marc son-of-Marc son-of-Marc around my yard—when she stopped cold. She pulled up straight, like a stack of stones, and her eyes rolled back in her head. Then she went toppling to the ground, like somebody tipped that stack of stones over. She lay on the ground, and I saw her pudgy little arms and legs shaking, and her teeth grinding

in her head. Scared the life out of me, it did. I ran screaming to Old Theresa, because she's the only one not out in
the fields. So we huddled over little Jeanne.

And then, the fit stopped. Jeanne's breathing was
ragged, but she weren't shaking no more. Theresa bent
over and roused the little girl. Cupped her wrinkled
hand behind Jeanne's head. Jeanne opened her eyes. Old
Theresa asked her what happened, how she was feeling,
that sort of thing. I'm leaning over them, wondering if
Jeanne's gonna be all right. And then Theresa asks, "Did
you see something, little one?" I don't know what she
means.

But finally Jeanne's face clears up, and she answers, "I
saw the rain."

And then, at that very moment, there's a clap of
thunder overhead and the sky opens up and the rain
starts to fall.

I swear it on my very life.

I crossed myself about a hundred times, and was
about to go tell the world the miracle I just witnessed,
when Theresa grabbed my wrist.

She had milky blue eyes, Theresa did. She held my
wrist tight. And she said, "Don't you tell no one about
what just happened." The rain was running down the
wrinkles in her face like they was streambeds. "Don't
you tell a soul. Not even her parents. Let me deal with it.
Swear to me."

Well, that's a hard thing to ask—see a little girl per-

form a miracle and not tell her parents or no one about it. But when Old Theresa grabs your wrist and stares at you with those pale blue eyes . . . Well, I swore.

After that, Jeanne spent a lot of time with Theresa. She had more fits, but she never did see the future again. Or if she did, she didn't tell no one what she saw.

Until one day, a few years later. I was with her and Theresa when Jeanne had another one of her fits—falling down, shaking, eyes rolling back in her head—and when she woke up, she said there was a giant coming. Theresa said that was nonsense and to hush. There were no giants in this part of France. But she said it again and again. I couldn't figure out why she was saying all this in front of me. Hadn't Theresa told her to keep her mouth shut?

But then Jeanne said that the giant was coming to take away Old Theresa.

That scared us. I admit it. Theresa got real quiet when she heard that.

The next day, sure enough, the giant came. I don't know if he were *really* a giant or just the biggest man I'd ever seen. But Marc son-of-Marc father-of-Marc, who's the tallest man in our town, only came up to the middle of his chest. The giant had wild red hair sticking up from his pate and wild red whiskers sticking out from his jowls. And he wore black robes—the black robes of a monk.

He called himself Michelangelo. Michelangelo di Bologna.

Little Jeanne had been working with her parents in the fields when word spread that the giant was come. She came to the edge of the fields. She saw the giant striding toward the village, his black robes billowing behind him.

Walking toward the giant, through the village, was my idiot brother-in-law, Charles the bailiff. He had Theresa by the arm, and he was bellowing some nonsense about new laws about rooting out heresy and pagan sorcery and some other fancy phrases he had just learned that week, I reckoned. He bowed deeply to the giant and then shoved Theresa at him, like she were a leper. The giant grabbed her thin wrist and began dragging Old Theresa out of town.

Jeanne ran down from the edge of the fields. "Charles!" she shouted. "What's happening? What's he doing with Theresa?"

Charles spoke as if Jeanne were a small child. "I don't know. But I imagine Michelangelo di Bologna is going to take her back to the holy Monastery Saint-Denis and burn her at the stake for pagan magic—for witchcraft. Burn her alive. Which is good and right and as it should be, my little pear pie."

Little Jeanne cast a look of hatred so pure and deep at Charles that I don't think he's forgotten it to this day. I know I haven't. Then she went sprinting out onto the road after the giant and Theresa, screaming and shouting, telling that giant to give Theresa back. You've never seen a girl so fierce and ferocious. "Give her back!" she cried. "Give her back!"

Old Theresa turned around. Her wrinkled face contorted with fear when she saw what little Jeanne was doing. "Jeanne!" she hissed. "Go! Quiet! Go back!"

But Jeanne would not quiet. "You stupid giant!" she screamed. She came up right behind them. "Stop it! Stop it you … you red … fat … wicked … giant!"

Slowly, the monk turned around.

His shadow engulfed the little girl.

He gazed down at her, his pale red eyes vaguely curious.

Jeanne looked right back up at him, like David facing Goliath. Except this Goliath looked like he was on fire.

And then the monk did something very frightening indeed.

He laughed.

He laughed at little Jeanne.

Then he dragged Old Theresa away.

And we never saw her again.

Jeanne ran home, her tears flying behind her. She threw open the thin wooden door of her house, collapsed on her bed, and cried.

Her mother came in just after her. Her footsteps were soft and reassuring on the dirt floor. She lowered herself onto the hay beside Jeanne and began to stroke her hair. "What's wrong, my girl?" she asked. "Are you scared for

Theresa?" She ran her fingers through Jeanne's tangled locks.

Jeanne turned over and looked through tears up at her mother. Her mother had a skin-colored mole just to the left of her mouth and mousy, messy hair like her daughter's. After a moment, Jeanne said, "I don't want to be burned alive."

Her mother's face changed. "Why would you be burned alive, Jeanne?"

Jeanne stared up at her mother. Her vision had come true. Wasn't that witchcraft?

Her mother's face came into focus. It wasn't comforting anymore. It looked ... angry. "Why would you be burned, Jeanne? Tell me!"

Jeanne hesitated. "I don't know," she mumbled. And she buried her face in the hay again.

"Why, Jeanne? Jeanne, answer me!"

But Jeanne was too afraid to speak.

From that day on, Jeanne was different. She still had her fits, a-course, but she never opened her mouth about what she saw. Not once. More than that, she weren't the happy little girl anymore. No more poking her head in our huts or chasing Marc son-of-Marc son-of-Marc around. She got seriouser. More watchful. Almost like she were scared. Not of other people, though.

Like she were scared of herself.

And then, about a week ago, some men came to our village, and they took Jeanne away.

———————

"And that's the end of my story."

I'm in the midst of taking a quaff of my ale and I nearly spit it all over the table.

"What?! That's it? They took her away? Why?" I sputter. "Who were they? And what about the *dog*? How did it come back to life?!"

"I can tell you."

This isn't Marie's voice. It's a nun at the next table. She's been listening to the story, obviously, and now she's leaning back on her little stool. "I know about Gwenforte and about the men who took little Jeanne." She's a tiny old woman, with silvery hair and bright blue eyes. And her accent is strange. It's as proper as any I've ever heard. But it's a little ... off. I can't quite say why.

"How would you know about Gwenforte and Jeanne?" Marie says. "You ain't never even been in our village!"

"But I do know," answers the nun.

"Then please," I say, "tell us."

CHAPTER 2

The Nun's Tale

Eight days ago, Jeanne lay in her bed of straw, staring through the smoke hole in her thatched roof. Her eyes followed the shifting stars as they twinkled in the early morning sky. She thought of her tasks for the next day—first collecting the eggs from the chickens, then walking out to the wide, cold fields to clear stones so her father could begin to break the land ahead of the planting. She wondered—

"Hey now!" Marie barks. "You don't know what she was thinking and wondering! You're just making that up!"

But the nun replies, "Maybe I'm making it up. Or perhaps I have my ways."

And she gives us a smile that makes the hair on my neck stand up.

"Shall I continue?"

I don't say a word. I think I'm frightened of her.

Jeanne wondered whether she'd be clearing her family's fields or the lord's—when her body went stiff, her muscles began to twitch and spasm, her teeth ground in her head, and her eyes saw things beyond the veil of this life. She saw:

The Holy Grove, where Gwenforte was buried.

Men, with axes and torches, coming to burn the grove to the ground.

And a white greyhound, standing on Gwenforte's grave.

When the fit was over, Jeanne lay in the dark. She was breathing hard.

Her fits always scared her. But this fit scared her more.

She lay in the darkness, waiting for the strength to return to her limbs. At last, when she felt she could move, she threw her woolen blanket to the floor, climbed from her straw bed, tiptoed through the single dark room where she, her parents, and the cow slept, and slipped out the door.

"You sleep with your cows?" I say to Marie.

"Only in winter," she replies.

"Oh," I say. "Obviously."

Jeanne walked out into the starry night, down the road through her village, and then into the forest that lay beyond. She found the path to the Holy Grove, for the moon was rising and it glowed a ghostly white.

She hurried down the path. The branches scratched her face. She came to a stream and took it in one leap. And then she was in the grove. The moonlight filtered through the trees.

Standing in the center of the clearing was a figure as white and shining as a ghost.

But it was not a ghost.

It was a dog.

A white greyhound, with a copper blaze on her forehead.

Jeanne could scarcely breathe.

She took a step into the clearing.

She whispered, "Gwenforte?"

The dog came closer.

"*Saint* Gwenforte?"

The dog sat down before her. Jeanne ran her hand over the dog's white coat.

She didn't remember the white greyhound that her parents had killed. But she had heard countless stories about her. She and her family often came to this very spot to send prayers of thanks for her life to the holy grey- hound.

Could *this* be Gwenforte?

The dog's big black eyes gazed up at Jeanne, as if awaiting a decision.

Just then, there came the sounds of branches breaking and voices in the distance. Jeanne peered into the trees.

Men.

With torches.

And axes.

Marching through the forest like an advancing army.

The first man Jeanne saw was thin, with long, dirty yellow hair, a patchy yellow beard, and a face like a weasel. Behind him trudged a short, bald man. Others were scattered through the trees.

The first man emerged into the clearing. "All right, you lady's maids! Hurry up and burn—"

He stopped. He had noticed Jeanne and Gwenforte, kneeling together in the center of the grove.

His men emerged from the wood behind him. They were knights. Jeanne could see that now. Swords in scabbards hung from their belts. Their tunics were leather. But everything about them was tattered and crusted in dust. And they had no horses. Perhaps they had left them somewhere. Jeanne hoped so. For a knight without a horse was a pathetic sight indeed. And a pathetic knight is a dangerous knight

The bald, squat one was fighting through a tangle of brambles. "Sir Fabian, do you want—"

"Will you shut up and use your piggy eyes?"

The bald one stopped struggling with the brambles. "*Jesus's boots . . .*," he swore.

A tall knight exclaimed, "Hey! It's a doggy!"

"I thought the dog was supposed to be dead," said the bald knight.

"That's what I was told," answered Sir Fabian.

"So what's it doing alive?"

Sir Fabian's thin hand drifted to the pommel of his sword. "I don't know," Fabian said. "But we can *make* it dead." He took a step toward Jeanne and pulled the sword from its leather sheath. Its long blade carved a semicircle in the air.

"Good doggy," he said. "Good peasant." He used the same voice for them both.

He stepped forward.

"Stay, doggy . . . stay, peasant . . ."

He stepped again.

Run, Jeanne thought. But her legs seemed to have grown roots into the forest floor.

The knight stepped forward once more.

Jeanne could not move.

He stepped forward one last time.

He raised his sword.

"NOW!" Jeanne screamed.

The dog ran.

I don't know if you've ever seen a greyhound run. If you have, you know that it is a mystical experience. They are so swift, so exactly proportioned and balanced. It is one of the few perfect things in this world.

Her legs extended, recoiled, extended again as she crossed the small green clearing. Then she disappeared into the forest.

For an instant Jeanne stood, mesmerized, and stared.

Then she took off in the opposite direction.

"Who should we go after?" asked the bald knight.

"For the love of God, both of them!" Fabian shouted. "Go!"

All of the knights started after the greyhound.

"Some of you go after the girl!" Sir Fabian cried.

And so the knights, with torches raised and swords drawn, charged into the wood after Jeanne and her dog, Gwenforte.

Not long after, Jeanne was crouching in the underbrush, at the edge of the little yard behind her house. The family hens were attacking the earth, searching for worms and insects, clucking and muttering to one another like proud, fat little abbesses.

Gwenforte nuzzled Jeanne's neck. They had found each other in the wood, and she had been content to walk by Jeanne's side all the way back to her village. As if she had known Jeanne for years. As if the village were her home.

Jeanne had no idea what to make of it.

Now they crouched together at the edge of her parents' yard. Jeanne suppressed a smile. What would her parents think?

Marc's old rooster cried his fifth cry of the night, and the village started to wake. Doors began to open down the road. Jeanne's neighbors were spilling into the sunlight, adjusting their brown woolen tunics, stretching, scratching their oily heads.

Jeanne heard the door of her own house open. She grabbed Gwenforte and whispered in her ear, "Lie down, and don't move." The greyhound lay down in the under-brush.

Jeanne stepped out into the yard just as her father appeared around the corner of the house, yawning and wiping his face, his hairy belly peeking out from under his shirt. He saw his daughter, exclaimed, "Jeanne!" and opened his arms. She ran to him and buried herself in his warmth and the tangy smell of his breath. He rubbed her back. "Cold?" he asked. "Hélène slept with us again last night."

"She always sleeps with you," Jeanne replied, pulling away and looking up at her father's scratchy chin.

He grinned. "It's because she likes me best."

Hélène was the cow.

Jeanne's mother's voice came from the front of the house. "Well? Is it back there?"

"Oh!" her father exclaimed. "My hoe! Today's my day on the *demesne*. Can't find my hoe."

This was not surprising. Jeanne's father could rarely find anything. The family owned no more than ten objects—two pots, three bowls, a hoe, a cow, some chickens—and a good five of them were regularly lost, thanks to her father.

Jeanne's mother appeared around the corner of the house. Jeanne stole a glance back at the greyhound. The dog lay hidden in the deep shade of the new spring leaves.

Jeanne's mother's green eyes were narrow, and her brown hair was all a-tangle. Her hands were planted on her hips, and her elbows stuck out sharply. "Well?"

Jeanne ran to her mother and hugged her, too. She smelled different from Jeanne's dad. Softer. Not so rough. Her mother kissed Jeanne's head. "You were up early. Where did you go off to?"

Jeanne looked from her mother to her father and then off to the woods. She couldn't help grinning. What would they think? Would they believe it was Gwenforte?

But before she had gone three steps, someone called her back. "Jeanne! Hey, Jeanne!" She turned. It was Marc son-of-Marc son-of-Marc, standing at the edge of their yard.

"Someone's looking for ya," he said.

"Who?" Jeanne asked.

"Men. With swords."

Jeanne's parents looked at her sharply. Without taking her eyes from her daughter, Jeanne's mother said to Marc, "Do the men know where she is?"

"I think so. Bailiff Charles is with them."

Jeanne's father swore: "God's hat!"

"Who are they?" her mother demanded. Marc shrugged. Her green gaze turned on her daughter.

"I saw them in the forest. I was at the Holy Grove. They were there with axes." Jeanne hesitated, unsure how much more to say. So she skipped to the end: "They chased me!"

Jeanne's mother's gaze lingered on her daughter

another moment, like an innkeeper waiting for the last drop of ale from the barrel tap. But Jeanne said no more.

So Jeanne's mother said, "Marc, run back to your father. Do not go to Bailiff Charles or the men. They are not our friends." Marc turned and ran.

"Into the woods with you," Jeanne's mother hissed. "Stay nearby, but hidden."

Jeanne's father rubbed her head and winked at her. Then Jeanne returned to the forest and the greyhound— no time to show the dog to her parents now—and knelt down in the thick foliage, pushing ragwort away from her bare arms.

Then, around the corner of the house, came Bailiff Charles, leading five dirty, angry men. Jeanne's stomach turned over hard, and sweat began to bead up on her lip.

The bald knight bellowed, "Peasants!" And now Jeanne could see the rest of the retinue. Following the bald knight was a knight with blond curly hair and a lazy eye. Beside him was a chubbier knight, with similar golden curls. Behind them stood two large, strong, stupid-looking men—one with a black unibrow running over his dull eyes, the other with a face like an anvil. Jeanne's neighbors had begun to gather around the edge of the yard or loiter in the road nearby.

"Peasants!" the bald knight repeated. "Have you a daughter?"

Jeanne's father hesitated. Then, without any warning, he spat—right on the bald knight's leather boots.

The world stood still. The peasants stared. Bailiff Charles gasped. The bald knight's eyebrows crawled up onto his shiny head.

He pulled his hand back to strike Jeanne's father.

But before he could make contact, Jeanne's mother pushed her husband backward. She began shouting.

At her husband.

"Oh, you wicked man!" she howled, in a voice just a little shriller than normal. "How dare you affront his lordship?! His worshipful lordship?!"

The knights looked surprised. She spun on them. "Oh, we do have a daughter, and a wicked one she is! Wicked like her father! She ran away this morning, the wicked devil!"

Jeanne stared, perplexed, from the cool green brush.

The bald knight squinted at the peasant woman. The tall one with the curly hair leaned forward and whispered, very loudly, *"Ask her if she knows where the girl's got to."*

The bald knight appraised Jeanne's mother and then nodded. "Where's your daughter got to?"

"Oh, she's here!" Jeanne's mother shrieked. "She came back home after seeing you in the wood!"

Jeanne nearly fell over.

Jeanne's father nearly fell over, too. "Yvette, be quiet!" he barked.

"Oh, stow it! These men are knights and lords! We can't lie to the gentle! We, but lowly peasants!"

The knights looked gratified. "She's right, you know,"

the bald one nodded. "Best not lie to the gentry. We can tell, can't we?"

"Oh, you can, you can! I always say so! No use lying to the gentle!"

"So?" the bald knight asked. "Where is she?"

Jeanne, her mouth hanging open in horror, watched her mother lean in and whisper into the knight's ear. She could not believe what she was seeing.

She made ready to run.

Jeanne's mother whispered so loudly everyone could hear it: *"She likes to hide in the dung heap!"*

"The dung heap?"

"Indeed!"

The bald knight looked at the other knights. The one with the lazy eye shrugged. "Peasants do like filth, don't they?"

The bald one scratched his neck. "I suppose they do."

"Oh, we do! We love it!" Jeanne's mother agreed. Her husband, and all the other villagers, watched her uncertainly. Jeanne's mother appealed to her neighbors. "The dung heap is where our little Jeanne is *always* hiding. Isn't that so?"

A few of them slowly nodded. Marc son-of-Marc son-of-Marc angled his head in confusion.

"All right," said the bald knight. "Where's the dung heap?"

"Oh, this way, sir! This way!" Jeanne's mother led them around the house and to the main road. She walked east, to where the refuse sat by the river. The knights followed her, and the peasants followed them. Some villagers, already out in the fields, stopped their hoeing and gazed at the strange procession as it passed.

Jeanne quietly rose to her feet, collected the grey-hound from where she lay, and led the dog gingerly along the shaded edge of the wood, keeping the knights in view.

After a few minutes' walk, the group arrived at the small river and, beside it, a hill—brown, fly infested, half solid and half liquid—reeking with the fetid smell of feces.

The bald knight approached it, covering his face with a thick, hairy hand. "Well?" he demanded. "Where is she?"

Jeanne's mother looked at him, so earnest and help-ful. "Why, she's inside it! That's where she's hiding! Right in the middle!" She appealed to her neighbors: "She's always just taking that dung and piling it up on top of her, isn't she?"

The other peasants hesitated—and then began nod-ding vigorously.

The knight with the lazy eye looked like he was going to be sick.

"So how do you get her out?" the bald knight wanted to know.

"Just stick your arms in there and feel around till you get her!"

The knights' eyes went wide.

"I'd help you," Jeanne's mother added. "But she'd just wriggle away from me. Knows my tricks too well, she does." Then Jeanne's mother added in a loud whisper,

"And don't bother with the other peasants. They'll just help the little devil escape. I've seen it before. You can't trust a peasant. As dishonest as they are stupid. Right?"

The bald knight nodded slowly, still eyeing the dung heap. At last, he said, "Okay, boys! Dig in!"

The knights stayed exactly where they were.

The bald one frowned at them. The chubby one raised his hands as if to say, *You're on your own, my friend.*

So the bald knight said, "Georges! Robert! Come on!"

The two large, particularly stupid-looking knights came forward. "Do Sir Fabian proud!" the bald one barked.

The knight with the heavy unibrow stuck out his chin and sighed. The one with the face like an anvil shrugged his shoulders and, without even rolling up his sleeves, shoved his arms into the dung with a squelch. A swarm of flies exploded from the heap's surface.

The other one pushed his woolen sleeves up above his elbows and plunged his hands in, too.

Jeanne, huddled in the nearest stretch of wood, watched in disbelief. She had to bury her face in her sleeve to prevent herself from laughing out loud. Beside her, Gwenforte yapped. Jeanne hushed her. The greyhound yapped again.

"*Shh!*" Jeanne giggled. "Don't laugh at them. It isn't nice."

But the dog turned toward the forest behind them and began to growl.

Jeanne's neighbors were hiding their smiles in their shirts now, trying not to give the game away.

"Are you sure this is necessary?" the chubby knight was asking, watching his comrades with disgust.

"Her own *mother* says she's in there," the bald knight snapped. "Peasants aren't smart enough to lie to the gentry. You heard her yourself." Suddenly, he had a thought. He turned to Jeanne's mother. "This is just animal refuse, right? You peasants do your own business somewhere else?"

Jeanne's mother smiled sweetly. "Oh no, sir. We do our squatting right here."

The bald knight glanced skyward. The lazy-eyed knight gagged. The two big blokes kept digging away. Their upper bodies were almost entirely submerged in feces. It looked like they were swimming.

Beside Jeanne, Gwenforte bristled, growling, staring into the forest. She barked. "Shh!" Jeanne hissed. "They'll hear you!" She wrapped her arms around Gwenforte and held her tightly.

And then, someone wrapped his arms around Jeanne.

She was lifted from her feet. Jeanne tried to scream, but a strong, calloused hand was clamped over her mouth.

Gwenforte spun and barked, and Jeanne kicked wildly. But the man's wiry arms were wrapped around her, pinning her own to her sides. An oily beard scratched her cheeks.

"*Got you, little girl,*" whispered Sir Fabian.

Gwenforte snapped at the knight's legs, but he kicked her in the face. The greyhound fell back, snarling. Fabian hoisted Jeanne under one arm, still holding her tightly.

With his free hand, he drew his sword and swung it at the dog. Gwenforte tried to bite him again, but the knight's long blade cut through air.

"Run, Gwenforte!" Jeanne cried. "Run!"

The greyhound stood, limbs aquiver, staring at little Jeanne. The sword flashed through the air again—and the dog had disappeared. Just a flash of fur, pelting through the forest and, in an instant, out of sight.

The knight carried Jeanne across a peasant's garden plot, scattering chickens as he went. His oily beard smelled. Jeanne tried to kick him, but her heels caught only air.

But as Fabian and Jeanne approached the main road, the knight slowed. Then stopped.

He gazed at his men, churning the village dung heap with their arms.

"Why," said Sir Fabian, "are my men swimming in crap?"

"Hey!" Marc son-of-Marc father-of-Marc cried. "Look!" Villagers turned from the spectacle of the dung heap to see little Jeanne, carried like a willful calf in the arms of the weasel-faced knight.

"Sir Fabian!" cried the bald one.

When her parents saw Jeanne, their faces went white as wool. Her mother's stupid-peasant act fell away. She ran for Jeanne, and Jeanne's father followed. The villagers went after, surging toward the little girl and her captor.

Behind them, the two big knights raised their heads from their fetid, stinking task. "Where's everyone going?" one asked. The other shrugged and got back to digging.

Sir Fabian held Jeanne tightly. His knights pushed past the villagers. "Stay back!" they cried. "Avaunt!" They interposed themselves between the peasants and their leader. Jeanne gave the bald one a swift kick from behind. He turned and growled at her.

"You put her down!" Jeanne's mother screamed. "You have no right! We are free peasants! I'll find a magistrate! You've no right!"

But Sir Fabian barked back, "I have every right! We are here on the orders of Saint-Denis."

The name momentarily halted the villagers' onslaught. Then Jeanne's mother cried, "You have orders to kidnap little girls?"

"We have orders to stamp out the pagan worship of a dog!"

"Who? What dog do we worship?" Jeanne's father objected.

"We would never!" someone shouted.

"But it's true!" Bailiff Charles piped up from the back. "You do worship a dog!"

"Gwenforte?" Marc son-of-Marc father-of-Marc called out. "We don't worship her! We venerate her proper! As the saint she is!"

And Marie the brewster said, "So do you, Charles! You bald-faced suck-up!"

Marie grinned. "So I did."

But Sir Fabian took on a superior air, as he squeezed
Jeanne with his thin, strong arms. "A dog can't be a
saint. That's blasphemy. We found this girl cavorting
with and protecting that dog. That's why we've the
right to take her. And anyone who tries to stop us will
be put to the sword!" The bald knight, following his
leader's cue, drew his and brandished it in the faces of
the villagers.

But the peasants had fallen silent.

Jeanne's mother said, "What dog?"

"Gwenforte, the greyhound," Fabian snapped. "You
peasants really *are* slow."

Bailiff Charles chewed on his mustache and stared at
the knight.

"Gwenforte is dead," Jeanne's father said. "She has
been for ten long years."

Sir Fabian heaved Jeanne higher to get a better grip
on her. "Then what was this little brat doing with a greyhound in your grove? A greyhound with a white coat and
a copper blaze on its nose? Is that not your holy dog?"

Jeanne's parents stood stock-still. Other villagers
crossed themselves. Some stepped back. They were staring at little Jeanne.

"What have you been doing, my girl?" Jeanne's father
whispered.

"I saw her during one of my fits!" Jeanne shouted, trying to tear herself from the knight's hard hands. She didn't mean to let the truth come pouring out of her. But, after all these years, it did. She was young, you see. And she was scared. "I saw Gwenforte during my fit, so I went to the grove. She was there! That's all! That's all I did!"

"Gwenforte was *there*?" her mother murmured.

Jeanne nodded, tears beginning to cloud her vision.

The villagers were now looking away from the little girl and her family. "Jeanne," her father said. "What have you done?"

"Mama! Papa!" Jeanne's voice was rising to a panicked pitch. "What did I do wrong?" But her parents did not answer. Her father bowed his head. Her mother looked away, tears in her eyes. "Mama!" Jeanne screamed.

"Practicing magic is a sin against God and a violation of the law," Sir Fabian announced. "We will take her to Saint-Denis to be tried."

"Mama!"

"And where she goes, maybe that damned dog will follow."

"Mama! Papa!" Jeanne's throat was straining, and tears were streaming down her face.

But her parents just stood there, staring. They were afraid.

"Mama! Papa!"

Afraid of their daughter.

Everyone at the table is leaning in, our lips open, our eyes wide.

"And then . . . ?" I ask.

The nun sits back on her rough stool. "They took her away! Just as Marie said. Isn't that true, Marie?"

The brewster nods thoughtfully. She's gazing at the little nun. "That's just how it happened," she murmurs. "Though I can't fathom how you know all that."

Instead of answering, the little nun picks up her mug and drains a long draft. When she puts it down, she has a foam mustache over her little mouth. "Maybe someone else could tell something. Perhaps about one of the boys?"

I study her impish smile and innocent eyes, and am about to press her for more information, when the innkeeper, who's been waddling around us, bringing fresh mugs to the nearby tables, says, "Brother Jerome, you said you knew the big boy, didn't you?"

We turn toward an old monk with a long white beard, sitting at the far end of the table. His thin hands are stained with ink.

The monk smiles and runs his hand over his whiskers. "Ah, I do, I do! I am the librarian at the monastery where the boy called William grew up. I know him rather well."

I can't believe my luck. As if all of these people had gathered together to make my job easy.

Which is great. I like easy. "Tell us about William," I say.

The monk inclines his white beard. "I shall—but I must warn you: This tale is darker and bloodier than the last. I wouldn't want to upset any of the present company." He gestures at the ladies.

I say, "Darker than a dog getting *killed*?"

"Indeed," says Jerome.

Marie tips her mug back, empties the last drops into her open mouth, and then slams it down, shaking everything on the table. "The bloodier the better!" she announces. And everyone laughs.

Old Jerome grins. "If you insist . . ."

HAPTER 3

The Librarian's Tale

I am the librarian at the Monastery Saint-Martin.

It is a simple monastery. A good place. Life there runs smoothly. At least, it did, until William arrived.

William was delivered to us as a baby. We get many infants that way. They are the sons of wealthy lords and ladies. Often they are younger sons, who will not inherit their father's lands. We teach them to read and write and love God, so they are ready for the universities at Paris or Bologna, and then for service in the courts of great men thereafter.

But a few of the children who will become our oblates—our young monks-in-training—are delivered to our doors in the dead of night. These are the sons of sin. And William was such a boy. His father is a great lord, fighting in Spain against the Muslim kings there. I believe William's mother must have come from Northern Africa, for her son looks like the people of that land—he has their hair, their coloring.

This makes him unique in our monastery. We have French and Italian monks, English and Flemish. But he is our first African.

But much more extraordinary than his color is his *size*. It is known that his father is a big man, and when William came to us he was already an unnaturally large baby. But the father cannot be as big as the son—for now that William is eleven years old, the tallest monk in the abbey barely reaches his collarbone.

He eats a great deal, of course. And he laughs a lot. And he talks. And talks. And talks. Which, you can imagine, is a *problem* at a monastery. We read, we pray, we do our tasks and our chores. That is all. We do not *make conversation*. But William is perpetually bursting with opinions, with questions, with ideas. To be blunt about it, he will not shut up.

And yet, I must admit, that I have never cared for an oblate more than I care for William.

He is as intelligent and inquisitive as any student I've ever known. He debates theology with me as if he were a master from Paris. He wants to read every page of every book in the library. And he makes me laugh.

Which is why I was heartbroken when I learned that William had been expelled from the monastery.

Things came to a head a week ago. The oblates had taken their places on the stone bench that runs along the walls of the chapter house. It was just after breakfast, and the frost was still visible on the grass at the center of the cloister.

Brother Bartholomew, the boys' teacher, shuffled in from the adjacent cloister and pulled back his hood, revealing his flabby face, tiny eyes, and permanent sneer. Heat rose from the thin hair atop his head. You should know that Brother Bartholomew hates children. He believes that they are closest to the state of original sin, and he tells them this. Constantly. He claims that the abbot assigned him his role because of his zeal for eradicating sinful thoughts from children's heads. I'm pretty sure that the abbot just doesn't like Bartholomew, and is torturing him intentionally.

"Today we shall discuss," Bartholomew began, his voice sharp and nasal, "the two kinds of people in the world."

William shifted on his stone bench. Already Bartholomew had uttered a falsehood. They would not "discuss" anything today. Bartholomew would harangue them until the bell tolled for sext, the midday prayers. William and the dozen other oblates would be expected to sit quietly and absorb the "wisdom" that Bartholomew bestowed upon them. He clenched his jaw and silently asked God for strength.

"The two kinds of people are these: those who are in league with the Devil, and those who stand on the side of God. There are no bystanders in this war, between evil and good, between God and the Devil. Do you understand? You are either on the side of the Devil or on the side of God!"

Brother Bartholomew shuffled toward a tiny Italian boy sitting at the far end of the stone bench. There is a small group of Italian oblates at our monastery. "You!" he shouted. Bartholomew always thinks the Italians understand him better when he shouts. "Are you on the side of God? Or the Devil? God? Or Devil? Understand?" He poked his finger into the boy's face. He also thinks it helps to poke his fingers into the Italians' faces and speak in broken sentences. "God? Or Devil?"

The boy stared up at Brother Bartholomew impassively. William always admired the Italian boys' way of looking up from under their eyebrows that was either totally respectful or utterly disrespectful, and you could never tell which. William told me once that he wanted to learn how to do it, but he never got a chance since he was too tall to look up at anyone.

Bartholomew strolled along the length of the bench. "The allies of the Devil are legion! Too many to number! There are murderers, of course! Criminals! There are liars! There are loafers and gluttons and tricksters! And peasants! All peasants are liars, loafers, or both!"

William nearly shouted when he heard this. Surely, *some* peasants were liars and loafers and allies of the Devil. But all? That was preposterous. Hadn't Pope Sylvester the Second started life as a peasant? For that matter, hadn't Jesus been born in a manger? The son of a carpenter? This was an excellent argument, and William decided that Brother Bartholomew really wouldn't mind hearing it. He opened his mouth to interrupt, but Bartholomew was already barreling past peasants.

"Jews, too, are in league with the Devil! For they deny the divinity of Christ!" Bartholomew's piggy eyes were flashing. "Jews are particularly dangerous, for while a peasant is made plain by his filthy clothes and the stench of farm animals, Jews can disguise themselves completely. Like the Devil himself! Beware the sneaky, evil, diabolical Jew!"

Now this was preposterous. Yes, Jews denied the divinity of Christ. But were they evil? All of them? Was Moses evil? Abraham? King David? And there were modern Jews who clearly were on the side of wisdom, instead of ignorance. William thought about the texts that he and I had read together—the great Rashi, who had shown our bishops the errors in our translations of the Hebrew Bible. And Rabbi Yehuda, who still writes to this day beautiful odes to God in His Glory. Not that I always agree with what he says about God . . . but in league with the Devil? William decided that it was time to interrupt and mention not just Jesus, but Rashi as well.

But it was too late, for Bartholomew had already moved on. "And women! The daughters of Eve, who tempted Adam to taste the forbidden fruit, and thus introduced evil into the world! The world was perfect before women came along and ruined it! Beware the daughters of Eve, for they indeed are in league with the Devil!"

Women? thought William, squirming so intensely he was in danger of falling off the bench and onto the floor. *All* women? Weren't we all born from women? Wasn't the great Hildegard of Bingen a woman? And Mary the Virgin? And Mary Magdalene? And more saints than William could count? Lucy and Elizabeth and Anne and Agatha and Abigail and—

Bartholomew was really getting worked up now. His face and neck were purple as a beet, and the spittle was flying all over the oblates as he spewed his sermon. "And of course, we should never forget *the Saracen!*"

He was looking directly at William.

William stopped squirming. All thought of women and Jews and peasants went straight out of his head.

Saracen is a word that William does not approve of. William likes precision. He likes clarity. He likes to understand things. The word *Saracen,* as you all know, means two completely different things. On the one hand, we use it to mean *Muslim,* a follower of Mohammed. On the other hand, we use it whenever we talk about someone who looks foreign. The Mongols are "Saracens," the pagan nomads of Arabia are "Saracens," the Muslims of Spain are "Saracens."

So is William a Saracen? He has devoted every waking moment to living a Christian life. And yet his brown skin and black hair have always set him apart.

"*Saracens,*" Brother Bartholomew said, dipping into the word like some savory sauce. "Saracens." He rolled it

around in his mouth. "If peasants are the Devil's slaves and if Jews are his emissaries and if women are his spies, Saracens are his foot soldiers. Are they not?"

William no longer controlled his throat or his tongue or any other organ used for speaking. Entirely against his will, he said, "Do you mean *Muslims*?"

Bartholomew grinned. He had provoked William. As he had intended all along, I imagine. "If you like. *Muslims* are Satan's foot soldiers, then." He beamed at William from his piggy little eyes.

"I do *not* like," William announced, and his voice bounced around the stone walls of the chapter house. "What of the great Muslim scholars, who saved Aristotle from oblivion?"

"What's Aristotle?" Bartholomew snapped.

William chose to ignore the staggering ignorance of the man who was supposed to be his teacher. "What about Algoritmi?" William went on. "Who introduced the idea of zero to the Western world?"

"Guess how much I care about that?" cried Bartholomew. "Zero! Ha!"

William's face was becoming hotter and hotter. "And last spring, when your urine was thick and dark as beef stew, how did Brother Jacques treat you? By consulting the work of Doctor Avicenna! You might be *dead* if not for that 'foot soldier of Satan'!"

Bartholomew, for once, was struck silent.

William's voice could now be heard throughout the

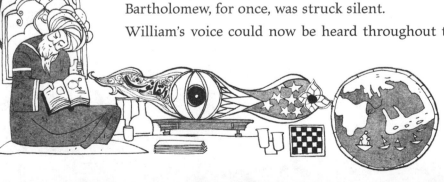

monastery: "Just as peasants can be popes and Jews can teach us the Bible and women can be disciples of Jesus, Muslims can *save your very life!*"

Bartholomew had, at last, recovered himself. His voice became quiet, and almost . . . sweet. "You want to defend the legions of Satan. I wonder why you would want to do such a thing?"

William held his breath.

"Why would you want to defend the allies of the Devil? You don't have to, you know. You might be a big brown bastard. But at least you're not a Saracen harlot, *like your mother.*"

William did not entirely understand what happened next. He saw white flecks of spittle on Bartholomew's red lips. He saw the sun on the frosted grass of the cloister. He heard distant monks, meditating in the covered walkway, muttering softly. He smelled his own sweat. He felt his hand come down, swiftly and with great force, on the stone bench.

There was a sharp cracking sound.

The bench shattered.

It was solid stone, carved into the wall. It was very sturdy and very expensive.

And it exploded when William hit it. Into a thousand pieces.

All the oblates went crashing to the floor.

Brother Bartholomew's mouth transformed from a smug smile to a great, wide O.

Jerome leans back on his stool and strokes his beard.

"The bench *exploded*?" I ask.

"I assure you, there is nothing left but shards and dust. The masons have no idea how to repair it. The whole wall may have to be rebuilt."

The innkeeper had taken a seat during Jerome's story, and now he says, "That Bartholomew is a pig. The abbot's going to let him keep teaching the children?"

"Funny you should ask," Jerome replies. "And funny you should make that comment about pigs. Our master of swine recently fell ill. So Bartholomew has been transferred. He now presides over the abbey sty. And, to be perfectly honest with you, I believe he prefers it."

When the laughter subsided, I said, "So William was expelled?"

"Indeed he was."

CHAPTER 4

The Second Part of the Librarian's Tale

William gazed through the small stone window down onto the cloister. Even in these early days of March, the grass was green. Three crows sat on the edge of the fountain, clacking at one another. Each looked just like the other, without freak or flaw. If God made them so uniform, why didn't He do the same for humans?

"William, are you listening?"

William's attention was jerked back to the abbot's gaunt face and long, ruddy nose. Our abbot's lips pouted, but in his sunken eyes, ringed with dark circles, I thought I detected pleasure. Or maybe it was relief.

"I'm afraid you can't stay here, William," the abbot said. "You don't fit. I promised your father I'd try, and try I have, but . . . I say, *look* at you! You eat three times as much as anyone else—we tried to feed you less when you were little, you know; you nearly died of starvation. You fight with your teacher Bartholomew constantly.

You squirm like a fox in a trap during services. And now you've shattered a very costly stone bench. Don't ask me *how* you shattered it ..."

I tried to suppress a chortle. I hadn't meant to laugh. It wasn't funny. It was just ... amazing.

The abbot shot me a dark look and went on. "No," he said with a sigh, "you don't fit here at all. So I am sending you to Saint-Denis. You'll have a donkey and some books that Abbot Hubert has requested. Hubert can figure out what to do with you. He's a good man. The best. As pious as any in France, save perhaps the king. Hubert will find the proper pasture for your tempestuous soul."

William blinked. Again. Once more. Saint-Denis? He was being sent to Saint-Denis? Saint-Denis was one of the greatest monasteries in the world! Second home of the kings of France! He'd thought he was going to be punished. This was hardly a punishment ...

The abbot gazed across his long red nose at William. "Try not to smirk like that, young brother. You'll make me change my mind."

"Yes, Father."

"Besides, you must do some penance. So you won't go straight to Saint-Denis. Instead, you'll take the long route. Through the forest of Malesherbes."

The legs of my chair slammed onto the stone floor of the library. "Henry, you aren't serious!"

"Indeed I am, Brother Jerome. I have often warned you that you coddle the boy."

"Malesherbes? They'll kill him! That's not penance! That's certain death!"

William sat up. His big feet spread wider on the floor. "Who'll kill me? I'd like to see them try!"

"Try they would, William," I scolded him, "and succeed, too. The Foul Fiends live in Malesherbes."

"Who?"

The abbot scoffed. "That's an old myth! Cold porridge left over from the Romans!"

"It certainly is not!" I exclaimed. "I have been to the forest of Malesherbes. I ventured in but a few leagues and feel very lucky to have escaped with my life. It is an entirely—"

William could not contain his curiosity. "What are the Foul Fiends, Brother Jerome?"

I must admit, despite myself, I smiled. Teaching William has been one of the great pleasures of my life. "The Foul Fiends, Brother William, are men and women—or they were, once. They refused to be governed by the laws of man or God. In the time of the Romans, a thousand years ago, they fled into the deep woods, to hide from God's sight. But no one can escape the sight of God. They have lived in wickedness for a hundred generations."

"What kind of wickedness?" William asked, leaning over the old wooden table.

"Watch it, Jerome," the abbot muttered.

"Every and any evil you can imagine. Theft, deceit, betrayal. And eventually, murder, too. A cabal of criminals, living without any laws or codes at all. Anything they felt like doing, anything against God, they did."

"With impunity," the abbot added.

"What's impunity?" William asked.

"You should know that, William," the abbot scolded. "It means 'without consequences.'"

"Oh, but there were consequences," said I. "Over the generations, these people changed. Their hearts became shriveled and black, like plums kept till Easter. Their skin became pale and their eyes pink from living in the darkest places. Just like you can breed dogs for friendship and faithfulness, these people bred for cruelty and viciousness and lack of human sympathy."

"They were evil," William said.

"Yes. So evil that from behind their heads there shines a black light. An inverted halo."

William gazed at me in the gray light of the little window. "Is that true?"

"I doubt it," said the abbot.

"I've seen them, Henry. It is true."

William sat back in his chair. It creaked so loudly the abbot flinched, expecting it to splinter under the boy's enormous weight. "I'm not afraid of them," William announced. "I'll cut their wicked heads from their wicked necks. Just give me a sword. Or an axe. Anything. I'm not afraid!"

I pulled at my beard, and the abbot said, "William, you have taken the vows. You wear the robe. You will soon be tonsured. You *may not* fight. Anyone. For any reason."

"If the Foul Fiends were to try to kill me, I couldn't fight back?" William asked, appalled.

"Even if they should threaten your very life, you could not fight back."

"And if they tried to take Abbot Hubert's books?"

"You may not fight."

"What if they wanted my robes? I would just have to take off my clothes for them?"

The abbot squinted. "I don't see why they would want your *robes*, William. But yes, even then, you could not fight back."

"Even if they wanted my underwear?"

"Why on *earth* would anyone want your underwear?" the abbot snapped.

But I laughed and wagged a finger at my abbot. "Actually, he has a point, there, Father. It is a sin to expose your nakedness to a stranger."

The abbot brooded on that for a moment, and then said, "Fine. If they try to take your underwear—though God knows why they would—you can fight back."

"So I'll need a sword!" William announced, like he'd just won a debate.

"Under no circumstances!" the abbot replied. "If you are forced to fight, you may use *nothing*. Nothing but flesh and bone."

"Fine," William said, grinning, tipping his stool back on two legs. "I'd like to see those Foul Fiends try me."

I leaned over the simple wooden table. The gray light

from the window cast spidery shadows across it. "No, William," I said. "You wouldn't."

The next day, we sent him on his way. I have not seen my young friend since.

———————

"But did he end up in that crazy forest?" Marie asks. "Did he see the Foul Fiends?"

Jerome shrugs. "I don't know. I'm not sure if we'll ever know."

For some reason—some reason that I cannot explain—my gaze slides to the little nun, whose face is buried in her mug at the end of the table. The innkeeper follows my gaze. So does Marie. Finally Jerome joins us. We're all staring at her.

After a moment, she looks up. "What?" she says. She's acting surprised. Definitely acting.

"Do you know, little Sister?" Jerome asks. "Do you know if William ventured into the Forest of Malesherbes? And if he did, do you know what happened there?"

"How should I know that?" she asks. She is suppressing a smile.

"I don't know, little Sister. But you seem to know more than you let on."

"Maybe I know," she says, after a space. She raises her cup. "And maybe my mug is empty."

The innkeeper pushes himself to his feet. "Ale for a tale. That's the fairest trade I know."

CHAPTER 5

The Second Part of the Nun's Tale

The night before William left, he lay in his narrow bed in the dormitory, staring into the darkness. The beds nearby were filled with boys snoring into the crooks of their arms. At the other end of the dormitory, the adults dreamt of rich food and friends from years gone by.

Once William was sure that his neighbors were asleep, he eased himself out of his wooden cot until he was kneeling on the cold stone floor. He reached through a hole in his mattress, into the hay. His hand closed around a belt.

William lifted his robes above his waist. He unbuckled the leather belt he used to keep up his underwear.

William slipped the belt that had been hidden in his mattress into the loops of his underwear. He hid his old leather belt in the mattress. He lay down again.

He smiled to himself in the darkness.

The next morning, William was given a donkey and two sacks of books for Abbot Hubert, of Saint-Denis. He began thumbing through a few of the titles: Isidore of Seville, an illuminated copy of *The Rule of Saint Benedict*, Saint Augustine's *Confessions*. Then, near the bottom of the first sack, William saw a strange book—it looked beat-up and flimsy, as if made not in a monastery but by some amateur hand. He began to reach for it, but the abbot, who was watching William carefully, stopped him. "Please don't dawdle, young William. You have a task ahead of you."

William replaced the books, said farewell to the abbot, and then to his dear Brother Jerome.

"Keep studying, William," Brother Jerome told him. "And be careful."

William replied, "I will."

"You will what?" said Brother Jerome.

William smiled. "I'll keep studying."

———————

Jerome bursts out laughing. "He did indeed say that! The scamp!" He shakes his white beard and sighs.

———————

The day was cold, the sky was as gray as wet wool, but William had never felt so free in his life. He could go *anywhere*. Do *anything*. Yes, he would go where the abbot told him to and do what he had been asked. But there was no one to watch him, no one to tell him he was doing it wrong. It was his responsibility entirely. It was the most incredible feeling in the world.

William passed peasants working the abbey's fields, and their little dark hovels, lining the road. He wondered what their lives were like. He wondered how many of them were liars and loafers, as Bartholomew said. Unexpectedly, a door to a hut opened, and a young woman emerged. *A daughter of Eve!* William thought. She was tall and her hair was thick and auburn and the very sight of her made William feel strange. Perhaps Bartholomew was right. Perhaps she did possess some Satanic power. He hurried on.

On to the forest of Malesherbes.

Nature has a way of warning you. *Don't come here, don't taste, don't touch.* Sometimes the warning is black-and-yellow stripes. Sometimes it's bared fangs. Sometimes, though, it is just a feeling. A feeling that says, "Go away. You are not wanted here."

The forest of Malesherbes is like that. Dark as twilight—even in the middle of the day. The trees brood over you, the streams don't babble—they growl, and each call of an animal seems like a dire warning of imminent danger.

You begin to notice the shadows. There are more than there should be. And they follow you.

Next, you see the eyes. Pink eyes, staring from the darkness. It is when you see the eyes that you want to

turn and flee. And indeed, most everyone does. But not
William. He pressed on.

Frogs croaked aggressively at the young oblate, each
croak like a curse. Large insects, like enormous walking
sticks, were frozen on the trees. More than once William
walked into a spider's web and frantically shook the tiny,
invisible spiders from his dark, curly hair.

As the forest's warning became louder, more plangent
and strident, William's buoyant mood shivered, quailed,
and fled like a routed army from the field. The walking-
stick bugs grew even larger—some of them four feet in
length. William put his arm around the donkey's neck.
Its neck quivered.

Suddenly, the donkey stopped walking.

William tried to drag the beast forward by its halter,
but it would not budge. He could have dragged it along
the path had he wanted to. He considered this. He put his
hands on his hips.

Then they fell to his sides.

There were pale figures ahead of him on the road.
Their shoulders were hunched. Their fingers curled like
claws. Darkness seemed to hover around their heads.

And then the shadows emerged from the trees.

A frigid sweat beaded up on William's forehead and
under his arms.

If Jerome had told the truth, and fiends had pink eyes
and pale skin and evil, wrinkled hearts, then these men
and women surrounding William now were, without any

question, fiends. They wore tattered rags. In their claw-like hands many of them gripped hatchets and maces with spiked heads. A few carried short bows, with quivers of arrows slung across their backs. And darkness hovered around their heads.

One of them, a stringy woman with a nose like a pig's, stepped forward. The other fiends seemed to shrink from her.

"I am the Wicked One," she announced. "And you will do what I say." Her voice sounded like breaking wood.

William did not move. He did not speak. He just stood there. The trees creaked, though there was no wind.

"Well?" he replied, after a moment. "What do you say?"

"We'll start with whatever's in those sacks," the Wicked One snarled, pointing a crooked finger at the sacks of books. "Give 'em over!"

William sighed grandly. "Oh, the books? Sure!" He laughed. "For a moment, I was worried you were going to ask for my robes!" He unfastened the two leather satchels from the donkey's back and tossed them into the dirt.

The Wicked One, as she had called herself, stared at William suspiciously. "Why would we want your robes?"

"No reason!" William replied quickly, and then he looked away into the trees.

The fiend grinned, showing off teeth as yellow and coarse as horns. "Well then, let's have your robes!" she rasped.

"Fine," William grumbled. "I guess you can have my

robes." He began to pull them up over his head. "As long
as you don't take my underwear."

The Wicked One laughed harshly. "Why would we
want your underw—" But then she stopped. For as William pulled up his robes past his midsection, she saw,
holding up his underwear, a belt inlaid with looping
whorls of gold.

"He has an underwear belt of GOLD?" I exclaim.

"Does he not?" the nun replies, looking to Jerome.

Jerome claps his hands. "Indeed he does! Indeed he
does. It's the only thing he has from his mother. Crafted by
the goldsmiths of Cordoba. It wasn't intended, of course,
as an underwear belt. And he was not allowed to wear it
at the monastery. He must have been thinking of that belt
all along . . ." Jerome smiles, shaking his head. "But what a
dangerous idea!"

"What idea?" I ask.

Instead of answering, Jerome turns back to the little nun.

When the Wicked One saw the belt inlaid with gold, she
cackled, "Oh ho! Now I see! Keeps his treasure in his underwear, does he? Well, give it over!"

"Ah," said William, sighing, "but I can't do that. To be
naked before strangers is a sin."

The Wicked One grinned. "Oh, you fools with your
morals and your sins. It doesn't much matter. We were going
to kill you anyway. We'll take the belt after you're dead."

"Oh," said William. "I hadn't thought of that. In that case, instead of my underwear, what if I give you this?"

William reached out and grabbed the heads of the two nearest fiends in his great palms. And he smashed their heads together with all his might. They exploded like melons. Deep red blood erupted from the collision, spattering William's bare skin.

For one instant, no one moved. The two fiends dropped, headless, to the earth.

William was as surprised at the explosion as the rest of the fiends. But he collected himself enough to say, "Anyone else want something from me?"

The Wicked One's pink eyes stared. Then she opened her hideous mouth and screamed, "KILL HIM!"

And the fiends converged on the enormous, nearly naked young monk.

William swung his mighty fist and a fiend's skull caved in on itself. He thrust out a leg like a horse would, straight back, and connected with a fiend's stomach, pulping its organs. Another fiend swung a hatchet with both hands. William caught the hatchet by the handle, gripped the fiend's arm, and broke it. He grabbed another by its long, sinewy neck and began swinging it around, knocking others to the earth. Around and around the fiend went, screaming to the treetops of Malesherbes. At last, William let go. The fiend flew over the heads of its comrades and smashed into a tree, and then slid down, leaving a streaked bloodstain on the bruised bark. Finally one

last fiend ran straight at William. William punched him in the face so hard that the fiend's neck snapped straight back, and he crumpled, lifeless, to the ground.

The fighting stopped. William stood in the center of the road, shoulders heaving, deep red blood spattered across his skin and face like war paint. Along the edges of the path, the fiends had fallen back, panting and staring. The Wicked One held an arm out, to stop the assault.

"You are strong," the Wicked One rasped. "Strong indeed. But may I ask—does your flesh repel arrows?"

Beside her, three fiends raised their short bows, arrows nocked, and aimed them at William's heart.

William took a step back. On the ground behind him lay a thick mace. He began to slowly reach for it, keeping his eyes trained on the archers.

And then he remembered the words of his abbot. No weapons. Nothing but flesh and bone.

William took a step back.

The bowstrings creaked.

Another step back.

The bows could not be pulled tighter.

William was up against the donkey now.

"FIRE!" the Wicked One screamed.

Just as she did, William reached down and grabbed the donkey's leg and yanked it as hard as he could.

The beast's leg was torn clean off its body.

Which sounds utterly horrific. But you will be glad

to know that the donkey did not feel a thing. It just stood there, gazing into the trees.

Quick as a flash of lightning, William whipped the leg around. The arrows thudded into the donkey's flesh.

The fiends were stunned. The donkey hobbled away placidly on three legs, to crop the ferns at the edge of the road.

William swung the donkey's fourth leg above his head and advanced on the fiends.

Brandishing his weapon. His weapon of flesh and bone.

Instantly, William was upon the fiends, swinging the leg like an enormous club. He smashed it across the right-most archer and sent him careening into the other two. Fiends closed around him again, and soon all anyone could see was a bristling mass of bodies and weapons and the donkey's leg rising and falling and the regular spatter of bright red donkey blood and deep red fiend blood.

Finally the Wicked One stood alone in the midst of the path.

William pulled the donkey's leg behind his head. He hesitated. "Well?" he said. "What do you say now?"

But the Wicked One didn't say anything. She just turned and ran.

So William stood there, amidst the carnage of fiends, wearing only his underwear and his golden belt. He looked around, said a prayer for the souls of the dead, picked up the blood-spattered leather satchels,

and finally walked over to the donkey. He pressed the donkey's leg to the place where it had once been.

It reattached itself. Instantly.

And then William wandered out of the forest of Malesherbes, leading the contented donkey behind him, and they continued on their way to Saint-Denis.

———————

Silence settles over the table. I say, "That did not happen."

The little nun shrugs. "Indeed it did."

"He beat them to death with a *donkey's leg*?"

"That's the craziest thing I ever heard," Marie puts in.

I try to sound nonchalant when I turn to the old monk. "Jerome, you're a man of God. Do you consider what William did—a *miracle*?"

He shrugs. "What else could you call it?"

Now I need to tread delicately. "Does that mean you think he's a *saint*?"

Jerome rubs his white beard. "Well, it takes a lifetime of miracles to be a saint," he says. "And then it requires death."

"Yes," I say. "It does."

"So we shall see when he dies, I suppose," Jerome concludes.

"If the king has his way, we may see rather soon."

The innkeeper puts his hands on Jerome's thin shoulders and announces he's bringing another round of ale.

"There's a third child, another boy," I say. "Does anyone know about him?"

At a nearby table, a thick man with heavy jowls and rough hands stands up. His beard is dark and curly. He strides over to us. "The third child, as you call him? Jacob is his name."

"You know him?"

"Why wouldn't I know him? Didn't he grow up in my village? Didn't he save my life, a week ago? I know him."

"What's your name?"

"My name? Aron. I'm a butcher in Nogent-sur-Oise. The Jewish side of town."

"Please," I say, "tell us about the boy."

So he does.

CHAPTER 6

The Butcher's Tale

First, let me set the scene: We're in the small house of Bathsheba and Moisé, and their son, Jacob. The wanted one.

I must tell you this about Jacob. He is not the most popular boy in our village. He's very gentle. He's very polite. But he's a little *strange*. Finds it easier to talk to adults than to other children, I gather. Anyway...

Who else is there? I'm there. Rabbi Isaac is there. And a young father called Levi, with his little boy.

Levi is nervous. His boy, no more than four years old, has a problem. This is why we're all gathered here. To see if we can help.

Levi is rocking back and forth from his heels to his toes. "He's done this for months now. I don't understand it. His mother doesn't understand it. *Her* mother doesn't understand it, and *she* understands *everything*."

Then it happens. The little boy, Levi's son, blinks hard,

and then opens his eyes very wide, like he's peering into another world.

"There!" his father shouts. "He's doing it!"

We watch, and I will admit, it looks so strange, so . . . *unnatural* . . . that we're afraid.

"Does he do this often?" I ask.

"All the time," says his father.

Rabbi Isaac is chewing on the end of his beard. "I fear to say it," says the rabbi. "But he could be *possessed*."

Levi moans and rocks harder, on his toes, on his heels, on his toes again.

But Bathsheba shushes the rabbi. "For shame! Superstitious old man! He's a little boy! He's not possessed!"

"He could have been possessed at night!" the rabbi replies. "An evil spirit could have slipped in through an open window!"

"Foolery!" Bathsheba scoffs. "Why would a spirit need to come through a window?"

Moisé murmurs, "The Christians speak of fiends in these forests. A race of men, older even than we, who steal infants and raise them as slaves, and leave their own wretched offspring in the infant's place. It could be a peasant's tale, but one never knows these days . . ."

"Are there evil spirits *or* fiends in the Torah?" Bathsheba objects. "What, God makes new plagues for us? The ancient ones weren't good enough?"

"There!" Rabbi Isaac points at the boy. Sure enough, he's doing it again. Blinking hard, then opening his eyes

so, so wide. I swear to you, the boy had to be possessed.
What other explanation could there be?

We, the elders of the village, stood there, yanking on
our beards. The rabbi chewed and chewed and chewed on
the end of his.

"May I ask something?"

It's a small voice, from one of the dark corners of the
room.

It belongs to Jacob.

The rabbi frowns. "What is it, my child?"

"I have a question."

"I have many questions, Jacob. You have but one?
What is it?"

But Jacob says, "It's not for you."

The rabbi looks offended. Jacob pushes past him and
past me and past Levi, until he's standing in front of the
little boy. He looks at him for a long time. And then Jacob
says to the little boy, "Where's your beard?"

"What kind of question is that?" Levi exclaims.

"Moisé, please," the rabbi objects. "What is this?"

But Jacob reaches out and rubs the little boy's face.
"I mean it! They all have beards. Why don't you?" He is
squinting and looking very seriously at the little boy.

"I don't have one," the boy says.

"I can see that. But why not?" Jacob puts his hands on
his hips like he's very confused.

The rabbi rolls his eyes. But the boy smiles. "Because
I'm just a little boy!" he says.

"You look pretty big to me," says Jacob.

"Not *that* big!" says the boy.

"So no beard yet?"

"No!"

"Soon?"

"No!" The little boy is laughing now, his dark eyes shining in the light of the fire. We're all getting impatient. What is Jacob doing?

Jacob shrugs. "I guess you just look older than you are." The little boy beams at him.

And then he does it. He blinks hard and opens his eyes very wide, like he's peering into some distant world.

No one moves a muscle.

And then, very quietly, Jacob says, "Tell me—why do you do that?"

The little boy shrugs.

And then he says, "My eyelashes get stuck together."

Not a word. Not even a breath in the little hut.

And then, everyone is laughing. We're laughing louder and louder. We can't believe it.

"His eyelashes!" we roar.

"Levi, his eyelashes!"

"You never asked him?"

"For *this* the sages of Nogent are cast into confusion? For eyelashes?"

We're making such a racket, the little boy starts to cry. Jacob puts his arm around the boy's shoulders. "Shh . . . ," he says. "They're not laughing at you. They're laughing at each other, for not knowing something a little boy knew all along." Jacob rubs the boy's cheek. "See? You should have a beard. You know more than all these old men put together."

And I hear Bathsheba whispering, "That's my boy. Thank you, God, that's my boy."

"But that's not a miracle!" I say. "Smart, yes. Empathic, absolutely. But the other children performed *miracles*. At least, so you all claim."

All Aron says is, "Wait."

The torches came that night. Jacob was curled up in the straw between his parents—I know this because he told me, later. He was listening to their breathing, when he heard, in the distance, an altogether different sound.

Voices were shouting. Young voices. They were laughing.

Then, he heard other voices crying out and livestock braying and the crackle of flames.

"Oh no . . . ," Marie mutters.

I look at old Jerome. He's covering his eyes.

Jacob leapt from the bed. "Wake up!" he cried, and immediately his parents were on their feet. He ran to the door of their house and threw it open.

Two big boys sprinted through the lane. Jacob

looked at them, hard, and then, like a flash of lightning illuminating the sky, he understood. Christian peasant boys. From the other side of town. They were laughing, but they were scared. This was some sort of prank, some sort of dare.

An eerie, flickering light illuminated the sky. Jacob looked up. The roofs were aflame.

They had dared each other to set our town on fire.

Bathsheba yanked her son back into the hut. Jacob looked at his parents. Their faces were wooden with fear.

"You stay here," Jacob's father whispered.

"But I can help!" Jacob said.

Just then, the door banged open. A boy with a leather cap and wide, wild eyes stood in the doorway. He was no more than fifteen. In one hand he held a torch. In the other, a hatchet. He pushed the torch at the walls. The straw sticking out of the mud started to smoke.

Bathsheba picked up an iron poker. Jacob expected her to attack the young man with it. But instead she attacked the opposite wall. With three thrusts she made a hole. The teenager was shoving the torch at the thatched roof now, because all the wall was doing was smoking. Jacob's father stared, frozen.

No. He wasn't frozen. Jacob could see his mouth moving. He was praying.

The hole in the wall was big enough for someone to crawl through. Bathsheba grabbed Jacob by the back of his neck and pushed him to it.

"Jacob," she said, her breath hot and sharp in his ear. "Run. Hide in the woods. We'll go, too. Meet us at the school, the *beit midrash,* tomorrow. If there's no *beit midrash* left, go to Cousin Yehuda's. Go!"

Jacob tried to object.

"Go!" She shoved him headfirst through the hole.

He tumbled into the alley behind their house. He scrambled to his knees and looked through the hole, into the house. "Mama!" he shouted.

His parents were gone. The roof was on fire.

"Mama! Papa!" he shouted again.

He didn't know where they were.

So he ran.

"Are you all right?" Aron says, looking around at us. All of us are sweating and rubbing our faces. Our mugs of ale sit untouched on the sticky table.

"Not really," the innkeeper says, and he wipes his face with his sleeve.

Jacob spent the whole night lying facedown in a streambed, shivering as the water trickled under his stomach. Long stems of yarrow hung from the bank over his head. He noticed this. Jacob had learned all the plants at a very young age. He seemed to have an affinity for plants. In the cold, lonely darkness, the yarrow gave him comfort.

The next morning, our community was gone. And

half the houses on the Christian side of town had burned, too. Stupid, stupid kids.

Jacob made his way through the wreckage, looking for the *beit midrash*. He didn't find it, for it had burned completely to the ground. He looked for his parents. He didn't find them, either.

But he did find me, lying beneath a collapsed wall. I was bleeding from my head. Jacob pulled the rubble off me, and then he did the strangest thing—he ran away.

I waited for death to come.

But then, Jacob came back, his hands dripping with yarrow root. He pressed it on my head and started to pray.

And this is the strangest part. He was halfway through the first line of the *Shema*, our holiest prayer, and my head stopped hurting. Halfway through the second line, and the blood was no longer running down my face. After he'd said the prayer once through, he pulled the yarrow root from my head.

We sat for a while together. I knew what he wanted to ask, but it took him a long time to finally say, "My parents?"

I shook my head and told him I hadn't seen them at all.

"I have to go to Yehuda's house," he said. "Ama said they'd meet me there."

I told him he was more likely to meet them in Heaven. But he didn't want to hear that. So he set off for Saint-Denis, where Yehuda lives.

There is a space, as we wait to see if the story will continue. But the silence is filled only with the clink of mugs at distant tables.

At last, Marie says, "Yarrow is a powerful healer."

I laugh. "Not that powerful." And then I ask Aron, "This was his miracle, then?"

"What else could it have been?" He pushes his black hair back to show us the scar. "How old does that scar look?"

"Years old," says Jerome.

"Days. It's days. I swear it on my life."

I'm studying Aron, considering.

Old Jerome, in turn, is studying me. "What are you here for?" he says suddenly.

I say, "What is everyone here for? I want to see the king and his troops. And, if I'm lucky, the three children and their—"

"No," Jerome interrupts me. "There's something else. You have a *motive*."

He holds me in his gaze. He has very red lips under his white beard.

At last, I shrug. "I collect stories," I say. "This seems a promising one."

The little nun at the end of the table is smiling at me in a most unsettling way.

"So," I say, because she is making me uncomfortable and because I want to hear more of the story, "as far as

I can tell, these children have *nothing* in common, don't know each other, and have no reason ever to meet. But they do meet, don't they? How? That's what I want to know."

The innkeeper grins. "Well, isn't that lucky? I can tell you that—because it happened right here."

CHAPTER 7

The Innkeeper's Tale

The first to arrive is William.

He's come out the other side of Malesherbes not much worse for wear—sure, under his robes he's spattered with blood, and I imagine he's a bit worn-out. But the day's fine and he's survived the forest. *More* than survived, really. His stride is long, and the breeze is cool and fresh and invigorating.

"How do *you* know all this?" I interrupt. I want to know if I'm sitting at a table filled with wizards and mind readers.

"Most of it I heard from those who was there," the innkeeper replies. "And some of it I take a guess at. I know what kind of day it was, I know how long his legs are, is it really so far a stretch to say his stride was long?"

I suppose it isn't.

"Besides, sometimes *elaborating* a little bit helps keep the ale flowing on a slow night."

William's been walking some time when, out ahead of him, he sees a group of pilgrims. They look wealthy—their cart is painted, they're dressed in brightly dyed tunics and gowns. They're a family of wealthy merchants, heading for the cathedral at Saint-Denis. This I know, because they came here later.

Two men and one woman are walking alongside the cart, and an old lady and a *really* old lady are riding inside it. William raises a big hand and waves at them. He's been walking alone for a while, and it would be nice to have someone to talk to. Yes, there are women there. But they're not peasants and, besides, they're old.

One of the old women sees him wave and says something to the men walking alongside the cart. The men turn, look back at William, and then peel off and stand in the middle of the road. The walking woman smacks the behind of the horse and hurries the cart ahead.

"Hail, friends!" William calls. The men are waiting for him. Silently. As William gets closer, he can see them better. The older one has a thick red beard. The younger has curly red hair. A father and his son. They look nervous. And William can't see their hands under their brightly colored cloaks.

"Hail," William says again. With less confidence this time.

"Halt," says the father. "Unmask yourself."

William comes to a stop about thirty paces away from them. "What?"

The bearded man looked nervously at his son, and then back to William. "Take off your mask, if you mean no harm."

William blinks at him. "What mask?"

The young man is biting his lip and staring. Suddenly, he pulls a short sword from beneath his cloak. "In the name of Christ, be away!"

William has *no idea* what is going on.

The older man draws a hatchet. "Be you brigand or be you devil, begone!"

William continues blinking at them. "I'm not a brigand or a devil. I'm a Benedictine brother. A monk."

The ruddy father and son are brandishing their weapons in an attempt to be menacing. They do not look menacing. They look afraid.

"I am a monk," William says again. "Devoted to God. Can we walk together on the road? I'm . . . kind of lonely."

The son's eyes are wild. "Begone!" He swings his sword at the air. William stumbles backward. He trips over his own sandal and lands—*smack*—on the road. "Begone!" the younger man shouts again.

"Fine," William says. "You're crazy—but fine."

The men start to back away, leaving William sitting on his derriere in the middle of the road.

And then he figures it out. He starts laughing.

If the men were scared before, now they're terrified. They turn and shout, "Spur the horse, Mathilde! Fly! Fly!" Mathilde smacks the horse, and the cart goes rumbling down the road, with the men running after it.

William's figured it out. They think he's a brigand because they think he's wearing a mask. They think he's wearing a mask because they've never seen someone with his color skin before. Hard to believe, I know. But what other explanation is there? William sighs, stands up, and brushes the mud from his enormous behind.

William starts out slowly now, so as not to overtake the pilgrims, but soon the cool air and swooping larks whip his mood into a fine, happy froth, and he completely forgets. It's not much later, then, that he comes across the paranoid pilgrims.

They are stopped in the middle of the road, and their cart is cocked half on its side. One of the cart's wheels is lying on the grassy edge of the road a few feet away. The small group is standing around the cart, staring at it like it's some strange fish, washed ashore. The women have their hands on their hips. The two men have their weapons drawn and are looking all around them like something's going to jump out of the woods and grab them.

And then that something comes walking down the road. When they see William they start shouting: "Away, brigand! Away!" The women stare, clutching each other for protection.

William sighs. He shakes his head. He keeps walking.

"Back!" the son cries. "Avaunt!"

William walks straight for him.

The young man swings his sword at the air. But William strides right at him, and the young man steps back. And back again. "Avaunt…," the young man mutters.

William walks past him. The travelers fall back. All except the oldest woman. She's wearing black wool, and her pale blue eyes fix William with the most evil stare he's ever seen. He tries to ignore her.

William walks up to the cart, puts his large hands on the axle where the wheel was attached, and lifts the cart up.

The pilgrims gape.

"Well?" William says. "Do you want to put the wheel back on or not?"

None of them move.

"I'm not a brigand. I'm a monk from the Abbey Saint-Martin. My mother was a Saracen"—he uses the word so they'll understand what he means—"that's why I have brown skin. But I'm a monk. A *monk*."

Still, they do not budge. Their mouths hang open stupidly.

"One last chance," William says. "Go pick up the wheel and put it on the axle. And don't go rushing down this road. It's too rutted and rocky to hurry down with a laden cart." He waits. "I'm going to drop it if you don't go get that wheel soon."

Not a person moves.

So William drops the cart. When it lands, there's a crack of wet wood. "I offered," William says, shrugging.

The old woman with the pale eyes mutters something about the anti-Christ. The men clutch the sweaty handles of their weapons and watch William warily. So the big oblate walks away. The cart lies in the middle of the road, broken and useless.

He gets here just before sunset. The yard out front is empty, except for my stable boy, Jacques. Jacques is sitting on a stump, whittling. William stands in front of him and says, "Excuse me." Jacques looks up, screams, and falls backward off the stump.

William instantly drops to one knee and says, "I am a brother of the Monastery Saint-Martin. I want only a place to sleep and some food, please."

Jacques stammers, backs away from him slowly, and then turns and runs inside to get me. Tells me there's a giant wearing a mask out in the yard, asking for a place to sleep. I come outside. I've seen Africans before. You see all sorts when you run an inn. But I've got to admit I've never seen anyone as big as William. Well, once. The Red Monk, Michelangelo di Bologna.

Anyway, I can't let William come inside.

———————

"And why not?" Jerome exclaims, his face flushing burgundy behind his beard.

———————

Look, Brother, he seems like a nice kid. I liked him. But he looks like something out of the Book of Revelation.

I mean, he has a nice face if you actually look at it, but most people don't really look. They just glance, get up, and leave. And I got an inn to run here.

So I offer to let him sleep in the stables. Free of charge. That's as fair as I can make it.

Then he asks for food. I ask for money. He doesn't have any, but he says he'll work for it. So I have him sweep up the stable. Good worker, that kid. When he's done, I bring him a big portion of the pigeon stew. He must have been famished, because he cleans out the whole bowl in about three bites.

Then I leave him in the stable, and pretty soon, he's snoring so loud I can hear him in the inn.

So William's here.

Not too long after, my door swings open, and a troop of filthy knights comes in. Petty knights. No horses. No lord either, except whoever's paying them that day. Just wandering around the countryside, pushing people around. I gotta tell you, the best thing about the Crusades is that morons like that have somewhere else to go to cause trouble.

Riffraff like them don't usually pay, so I'm on my guard already. I try to tell them to wipe their feet. They don't care. They're filing in—one, two, three, four, five of them. I end up learning their names as they sit there, drinking. There's Baldwin, who's short and bald—so that's easy to remember. There's Georges and Robert. I can't tell which is which, because they're the muscle. Each big as hills, and neither as smart as one. Then there are two brothers, with curly golden hair. One is tall and skinny, with a big Adam's apple and a lazy eye. Haye, his name is. And his brother is chubbier and called Marmeluc, which is a ridiculous name if you ask me.

Finally their leader walks in. Small and wiry, with long, ratty yellow hair and a face like a weasel. Sir Fabian, they call him. Fabian is holding a rope that trails behind him and out the door.

I'm just trying to figure out what the rope is for when the door opens one last time.

There is a girl at the end of the rope.

A peasant girl. The rope is tied around her neck. It's left a red ring on her skin. The girl looks dusty and bruised and exhausted.

But there's something about her. Something . . . I don't know. If I were those knights, I wouldn't want to keep her tied up. There's something about her that looks like it can't be caged or bound—at least not for long.

Well, Sir Fabian the Weasel makes her sit on the floor, and he ties the rope around his ankle. "In case I get too drunk to look after you," he says. And then he and the rest of them start drinking.

So Jeanne's here, too.

Twilight's settling over the forest. A boy creeps up to the inn. He's afraid. He's not sure he's welcome here. After

what's happened to his village, I don't blame him. He sees Jacques, peeling carrots in the yard. He stares for a moment and decides that Jacques looks jumpy.

So the boy—Jacob—creeps around back, where he finds the pig's trough. In the trough, among the slop and the stale beer, there's an old carrot and a withered apple. They don't look very good, but the boy hasn't eaten, and hasn't slept, in more than a day. He takes them.

"Hey!" says a voice. Jacob drops the food.

The bald knight stands up out of the bushes. He was relieving himself. "Are you stealing?" says the knight. "Are you a thief?"

Jacob hesitates for a moment and then decides his best bet is to try to simply walk away. He does it real calm, real slow. But Baldwin hikes up his pants and hurries to catch up with him. He grabs Jacob, hard, by the arm. "Hey!" he shouts to nobody. "I caught a thief! I caught a thief!" His fingers dig like screws into Jacob's arm. The little boy winces and tries to regain his footing as he's dragged around the corner of the inn, into the yard. I don't know if any of you ever got dragged around by a bully when you were kids. I did. There ain't nothing scarier. They got total power over you. You can't run, fighting back won't do any good at all, and pleading makes them laugh. Just remembering it makes me feel sick and scared all over again.

Well, I figure that's just about how Jacob was feeling. And after his long and terrible day, if I were him, I would have been about ready to cry.

In front of the inn, a couple of knights are out enjoying the fresh air and the sunset—Haye, Georges, and Robert.

"Look!" Baldwin says. "I caught a thief! Stealing from the pig's trough!"

"I'm not a thief!" Jacob exclaims.

"Thieves are bad," says Georges. Because he's really smart.

Baldwin says, "What should we do with him?"

Jacob's heart is pounding as he looks between the cruel men with their lazy sneers.

Haye smiles. "I want to play ball."

"Good." Baldwin grins. "Let's play."

Now all three children are here. Jeanne, William, and Jacob.

Baldwin pushes the kid. Hard. Jacob's neck snaps backward, and he goes careening into the chest of one of the big knights.

Robert stares down from under the black brow that stretches over both of his eyes. Then he pushes, and Jacob's feet go out from under him and he hits the ground. The wind is knocked out of him. Jacob writhes in the dirt, trying to get some air into his lungs, squirming like a fish in a boat.

Just as Jacob gets his breath back, Haye grabs his shirt and yanks him up. The little boy stares into the knight's wide blue eyes. Only one looks back at him.

He shoves Jacob to the anvil-faced knight, Georges. Georges grabs Jacob around the neck. "Kill the thief," Georges says.

Nobody contradicts him.

Jeanne, meanwhile, is sitting on the floor next to Fabian's feet—under that table over there.

She stares up at Fabian as he sucks on a chicken bone. Beside him, Sir Marmeluc takes deep drafts of ale.

Jeanne watches them, disgusted.

Then Baldwin pokes his head in the front door. "Fabian!" he says. "We caught a thief!"

Fabian continues to suck on the chicken bone. Slowly, he puts it down. A line of saliva trails from his lower lip to the bone. "So?" he says.

"I think Georges is gonna kill it. Wanna watch?"

Well, I start shouting. I don't know who this thief is or who he's supposed to have stolen from, but no one is going to kill anyone on my property. Terrible for business.

But Fabian doesn't give a pig's nose about my business or what I'm saying. He gets up, knocks his stool over, and goes to the door. The rope around Jeanne's neck gets tight. He kicks his foot out, jerking her head forward. She crawls to her feet and, because she has no choice, she follows Fabian outside. So do I.

In the yard in the falling dusk we see a boy with curly brown hair. Georges is choking him. His face is red and turning blue, and his little legs are kicking the air.

And then a voice cuts through the yard, bright and commanding and clear. Like a war trumpet or some-thing.

"Stop it! Leave him alone!"

We all turn and look. The knights, too.

It's Jeanne. A little peasant girl, with a rope around her neck. Telling a bunch of knights what to do.

Georges is confused enough to drop Jacob—just *bam*. Drops him. Jacob bounces. Then he lies still in the dust.

The knights look at Jeanne. Then they look at Fabian.

Fabian shrugs. "Get it over with already."

Baldwin draws his sword. He advances on Jacob.

"Hey!" I shout. "Don't!"

"We can take him to the woods to kill him if you want," says Sir Haye, shrugging.

"Don't kill him at all!" I cry.

And Jeanne is shrieking, "Stop! STOP!"

Inside the stable, William opens his eyes and pushes straw from his face.

People are screaming in the yard.

Why are people screaming in the yard?

He sits up—and finds his face very close to his don-key's rear end. He plants a big hand on the donkey and pushes it away.

More screaming. William pulls himself to his feet. He's covered in hay. He dusts off his habit and groggily makes his way to the door of the stable. When he gets there, he can't figure out how to open it. He pushes it to the left, but it won't budge. He pushes harder. It still won't open. More screaming outside. William wonders, *Did they lock me in?* He leans all his very considerable weight against the door. Nothing.

The screaming continues.

William decides to pull the door to the right.

It slides open.

William chuckles at himself and leans out into the dusk.

In the yard he sees a cluster of men. They have swords. One is drawn. He sees me shouting. Nearby, he sees an ugly little man with long yellow hair and a face like a wea- sel. And a little peasant girl. A dirty, angry peasant girl. With a rope around her neck.

"Let him go!" she's screaming.

Let who go? William wonders. And then he sees it. A bald man has his foot on the neck of a little boy. His sword is pointed at the place where the boy's spine meets his skull.

What is everybody screaming about? Why does that peasant have a rope around her neck? And why is a grown man standing on a little boy? William doesn't know the answer to any of these questions. But he does know how to find out.

Jacob is trying to pray. I can see it. He's gasping for breath and mouthing words, but he can't get the prayer out. He's said the first verse: *"Shema yisrael, adonai elohainu, adonai echad..."*

"How do you know the *Shema*?" Aron cuts in.

The innkeeper tugs at the fat of his neck. "My grandmother taught it to me," he says.

"Was she...?"

"She was."

Jacob is trying to remember the rest of the *Shema*. The first verse is out—*Hear, O Israel, the Lord Our God, the Lord is One.* Normally, the rest rolls off his tongue as easily as his own name. But his mouth is fumbling the words, and his throat is choked with dust and tears, and a foot is pressing hard on the bones in the back of his neck. Frantically, he tries to remember: "Blessed are you—" he mutters. "Blessed be you, Oh God... Adonai... Blessed... Blessed be—" Tears are running down his cheeks. "Blessed—"

And then, the ground under his face begins to tremble. It trembles again. And again. And again. Faster and faster. Like a summer lightning storm, speeding across the horizon. Jacob tries to crane his head around, under the weight of the leather shoe-sole, pinning his neck. He catches a fleeting glimpse of something—something enormous and dark—flying across the yard of the inn.

And then—blessed relief. The foot is off his neck.

And the words come back to him like summer rain pouring from the sky: *Blessed be the name of God's Kingdom forever
and ever. And you shall love the Lord your God with all your heart
and all your soul and all your might. And these words I command
you this day . . .*

Jeanne has been screaming—but she stops when she sees
a dark shape, storming out of the stable. What is it? It's
moving too fast to tell. It thunders across the yard—just
a thunderhead of black robes.

She blinks, and suddenly the bald knight is sprawling
through the dust.

The great thing comes to rest. It stands upright. It
may be the largest thing Jeanne has ever seen.

But it's not a thing.

It's a boy.

And his name is William.

William gazes around the yard. The knights are ogling
him. They're dumbstruck.

He reaches down and pulls Jacob to his feet. "You
okay?" he asks. Jacob nods, but he's staring up at William,
just as dumbstruck as everybody else.

And then, from the side of his eye, William sees a
flash of silver.

Sir Fabian is brandishing his sword above his head,
running at William and Jacob. "I don't know what you
are," Fabian is saying, "but you're about to be dead."

William raises his arm to shield himself and Jacob.

Fabian is on them now. He swings his sword—and falls, facefirst, into the dirt.

The rope attached to his ankle is stretched to the door of the inn.

While no one was looking, Jeanne had wrapped it around the door handle.

Fabian, sprawling in the dirt, shouts at someone to cut the rope. Haye rushes over, pushes Jeanne out of the way, and hacks the rope in two.

Fabian gets to his feet. He swings his sword at the boys, slicing the air. He swings it again, getting closer and closer. I'm shouting for him to stop—but he won't listen. He's coming for the boys.

I close my eyes. This is something I cannot watch.

I hear William scream.

Someone is running past me. I open my eyes. William, holding Jacob's hand. Jacob grabs Jeanne, and they keep running.

William looks uninjured. So who's screaming?

I turn to the yard. A white greyhound is gnawing on Fabian's leg. Fabian is screaming and trying to get it off. The kids are running into the forest. Jeanne shouts, "Gwenforte!"

The greyhound lets go of Fabian, who crumples to the ground, and the dog is off running, first trying to catch the kids, and then alongside them, and then out in front.

They disappear into the woods.

Fabian is lying on the ground, howling in pain and fury.

And then, from the woods, his howl is answered. First by the dog. Then by the kids. They're howling, just like Fabian. But theirs is a howl of triumph.

The innkeeper leans back and throws up his hands. "Well, that's my part of the story."

The inn has become quiet. The diners and drinkers at neighboring tables have, over the course of the innkeeper's tale, let their own conversations fall to the wayside and have begun listening to ours.

A handsome man with dark curls stands up and asks if he can sit with us. His are simple traveling clothes, and yet they're the finest traveling clothes I've ever seen. Subtle: just browns and yellows and hints of pale blue, but stitched with an attention to detail good enough for the king himself. A small detail, but I notice—anyone of my profession would.

The little nun says, "I know the next part. Would you like to hear it?"

Of course we would.

CHAPTER 8

The Third Part of the Nun's Tale

Three children—so different, so far from home, and, up until recently, so very alone—sat on the bank of a small stream. Jeanne stroked Gwenforte's white coat. William had taken off his leather sandals and plunged his feet into the cold water. Jacob was hugging his legs to his body and staring up at the gently shifting trees—he could identify them by the silhouettes of their leaves—and beyond them, to the stars he could not name.

Each child glanced at the others. No one spoke.

The excitement of their escape had burned hot and then died, like a birchwood fire.

I am in a dark wood with a giant monk, Jeanne thought. She did not trust monks and she did not trust giants, and the last time she'd seen a giant monk, her friend Theresa had been taken away to be burned at the stake. So she would not speak to this huge brown boy, lest her secret slip. She decided, in fact, that it would be safest not to speak at all.

Jacob was shivering. He could not tell if it was the cold or the fact that his village had been destroyed; he didn't know where his parents were and he was alone in a forest in the middle of the night with two young Christians. He had not had good luck, recently, with young Christians. These two *seemed* rather different from those teenagers who had set fire to his village. Even so, he could not be sure. The shivering spread from his arms to his chest.

William was thinking, *I am in a dark wood with a girl. A GIRL.* William had never been this close to a girl before. Or a woman. Well, as an infant he had been. Necessarily. Given where babies come from. But not since. The closest he'd been to a daughter of Eve was seeing that peasant across the field. Yes, he had defended girls-as-an-idea in front of Bartholomew. That was one thing. Spending a night in a dark wood with one—and, moreover, a *peasant* girl—well, that was a different matter altogether. *Do not close your eyes on her.*

So the children sat in silent fear of one another.

Well, for the space of about ten breaths.

And then William spoke, because ten breaths was about as long as he could go without talking.

"What's your dog's name?" he asked the girl. *What are you doing?* he thought. *Beware the daughters of Eve!*

Jeanne said, "Gwenforte, the Holy Greyhound." *Be quiet!* she shouted at herself. *Why would you say that?*

Jacob smirked. "The *holy* greyhound? A holy *dog*? Christians worship dogs?" Instantly he regretted it. *God be merciful, what did you just say? Are you trying to get yourself killed?*

Jeanne and William turned on him.

"What do you mean, *Christians*?" William asked. "You're not a Christian?"

"Then what *are* you?" Jeanne said. She didn't really know any alternatives to being Christian. Everyone she had ever met was Christian.

Jacob peered into William's face. Then he peered into Jeanne's. He made a decision. "I'm a Jew."

Jeanne laughed. "No you're not!"

"Uh . . . yes I am."

"No you're not!" she insisted.

Jacob was completely confused. William was, too.

"Why am I not a Jew?" he asked.

"You don't look like one!" Jeanne said.

Jacob said, "What is a Jew supposed to look like?"

"I don't know. Different!"

William said to Jeanne, "You don't know very much about Jews."

Quick as a flame catching a wick, Jeanne spat, "You don't know what I know!"

"I know you think you have a holy dog." He turned to Jacob. "Do they worship dogs in your heathen religion?"

"I am *not* a heathen. And no. There are no holy dogs in the *Tanakh*."

William turned to Jeanne. "See? Even the *Jews* don't believe in them."

"She *is* holy," Jeanne said, and the sharpness of her voice cut through William's teasing like a scythe through summer hay.

The boys fell silent. The ash trees creaked and the stream sang. The wood smelled cold.

"Okay, peasant. Prove it," said William.

Jeanne glowered at him. She did not like how he said *peasant*. It sounded like a curse.

"You can't claim that she's holy," William said, "and not tell us *why*."

Jeanne crooked an eyebrow. "I can do what I like, *monk*." She tried to make it sound like a curse, too.

Jacob chuckled. "Oh, come on."

Jeanne glared at him.

"Please?"

But Jeanne had turned away from them, pulling Gwenforte with her. She had already violated her rule. Never tell. Never.

Jeanne, William, and Jacob lay down under the slowly shifting stars and swaying branches of the ashes. Gwenforte was curled under Jeanne's arm. At first, each child refused to sleep, afraid of the other two. But soon, the events of the day weighed so heavily on their eyelids that they could no longer resist.

. . .

At dawn, a frog began croaking belligerently from the streambed. Jeanne shifted and woke.

The light was soft in the wood. Jeanne descended the small bank of the brook and splashed water on her cheeks and neck. The frog hopped a ways off and continued his bellowing.

She heard movement behind her, up on the bank. She spun. Jacob was kneeling, eyes closed, whispering. Jeanne watched him. He might be destined for Hell, but he certainly looked like a Christian when he prayed. Even his curly hair and splatter of freckles could have belonged to any boy in her village. At last, he opened his eyes. He saw her looking at him, and he smiled. "What are you furrowing your brow about?" he said softly.

Jeanne shrugged and climbed up on the bank beside him. William had rolled onto his stomach and stretched out his arm so it hung limply over Gwenforte's white flank.

"What are you doing on the road?" Jeanne asked, her voice soft and scratchy in the early morning. "Where are your parents?"

Jacob fingered a patch of dead raspberry leaves. "I don't know where they are right now."

"Why not?"

"A fire in my village. Some boys burned it down."

"Oh God . . ." Jeanne put her brown fingernails in her mouth.

"Christian boys," Jacob added.

Jeanne nodded, her nails still between her teeth.

"I got separated from my parents. They told me to meet them at Saint-Denis. How about you? Where are you going?"

Jeanne was still nodding, still chewing on her fingernails. "I . . . I'm not sure yet."

"Why not? Aren't your parents waiting for you somewhere?"

Jeanne hesitated. Jacob was looking at her intently. Like he was trying to look past her skin. "It's not important," she said at last.

There was a pause. And then Jacob said, "I bet it's important to you."

Jeanne looked at the earth. But she was smiling.

Then Jacob said, "I wonder where *he's* headed." He gestured at the enormous, snoring William.

Jeanne pushed herself to her feet. "Let's find out."

She approached the cacophonous sleeper, now on his side. She knelt down and tapped on his arm. William did not respond.

Jacob came over, bent down, and whispered in William's ear, "Wake up!"

Nothing.

Jacob grabbed the enormous hock of meat that passed for William's shoulder and shook it.

The big boy's eyelids did not stir.

"Do you think something's wrong with him?" Jeanne wondered.

Jacob shrugged. "Some people live violently and sleep violently. Kick him."

"What?"

"He'll be fine. Just try it."

Jeanne was reluctant. So Jacob kicked one of William's log-like legs.

No response.

Jacob dug his toe into William's back.

William continued to snore.

So Jeanne gave a swift, not-quite-as-gentle-as-she-had-intended kick to William's stomach. Actually, it was rather hard.

Gwenforte leapt to her feet.

"What?" William groaned sleepily, rolling onto his back. "What is it?"

"Did you really sleep through all that? We kicked you a lot of times."

William wiped his face with his sleeve and did not open his eyes. "Then I don't see why I should wake up, if you're going to abuse me."

But Gwenforte had decided that it was indeed time to get up—either that, or she liked the salty taste of William's sweat—because she began licking his ears and forehead.

"Stop! Stop!" William shouted. Jeanne and Jacob grinned. "Stop it!" He tried to push the long dog-face away, but Gwenforte kept finding new openings to attack.

More in self-defense than out of any decision to wake

up, William pulled himself to his feet—like a tree falling in reverse—and stretched his long arms over his head. Jacob and Jeanne marveled at him, unfurled to his full length.

"Were your parents giants?" Jacob asked.

William yawned. "No. My mother was a Muslim. My father is a Christian lord. He fights in the *Reconquista*."

He pushed past them, sat on his rear, and slid down the short, steep bank to the brook. Black branches overhead framed a gray-blue morning. Jeanne and Jacob moved to the verge of the bank and sat down. Their eyes were about level with William's now.

"The what?" Jeanne asked.

"The *Reconquista*. Christians taking back Spain from the Muslims. Trying to push them all the way back to Africa."

"Your mom is *African*?"

"I don't know. I never met her. Never met my dad either, actually."

Jacob watched as William splashed water on his face. "Do you want to?"

"Meet my parents?" William shrugged. "I don't know. I bet my mom died in childbirth."

Jeanne was horrified. "You shouldn't say that!"

"And my father's too important. I'm sure he's got a hundred sons like me."

Jacob smirked. "Probably not *exactly* like you."

William grabbed the hem of his monk's habit. Then he

hesitated. He looked at Jeanne. "Would you turn around? I need to wash my chest." Jeanne turned around. William watched to make sure she wouldn't do something evil and daughter-of-Eve-like. She seemed to have no intention of doing anything of the sort. So he pulled the habit over his head.

"Holy Moses!" Jacob exclaimed.

"What?" said William.

"What?" said Jeanne, turning around.

"Turn around!" William shouted at her.

She turned back around. But she tried to crane her neck to see what Jacob was talking about.

"You're covered in blood!" Jacob said.

Jeanne spun around again so she could see.

It was true. William was caked with dark blood all over his chest and stomach and back. Also, he wore a leather belt inlaid with shining gold through the loops of his underwear. But mostly, the kids were staring at the blood.

"Oh, that?" William laughed. "Don't worry. It's not mine."

"That doesn't make me feel any better," Jacob said.

"No, it's not like that. It's not even human blood."

"What kind of blood is it?" Jeanne asked.

"Fiend blood."

"What?"

"It's the blood of the Foul Fiends of the forest of Malesherbes."

Jacob turned to Jeanne. "Do you understand what he just said?"

"No."

"Just checking."

William said, "Let me wash up, and then I'll tell you. And you, peasant, turn around."

"My pleasure, *monk*."

Despite himself, William laughed.

When he had washed, William sat beside Jacob and Jeanne on the bank and told them of his expulsion from the monastery of Saint-Martin—"You broke a stone bench with your bare hands?" Jeanne said. "Really? Actually really?"—and then of his journey through the forest of Malesherbes—"Their heads *exploded*? That can't be true. Though there was a *lot* of blood on you . . ."—When he got to the part with the donkey's leg, they both began stammering at once. "What?" "No!" "Truly?" "It can't be!"

But William swore it all was true.

As Jeanne listened to the tale, she began to think. Hard.

When he was done, William turned to Jacob. "I've told my story. How do you come to be here, my good Jew?"

"Well, my good Christian," Jacob replied, eliciting a smirk from Jeanne, "it was because of a fire."

Jacob told William what he had told Jeanne. William was less horrified than Jeanne—and more furious. "Do you know where those Christian boys live? Let's go find them! I'll tear them limb from—"

But Jacob said, "No. I'm sure you could. But don't." And then he told of his parents disappearing and finding the butcher lying beneath the wall and of healing his head with yarrow.

"It closed instantly?" William wanted to know.

"The time it took to say the *Shema*. A few lines."

Jeanne's mind was racing now.

The boys turned to her.

"Well?" said William. "Will you tell us why you're here?"

"And, maybe, about that dog of yours?"

Gwenforte had been sleeping in a sunbeam, but now she stood up, shook herself, and padded over to Jeanne. The greyhound yawned, her tongue rising like a hill in her mouth, then shook herself, sat down, and looked at Jeanne as if she, too, wanted to hear the story.

Jeanne thought for a moment about the stories they had just told her. Then she pulled Gwenforte's head into her lap and began stroking her long copper blaze.

Jeanne's rustic peasant accent suited tale-telling well. The boys sat up, wrapped their arms around their knees, and watched the little girl stroke the dog. And they listened. She told them everything that we've heard already. Including about her visions.

Because, she realized, if she was going to be burned at the stake for magic—well, they would be, too.

When she told them about seeing the greyhound on Gwenforte's grave, the boys stopped listening altogether

and turned their attention entirely to the white greyhound. Suddenly, William whispered, "Hey, Brutus!"

The kids looked at him, but he was staring at the dog.
She continued to lie in Jeanne's lap.

"Here, Cassandra! Fido! Weston! Elsie!" The dog's ears
twitched with each call, but she lay still. At last, William
said, "Gwenforte!"

The greyhound sat straight up and stared at him.

"That is weird ...," Jacob murmured.

"That is beyond weird," William said. "That is a miracle."

"And then the knights showed up in the grove," Jeanne
said. "And they captured me."

"And they brought you to the inn," William concluded.
"So now, will you take the greyhound home?"

Jeanne hesitated. "I . . . I don't think so."

"Why not?"

"The people in my village. They wouldn't understand."

"But your parents?"

"Don't understand." The memory of their faces, the
last moment she'd seen them, made her feel like she'd
drunk a bowlful of sour milk.

The boys were silent. The woods creaked in the morning wind. At last, Jacob said, "Well, you can always come
with me to Saint-Denis."

William bellowed, "Saint-Denis? My ass!"

Jacob and Jeanne both blinked and stared at William.
"What?"

"Where is my ass?" William shouted.

Jacob started to giggle. "Say that again?"

"Where in God's name is my ass!?" William bellowed, standing up. "What did you do with it?"

Jeanne and Jacob were both giggling now. Jeanne managed to say, "What are you talking about?"

"My donkey! Where is my donkey?"

Jeanne's and Jacob's laughter began to subside. Jeanne said, "What donkey?"

William slapped his forehead with one huge hand. "I left my ass at the inn!"

Jeanne and Jacob burst out laughing again.

But William wasn't laughing. "We must retrieve it!"

"What?" Jacob said.

"What?" Jeanne said, at exactly the same moment, in exactly the same tone.

"My donkey had two satchels full of books for Saint-Denis. That's where I'm going, too! To Abbot Hubert, at Saint-Denis! So first we'll go retrieve the books, and then we'll all go to Saint-Denis together!"

But Jeanne was shaking her head. "That's the last place I'd go. That's where the knights came from. That's where they wanted to take me. To Michelangelo di Bologna."

Suddenly, William's face had an expression that neither Jeanne nor Jacob had seen on it before. He said, "That is not good."

"Who are we talking about?" said Jacob.

William explained, "Michelangelo di Bolonga is the most evil monk in all of France. Red, Fat, and Wicked—

that's what they call him. He's bigger even than I am, they say. And meaner than a hungry bear."

"He took my best friend, Old Theresa, away to be burned at the stake. He lives at Saint-Denis."

"And that's *exactly* why you should go there!" William exclaimed. "Straight into the lion's den!"

"That makes no sense," said Jeanne. Jacob agreed.

"But it does!" William insisted. "For this lion is not the king of beasts! There is one greater than him. His abbot, Hubert the Good. Do you want to tame the lion? Go to his master!"

"And say what?"

"Ask for pardon, for you and for Gwenforte." The greyhound looked up, cocked her head at William, and then laid her head back in Jeanne's lap.

"That's crazy," Jeanne said.

"If Michelangelo wants to find you, do you think you can escape him? He strikes terror into the heart of every peasant, monk, and noble. Once he knows you've escaped from the knights, he'll hunt you down. You stand no chance."

Jeanne frowned down at Gwenforte. Then she looked to Jacob.

He shrugged. "It's not a bad argument."

"Go to his master. Hubert's wisdom and piety are famous across Christendom. I'm bringing some books to him anyway. Come with me, and we'll tell him all about the crimes of the wicked Michelangelo."

Every one of Jeanne's instincts told her to refuse.

Don't trust this monk. Don't go to Saint-Denis. Don't put your life in the hands of an abbot you've never met. Don't get any closer to Michelangelo than you have to.

Every instinct, that is, but one. The two boys gazed at her like they wanted her to come with them. Like they wanted her.

Her voice was quieter than the wind in the ashes. "You'll stay with me?"

William grinned. "I swear it on my life."

"All right."

"All right?"

"All right."

"So we're all going to Saint-Denis?" Jacob said.

"We're all going to Saint-Denis," Jeanne conceded.

"But first," cried William, "my ass!"

The sun was warming, and the children could hear the scattered chirruping of the first birds, returned from the south.

They tramped one after the other, trying to find their way back to the inn. Their flight last night had been wild and at random. No one was quite sure in which direction the inn lay.

William started in front—it seemed to be in his na-ture. Jeanne and Jacob were noticing this—always to be loudest, biggest, first. Strangely, though, it wasn't annoy-ing. Some children push themselves ahead just to lord it over other children, because they're insecure or selfish.

But William was not like that. He just burned with enthusiasm from within. He was always out in front because
he could not wait to see what was next.

But they quickly moved him to the back. First, because he was by far the easiest to spot; the children
wanted to see the knights before the knights saw them.
And second, because he was so large that every branch
he passed snapped back violently. After both Jacob and
Jeanne had taken turns receiving lashes to their eyes
and cheeks and chins, they made William walk in the
rear. Gwenforte walked beside Jeanne, rubbing her white
flank up against the little girl who she had loved so
much and lost for so long.

They continued to talk as they made their way
through the forest. Their accents were unique. Jacob's
was inflected with the rhythms of the Hebrew Bible
and the *beit midrash* where the men of his village studied
and argued. William, on the other hand, spoke the high
French of the monastery, which was infused with Latin.
Jeanne's speech was broad and flat like the fields her
people tilled.

They told one another about where they were from,
what their lives were like, their friends back home—
though they discovered, to their mutual surprise, that
none of them really had any friends back home. Each of
them seemed nice to the others, easy to get along with.
But at home, it turned out, they had all felt the same way:
as if they were different from the other children. As if

they had thoughts buzzing around in their heads that, if said aloud, would make them seem strange.

They laughed to hear one another describe this feeling they had all felt, but never before put into words. William, Jacob, and Jeanne, despite their differences, found it remarkably easy to talk to one another. As if, despite their different accents, they had finally met someone who spoke their native tongue.

Soon, they came to a broad road and saw an inn. Peering from the trees, across the road, though, it was quite obvious that this was *not* the inn they had come from.

"I think we're lost," Jacob announced.

"We are definitely lost," agreed Jeanne.

"We're not!" William, who had been choosing their path, even from behind, objected. "We're just taking a different route."

"A route so different it takes us to a different inn?" Jacob asked.

Jeanne laughed, and William blushed. A familiar feeling crept over him. Two children, pink skinned and of the same size, laughing together. At William. "I meant to take us here!" he growled.

Jeanne said, "Look!" She put her hand on William's arm. William recoiled. He had been touched by a daughter of Eve! He was about to snap at her—when he saw where she was pointing. He followed the line of her finger, past the mottled, mossy tree trunks.

Down the road, there was a market, bustling with

buyers and sellers. The sounds of bargaining and laughter echoed over the road.

"There," said Jeanne. "Let's go there and ask how to get back to the inn."

"Good idea!" William agreed. He took a step toward the road.

Jeanne stopped him. "Not you! If the knights are any-where nearby, they'll spot you from a mile away. Gwen-forte, too. Stay here with her. Jacob and I will find out where the inn is, and be right back."

The nun stops talking.

Someone is standing at my elbow. I turn—and see that he doesn't reach my shoulder. And I'm sitting down. His hair is so red it looks like it's on fire. And his face is all freckles. He grins at me, and his two front teeth are broken.

"I know somefing," he says. "Saw it all, I did. Saw what happened to those poor kids. Saw what *he* did and what *they* did and all the terrible fings that happened after that."

He's a child. But he looks like the kind of child who has seen too much of life, who's seen more than most adults. His eyes are both sharp and dead at the same time. As if he won't miss anything, because he's seen it all already.

"But if you want somefing, you gotta give somefing, know what I mean?"

"Get out!" the innkeeper says, rising to his feet. "I told you twenty times, Renard, you don't come in here! Never again! I will skin you with a branch if I gotta!" The innkeeper's jowly face is turning as red as the boy's hair. I stand up and grab the innkeeper's arm and guide him back to his stool.

"I want to hear his story," I say.

"Don't you believe a thing he says," the innkeeper spits. "This kid will steal the shoes off your feet while you're running after him to get your purse back."

The boy—Renard—looks hurt. I say, "That may be. But I need to hear the rest of the story. And if he knows it, I'll listen."

Renard winks at me. "Get me a mug of ale—the strong stuff—and the story's yours."

"No!" the innkeeper says.

I add, "No ale. But you can have a plate of food. On me."

The innkeeper scowls, but I'm already pulling up a stool to the table for the flame-haired boy.

CHAPTER 9

The Jongleur's Tale

I'm a jongleur. I'll set me up in a market on market day, sing songs, juggle a little, whatever it takes to make a penny or two for a poor boy like meself.

So I was set up in the weekly market just south of Belair-sur-Oise, and I was keepin' the people entertained, as I do, when I notice the strangest sight. There's some woods next to where they set up the market. And I see, lurking in them woods, a white dog, wif a copper blaze down her snout. And then, beside her, I see the biggest bloke I ever saw. And browner than a serf in summer, I swear it. I nearly forgot the song I was singing, 'alfway frew. That's how surprised I was. And then, next to the big boy, I see two kids about my age, a boy and a girl, and I'm pretty sure the boy's a Jew. Not that he looks all that different. But you know, being a jongleur, you gotta know people. Where they're from, what kind of jokes they'll like, which God to make fun of, where they keep their purse—that sort of fing.

Next fing I know, the Jew and the peasant are out in the market. They look like they're having a grand ol' time. I mean, I fink they're out on a mission—trying to figure out where they are or somefing. But the market—that's an intoxicating place, isn't it? You got every maker and craftsman from every little town nearby, settin' out their blankets, settin' out their wares. You got honey and bees-wax, you got ale from brewers and brewsters like Marie here, you've got leather and horn and blacksmiffs and cheese like any good Frenchman could never say no to.

And the best part of the market—and I know this personal—is there ain't no lords nor priests as to tell you what to do. You come to the market wif your own labor, your own money, to buy and sell what you can. That's the life for me, I tell you. None of this sweating in the fields. You earn what earn as you can. By hook or by crook, by spit or by wit. It don't matter.

And Jeanne and Jacob—those were their names, I know now—they felt it. As they walked into the market, they began to feel freer, more fresh wif life. That's what a market'll do to you. They're looking at all the stalls. Jacob picks up some spun wool and twirls it between his fingers. Jeanne pushes around some new nails on a smith's table.

The big boy watched from the woods, and I could just about feel the envy and insecurity rising from him. I don't blame him. He probably feels left out all the time, looking like he does.

After a while, Jeanne and Jacob seem to remember what they're about. They stop by a lady selling goose eggs and ask her if she knows a Holy Cross-Roads Inn. She don't. They ask a fat man who'd been listening to my song. He wipes his brow and says he don't know neither. They turn to a little lady, about to ask her the same question.

Which is when Jeanne saw him.

Time changed. I felt it—like a plunging rock hitting the surface of a stream and slowly starting to sink. Dust hung in the air. Peasants practically froze. And there, in the middle of them all, was a *huge* man.

He's taller than every other man there by a head, or more.

He's got bushy red whiskers and orange-red hair, sticking up at crazy angles from his scalp.

His big ol' cheeks are crimson.

And his tiny red eyes, buried in fat, are trained wif a mixture of wonder and fury on Jeanne.

Yeah, you know who it is.

It's Red, Fat, and Wicked himself. Michelangelo di Bologna.

Suddenly, he's pushing people, just shoving 'em out the way, bellowing at the top of his lungs, "Stop! Stop those children!"

Jeanne don't wait. She bolts off in the opposite direction, grabbing Jacob and yanking him behind her.

At first, she seems headed for the forest, where the big boy and the dog are hiding, but then she finks better of it—why lead Red, Fat, and Wicked right for the dog?—and zigzags off in another direction.

Jacob is struggling to keep up, trying to duck and weave past all the peasants and peddlers in the road. Jeanne is jumping over blankets wif wares on 'em, provoking the nastiest curses from the merchants. Until Michelangelo comes, that is, and then their curses are worse, because he just stomps straight over whatever they're trying to sell. I sawed him mash some crockery to shards. And he's gaining on the kids.

But Jeanne gets clever now. She ducks down, real low, so she's hidden among all the bodies in the market. Jacob does the same. And now Red, Fat, and Wicked is lost. He's turning around and around, trying to clap eyes on 'em again.

Meanwhile, they're sneaking out the back of the market and onto the road heading souf.

Well, I see me a little opportunity here. I slip out of the market after 'em and head down the road. I look back. Michelangelo is spinning around like a top, trying to find the kids. Off in the woods, I bet the big boy is wondering what on earf he should do.

Jeanne and Jacob get around the bend in the road as quick as they can. But they don't slow. Jeanne keeps running, and she calls out to Jacob, "Faster!" She's lost her wits a bit, I fink. Everyone's scared of Red, Fat, and Wicked. But she seems particularly scared. I'm hurrying after 'em. They don't notice a fing.

Jacob calls out, "What about William?"

"We'll come back for him!"

Straight ahead on the road are six men. They got swords hanging from their belts. That tells me quite a bit. If you've got a sword and no horse, you're either a brig-and or a poor knight indeed.

Well, Jeanne must've seen it when I did, because she shouts, "Off the road!" She turns right, hard. She leaps over this mound of dirt that runs along the side of the way.

And she screams.

Jacob follows her—I don't know why. I see him try to stop himself once he clears the mound. Because that mound separates the road from the Oise River, don't it?

Jeanne and Jacob go tumbling, heels over head, into the river. Just—*skid, skid, crunch, SPLASH!* Just like that.

I been in that part of the Oise. Not some lovely stream that is. Reeks of manure and dead fish.

And it ain't shallow neither.

Jeanne is swimming, or trying to swim. But she don't know how. Who does? Mostly she's just flailing and shouting. Then Jacob plows right into her, from above, and they're grabbing each other, pulling each other down, swallowing water, grabbing each other's hair to stay above the surface. Drowning. That's what they're doing.

And then, I see this big knight—he's got a face like a shield, I'd say, just as flat and dumb—and he jumps down into the water, and it only comes up to his shoulders, and he's lifting 'em out of the river, up above his head, and they're still kicking and fighting.

He carries 'em up the bank and drops 'em—hard—in the dirt. They're flopping around, coughing and spluttering like fish.

Finally they regain themselves. And they look up.

And this skinny knight wif long blond hair and a face like a weasel is staring right down at them.

And he's grinning like the Devil himself.

The innkeeper puts a plate of cold pie down in front of the boy. The jongleur looks up at him and grins. "Well?" he says. "Weren't that worth a spot of pie?"

The innkeeper grunts. But I say, "Indeed it was. Was that all you saw?"

"Oh no!" he says, picking chunks of crust and meat up between his filthy fingers and shoveling them into his mouth. "I followed 'em, didn't I? A big muck like Red, Fat, and Wicked wants to find 'em! That could be worth some money, couldn't it?"

Jerome exclaims, "You would betray them? For money? That's despicable!"

"Now, now, I gotta earn a living, don't I? I don't have some fancy monastery, giving me food, do I?" He turns to the handsome man. "Nor do I have some fancy lord to give me the clothes on my back!" The man frowns at him. "No! I got to earn my keep! However I can! And if you were in my position, you'd do the very same fing."

He continues to eat his pie like he's afraid someone might steal it from him, one arm curled around the plate, the opposite hand shoveling food into his mouth. Then he says, "For a mug of strong ale, I'll tell you what happened next."

I hesitate. I don't like giving strong ale to children. That's what the weak ale is for—children and clerics.

The little nun says, "How about a nice cup of water?"

Everyone around the table makes a face. "You don't drink *water*, do you?" says the innkeeper.

"That's disgusting!" agrees Marie.

"Nor is it sanitary!" adds Aron.

The little nun shrugs. "If God made it, can it be so bad?"

Aron leans forward, raises one finger in front of his face, and says, "God made urine, too, Sister."

I order the jongleur a mug of the weak ale, the innkeeper brings it, and the boy goes on.

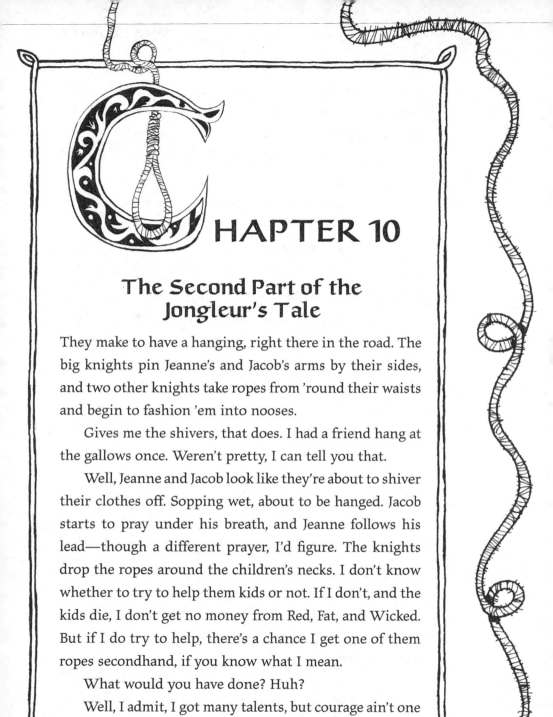

CHAPTER 10

The Second Part of the Jongleur's Tale

They make to have a hanging, right there in the road. The big knights pin Jeanne's and Jacob's arms by their sides, and two other knights take ropes from 'round their waists and begin to fashion 'em into nooses.

Gives me the shivers, that does. I had a friend hang at the gallows once. Weren't pretty, I can tell you that.

Well, Jeanne and Jacob look like they're about to shiver their clothes off. Sopping wet, about to be hanged. Jacob starts to pray under his breath, and Jeanne follows his lead—though a different prayer, I'd figure. The knights drop the ropes around the children's necks. I don't know whether to try to help them kids or not. If I don't, and the kids die, I don't get no money from Red, Fat, and Wicked. But if I do try to help, there's a chance I get one of them ropes secondhand, if you know what I mean.

What would you have done? Huh?

Well, I admit, I got many talents, but courage ain't one

of 'em. So I watch as the ropes get pulled tight around the kids' necks. They're praying hard now. I can hear 'em.

And then—they get yanked down the road.

The knights are walking, dragging the kids behind 'em like dogs.

Them ropes weren't nooses. They're leashes.

The knights lead the kids off the main road, onto a little way that crosses the Oise and heads west. I go that way, too, but it's too small a road for me to be following 'em. They'll get suspicious, won't they?

I hurry to catch up. Best place to hide is in plain sight. That's what I always say.

"Excuse me!" I call. "You going this way?"

One of 'em says, "Of course we are. Why would we take this road if we weren't?" He's got a lazy eye, and he's holding the rope that's tied to Jacob's neck.

"Well, mind if I come wif you? I'm going this way meself, and it's a lonely road."

"Shove off!" says the weasel-faced one. They all talk like rich boys. But rich boys who've been to the wars, you know? Not proper at all. But still rich. Know what I mean?

Anyway, I say I'll sing for my supper. The weasel don't want to hear it, but the other knights do. So I sing a bawdy song. One of the good ones, where all the bad words rhyme.

Jeanne turns red as a beet, and Jacob looks mighty uncomfortable, but the knights are laughing. Most of 'em, anyway. They decide to let me walk wif 'em. It's useful to know a dirty song or two, I always say.

So I've got my plan. Soon as I know where they're going, I'll double back and see if I can't get a few coin out of Red, Fat, and Wicked in exchange for information about the kids. Who, I gotta admit, I'm feeling bad for. Jacob is limping along, like he's in a lot of pain. Jeanne manages to loosen her noose a little, but when Jacob tries to do the same, the knight with the lazy eye yanks the rope so tight Jacob goes choking and staggering to his knees.

"Get up!" the knight growls, and he hoists Jacob to his feet by the rope.

Jeanne cries, "Stop it, you ugly Viking!" I expect her to get yanked by the throat for the insult, but the chubby knight who's got her rope just laughs.

I start to learn the knights' names—and give 'em nicknames in me head. Fabian the Weasel, Baldwin the Bald, Haye the Lazy-Eyed, Haye's chubby brother, Marmeluc, and Georges and Robert, who're bigger than mill wheels and twice as slow.

After some time walking, Marmeluc says, "What kind of prayer was that you were saying?"

Over his shoulder, Fabian the Weasel says, "Don't talk to the prisoners."

But Marmeluc ignores him. "It sounded Jewish," he says. But he don't say it mean like. He sounds—curious, I guess.

Jacob turns his head, ever so slightly, to clap an eye on Marmeluc, but he don't say nuffing.

After a moment, Marmeluc says, "Are you Jewish?"

Jacob looks like he's finking about what to say. And then, he kind of gives in. "Yeah, I am."

"Really?" says Marmeluc.

Jacob, real flat-like, replies, "Why would I lie about being Jewish?"

Suddenly, the rope around his neck is jerked hard, and Jacob's staggering around and coughing, grabbing his throat.

"Don't be clever with my brother," Haye snarls.

Marmeluc waits until Jacob recovers. Then he says, "So you don't believe in God?"

The Weasel glances over his shoulder at Marmeluc, and his look says, *What in God's name are you doing?*

Jacob—real carefully this time, and his voice all raspy now—says, "I do believe in God."

"You do not!" barks Haye. But he lets the rope hang limp.

Marmeluc says, "You pray to Jesus? Say the Creed?"

"No," says Jacob. "I don't believe in Jesus. But I believe in God."

"Jesus *is* God, you filthy heathen," Sir Fabian mutters, not even bothering to turn around.

But Marmeluc says, "How can you believe in God but not Jesus?" He sounds really curious now.

Jacob finks for a moment. I can tell he's scared—I can

smell his sweat. Scared sweat smells different. A knight's got him by the throat, and he's expected to debate feology. Course, that's how Jews are mostly expected to debate feology these days. Sad state of affairs, but true enough.

Jacob seems to have weighed his options carefully. The swords on the knights' belts are waggling all around him as we walk. He says, no more than a murmur, "You believe in the Trinity. The Father, the Son, and the Holy Spirit. I just believe in the Father."

Marmeluc asks, "Are there Jews who believe in other parts of the Trinity?"

His brother scowls at him and says, "What is wrong with you?"

But Marmeluc answers, "I've never talked to a Jew. I just want to know."

Jacob, warily, replies, "No. We just believe in the Father. That's what makes us Jews, I guess."

"Huh," says Marmeluc. Fabian looks at the other knights and rolls his eyes.

We make camp on the side of the road. The sun is touching the hills and spreading its red guts all over 'em.

Georges and Robert make a fire wif pine needles and sticks. The pine needles don't do nuffing but smoke, 'cause they're green. Like I said, slower than a mill wheel, those two are. Eventually, Baldwin gets it going.

The knights all tuck in to dried sausages they've had in their satchels. I offer to sing a song for some sausage,

but Fabian throws me the butt of one and tells me that's for *not* singing. I heard that joke a hundred times. I still fink it's funny though—'cause I get paid for not doing nuffing. Jeanne and Jacob, they don't get offered no food at all. They look as tired, hungry, and miserable as any two children I ever saw.

Eventually, we spread out on the ground to sleep. Except Marmeluc—he's gotta keep watch—and the kids, who stay by the fire, the ropes still dangling from their necks.

I lie down and pretend to sleep, because I don't want to lose those kids any more than the knights do. Besides, you hear lots of useful fings when people fink you're sleeping.

So Marmeluc and the kids are staring into the fire, and there's the sound of the crackling logs and the light of their burning orange cores. Away from the fire, the night is dark—clouds are covering the stars, and there ain't no moon. The night sounds get going—crickets, yes. But also wind in the faraway trees. And other sounds. Ones I don't know. Eerie sounds.

Around the fire, Jeanne and Jacob start to look over their shoulders. The wild beasts roam in the darkness. Wolf packs, starving bears just rising from their hibernation. And worse fings. Ghosts. Spirits. Draugrs, the blood-hungry undead. The sounds stand up the hair on my neck.

And then, suddenly, there's this wail. Long and high and thin. I would say it sounded like somefing dying—

but it's no fing that should live on this earf. Jeanne and Jacob sit straight up and stare out into the hills.

Jeanne says, "Sir Marmeluc, do you hear that?"

Marmeluc looks up at her across the fire. He don't look scared at all. He looks . . . sad. He nods. And then he whispers, "That's just Fabian. He cries in his sleep. We're all used to it now."

I can't believe what I'm hearing. The Weasel cries in his sleep?

Jacob looks like he don't believe that sound is just Fabian. He's glancing over his shoulders into the darkness, ready for the draugr to come get him. But Jeanne says, "So why don't you wake him?"

"Georges did the first time. Fabian beat him so bad for accusing him of crying that we never did it again."

"Fabian can beat up Georges?"

"Fabian is a scary man."

"So why does he cry, do you think?"

Marmeluc looks across the fire at the children. Then he does somefing very strange indeed.

He looks around the camp.

He calls the name of each knight in a whisper, one by one. No one stirs.

Then he stretches his back, rubs his hands togevver against the cold, looks out at the heavy curtain of darkness, and tells us a truly frightening tale.

"We were on Crusade. We set out with two hundred knights, under the command of Lord Montjoie, for the

Holy Land, to liberate it from the rule of the Saracen king. Spirits are high. We've been told that the Saracens are cowards and idiots, and that flying the banner of Christ, we cannot lose. We believe that." Marmeluc's face is lit from below by the smoldering campfire.

"Upon arrival, we march straight for Damascus, the first city we plan to liberate. We will liberate it, of course, by killing everyone inside. We lay siege to the city—and immediately, the Saracens turn the siege around on us. We are surrounded, pinned to the city walls. We are out-numbered and cut off from any escape route. Rather than fight us, though, they decided to let us starve. Cowards, maybe. But the only idiots there were the rich boys who'd left their comfortable French homes for this Hell.

"We starved for nearly a month. Soldiers were dying in every platoon. Lord Montjoie had a camp at the center, and he wasn't seen going in or out for weeks. There was a rumor that he was dying, or already dead. The earth there was so dry we couldn't properly bury the bodies of those who died of hunger or sickness—they'd stink from underground—so we took to burning them in our bonfires. The whole camp stunk of burning flesh. It was unbearable."

Sir Fabian's sobs are receding. They now sound like choking, or a bullfrog's croak.

"Eventually, seven of us decided to flee. We crept up to the edge of the camp one night and set out running. When we came to the enemy lines we crawled through the patches of darkness on our bellies. I've never been so scared in my life. But it was better than being stuck in that camp. By dawn, we were clear of the Saracen forces. At the time, I thought God Himself had guided our path. Now, I'm not so sure. We found a road that led north and followed it, trying to make our way back to France.

"The journey takes months by land. If you can go by ship from the Holy Land back to Venice, which is how we came, it's half the time. But we had no money for the passage. So Fabian decided we should, just temporarily, turn brigand. I fought him on it, I swear I did. But the rest of them agreed, and I couldn't very well survive out there alone, could I?"

The young knight looks at Jeanne, and then at Jacob, straight into their eyes, as if he really wanted them to agree. As if it would help, somehow.

And, bless their hearts, they nodded. He goes on:

"Right. So one morning, we hid among the rocks of a canyon, where the road from Jerusalem to Constantinople passed through. A few small groups went by. Fabian held us back.

"He's our leader. I don't know how that happened. Some people just talk and talk and everyone listens. Other people talk and no one does.

"Eventually a four-wheeler came through the canyon. Fabian signaled to us all. When the cart was abreast of us, we leapt out and cried, 'Jowls to the ground!' like real French brigands. Well, they didn't understand our words, but they

understood our swords well enough. They lay down on the road. We stepped over them as we made for the cart. Fabian threw open a side door. Inside were spices like you've never seen. Heaps of purple and orange in sacks. And dates— which are like prunes, but drier and sweeter. We took it all.

"And then . . ." Marmeluc sighs. It's the deepest, sad-dest sigh I ever heard. He says, "Fabian killed the men. Said they'd raise the alarm on us. I couldn't watch.

"Only once they were dead did we see that they wore the seal of the Knights Hospitalier. They're the ones who care for wounded Christians on Crusade. They devote their lives to it. Healing monks, is what they are. Barely knights at all. Healers of Christian soldiers, really.

"I was sick, right there on the side of the road to Con-stantinople."

He gets silent again. Looks as if he can still taste the sick in his mouth. Then he says, "We traded the cart and its contents for passage to Venice. When we got to France, our seventh companion, a knight called Guy-Francois, disappeared. That made us uneasy. We were right to be. When we returned to the es-tates where we had each grown up, we discovered that Guy-Francois had betrayed us. He'd come home and told of what we'd done and entered a monas-tery to repent. My father, Lord Marmeluc de Li-mors, a rich and powerful man, called me and my brother murderers. To our faces. I fell to my knees and begged him to listen, that it had been Fabian, not we, to kill the good Hospitaliers. He just raged louder. Now our littlest brother will inherit my father's lands. And I am forbidden from returning home ever again."

Fabian's crying has stopped now. The crickets are humming.

And then Marmeluc says, "I miss my mother."

The kids watch him chew on his lips and stare into the fire.

Finally Jacob says, "Is that why Fabian cries? Because he can't go home?"

And Marmeluc answers, "He has a twin sister. She would not speak to him when he returned. I believe he cries for his sister."

The next morning, everyone's a bit groggy, a bit surly, as men'll be of a morning. They pass around some sacks of vinegary wine to wash the funk from their mouths. I steal a sip wifout Fabian noticing.

We get out on the road, still heading west. As the sun climbs in the sky, we find ourselves among wide brown pastures. No one's talking much. Just watching the sheep cropping on the hillsides.

Which is how Haye spots it.

He leaves the road—he don't say why—and walks to the stone wall at the edge of the pasture. His brow's all furrowed and wrinkled up. I'm curious, ain't I? So I follow him.

We see the strangest fing. There's a deep cut in the earf. Not just in the dirt. Deeper. Into the stone below, like. And even the stone looks like it's been cut into—I tell you, it looks like claw marks to me. The biggest claw marks you ever saw. Beside it is a long track of burned grass.

Well, we're all staring at it, trying to figure out where it come from, what it could be, when Jeanne starts shaking like dice in a cup.

Jacob says, "Jeanne. Jeanne, are you okay?"

She don't answer.

"Jeanne!" he says again. "Jeanne!"

I look a little closer. Her teef are grinding in her head. Her neck looks like it's got tree roots running up and down it. Her arms are shaking. And then, she topples over like a tree cut down wif an axe. Luckily, Jacob catches her and eases her to the ground. She lies there, trembling and shaking like nuffing I've ever seen.

Fabian starts shouting, "What's going on? What is this?"

Jacob says, "I think she's having a fit."

Fabian gets down right beside Jeanne and starts yelling in her face. "Peasant! PEASANT! Get up! You're not fooling anyone!"

But she can't hear him any more than the stone wall can. That's clear as the morning.

He stands up. "Georges. You carry her the rest of the way to Lord Bertulf's if she won't walk herself."

"She don't look so good."

"She's fine. Carry her."

But Georges says, "This is weird. I don't like it."

Then, with no warning, Jeanne's body stops trembling and goes limp. We all see it. She's not faking it—I can tell. I've faked a number of medical conditions in my time. That weren't no fake.

Jacob gets right down close to her and says, "Jeanne, are you all right?"

She's heaving and sweating, like she's got a fever.

We're all staring at her. Baldwin in particular looks terrified.

"Did you see something?" Jacob asks.

Jeanne nods.

"What?"

When she finally speaks, it sounds like her breaf is being torn from her froat.

And all she can say is, "I saw a dragon."

Renard leans back on his stool. "That's it!"

"What? You can't stop now!" I say. "Was there a dragon? Did you see it?"

The jongleur looks at me like I'm insane. "You fink I stayed around after this girl says there's a *dragon* about? Are you out of your mind?"

Marie laughs.

"I knew where they was going now, didn't I? Didn't he say Lord Bertulf's? So what reason on God's green earf could you give for me for sticking around after hearing there's a dragon about?"

"So you believed she was having a vision? Foretelling the future?"

"What do *you* fink she was doing? Jigging a lark?"

"I don't know what that means. So you left to tell Michelangelo di Bologna. Did you find him?"

"Who—Red, Fat, and Wicked? I couldn't find him, could I? Big as a mountain he is, and I still couldn't find him."

"And would you really have told him where they were if you had?"

The jongleur sticks his tongue out. "Don't bring your morality around me. Morals is for people who's already got food. Sure I would have. And then I probably would have helped 'em bust out of prison before they was executed, wouldn't I? Because a friend alive is more valuable than an enemy dead, ain't he?"

The innkeeper pushes himself to his feet. "Yeah, that's about as far as my hospitality extends, Renard. Everybody check your purses. Renard, you want to stay, you can sleep in the stables."

"Look, I fink I've been a very sociable member of this little—"

The innkeeper grabs Renard by the arm, lifts him off the ground, and carries him to the door.

"It was a pleasure to meet you all, ladies and gentlemen!" the jongleur is shouting over the innkeeper's shoulder. "If we should meet again, I beg that you look kindly on a poor jongleur, and share some—"

He is thrown out into the darkness.

Aron the butcher says to me, "You believe this story? That she foretold a dragon? You think such things really exist?"

"I don't know."

And then, a figure approaches the table. He is tall and thin. He peers down from tiny round eyes over a long equine nose. "I can answer your question."

The man has the strangest accent. His *r*'s roll like hills.

I invite him to pull up a stool. He does. Even sitting, he's taller than any of us. His cheeks are so hollowed and pitted, he looks like he subsists entirely on turnips. He smells that way, too.

"I am Brother Geraldus Scotus—Gerald the Scot. I come from Aberdeen. Do you know Aberdeen?"

I've heard of it. The far north of the Isle of Britain. The farthest reaches of Christendom. This Gerald comes from the edge of the earth.

"I've traveled from the Hebrides, down the coast of England, across the Channel, to the Low Countries, and then followed a peripatetic path to this very place. Wherever I go, I write down what I see. I am making a chronicle of our times. I have seen many a strange thing. Strange beasts. Strange sights. Strange men. But never have I seen anything so strange as what I saw when I met these children you're asking about."

"What did you see?"

He smiled and sniffed through his huge red nostrils.

"My brothers and sisters, have you ever heard of the Dragon of the Deadly Farts? No? Then let me tell you."

CHAPTER 11

The Chronicler's Tale

I first met the children in the hall of Lord Bertulf and Lady Galbert-Bertulf.

Lord Bertulf, as you may know, is a great man. By that, I mean he's very chunky. He's about as round as he is tall. And he has no hair on him. Not anywhere. His eyebrows are bare, his head is bare, his cheeks are bare as a baby's bottom—but chubbier. He's not a great lord. He's not even really a middling lord. He's got an estate and a stone keep and a wall around his bailey—but the wall is made of wood and isn't all that high. He hails from Flanders, which means he has an accent even stranger than mine. His esses are like zeds, and his effs are like vees. He's a weird little man, if I'm to be honest with you. And I always am. It's my vocation.

His wife, Lady Galbert-Bertulf, is from a fine family here in the valley Oise. She is even shorter than her husband. She looks like a little vole, really. And she's very warm, and very kind. Until you threaten her money, that is. Then she shuts up like a clam, she does. And bites like a badger.

On the evening in question, I was sitting at their high table with them in their great hall. It is a low and musty place, with a dozen tables on a dirt floor and a raised dais with a moldy tapestry behind the high table.

Six dirty knights came striding in like they were the most important people in the world. Behind them, slinking like beaten cats, were two children. I noticed the red marks of ropes recently removed from their throats.

The lord and lady welcomed the knights warmly. Well, the lady did. Lord Bertulf just sat in his chair behind the table, like a stick of butter slowly melting.

"Come here! Come here!" the lady cried, leaping down from the dais and bustling from knight to knight. Then she swept Fabian up to the high table, asking him for his "report."

I saw the boy, Jacob, lean over to the girl, Jeanne. "Fabian works for *them*?" he whispered. "I thought he was working for Michelangelo di Bologna?" Jeanne also looked perplexed. Then she was grabbed by her arm, and Jacob was grabbed by his, and the knights took them to the nearest corner, out of earshot of Fabian and the Bertulfs. Jacob wrinkled his nose, and Jeanne covered her mouth. This was the corner where the lord and lady relieved themselves during dinners and banquets.

I watched from the floor as Bertulf and his wife

huddled with Sir Fabian. At first, the knight was talking and gesticulating, pointing at the two children. But then Lady Galbert-Bertulf took over and Fabian's eyes went wider and wider as she spoke. Finally he stood up like a bolt, toppling his bench over, staring at Jeanne and pointing. "She's a witch!" he's shouting. "A sorceress! A pagan witch!"

For Jeanne, the world stopped moving. I could see it in her face. Fabian was frozen for her, and his words were echoing, over and over, in her ears.

The bald knight was saying, "What is it, Fabian? What's happened?"

And Fabian answered, "There *is* a dragon..."

We stood on the ramparts of the keep, looking out between the stone crenellations at the bare trees and scarred hills of Bertulf's domain. The air was still and warm for early March. A yellow haze had descended on the horizon.

Lord Bertulf pointed at me with a finger like a butter churn. "You!" he barks, his accent more Flemish than French. "Tell vat you know of de dragon!"

The knights and the children, the lord and the lady, they all turn to me, and listen.

"Last month, I arrived from Scotland, looking to chronicle all that is weird and worthy of being written down. Soon after my arrival, I was told of a horrible beast that was terrorizing the people of Flanders.

"It was a wingless dragon, and they said it came

up out of the sea. That may be so, for it is black and sea-green and spattered with sharp white bumps like barnacles. It began by attacking small creatures— chickens and cats mostly. But it grew, and it grew. It moved on to sheep. Now it's so large it can kill and devour a bull in an afternoon. Nor does it only kill animals. It has killed many a brave knight who has tried to challenge it.

"At first, it killed with its teeth and its claws, which are large and deadly enough. But it has of late developed a new diabolical power. I first witnessed it in Burgundy. I had followed the beast there, chronicling its devastation. In Burgundy, the great knight Sir Ewan the Bold set out to fight the dragon. He was shimmering in his armor, his red crest shining like the rising sun. A group of us followed, intent to see the great champion bring down the beast. He discovered it in the ruins of a famous inn, the Ale and Cheese. The patrons and innkeeper were all scattered or dead, and the dragon was making quick work of the provision they'd left behind.

"Sir Ewan drove the dragon from the inn by setting the ruins ablaze. Then, in the pasture beyond, they fought. Sir Ewan spurred his horse and charged the beast. He leveled his lance, aiming right between the dragon's eyes. The dragon faced him—and then, in a moment of cowardice or treachery, he turned and expelled a great and thunderous fart.

"I must admit, we, the spectators, laughed at first. But when the wave of that fart hit brave Sir Ewan, he and his horse, his armor and his lance, all burst into flames. He screamed, and the dragon fled, and we stood powerless as Sir Ewan roasted in his own armor."

At that point, Jacob interrupted me.

"Wait. You're saying it kills people by *farting* on them?"

I nodded gravely.

"It has deadly farts?"

"Yes."

"Poisonous gas-passing?"

Jeanne muttered, "We get it, Jacob."

"Its farts are so smelly, you *burst into flames*?"

"I don't know why you find this so hard to believe."

"I don't know why you *don't* find this so hard to believe."

Lord Bertulf held up a flabby white hand. He turned to Jeanne. "All dis you foresaw, little vitch?"

Jeanne hesitated. She looked at me. Then little Jacob reached out and took her hand. She looked down, surprised. Now that I know more about Jacob, I understand why—I'd never seen a Jew and a Christian holding hands before, either.

But Jeanne seemed to take strength from it. She said, "I didn't foresee it all. But the dragon I did. Also, I foresaw a sickness in the land."

"Dere your magic fails you, little sorceress," Bertulf

replied. "Dere is no sickness here." He turned to Fabian. "Zo, vill you fight it?"

Fabian took a step back. "What? Fight it? You're joking."

"Vat, are you scared?"

"No," said Fabian, looking very scared indeed. "I just... why should I?"

"Dere vould be a great revard!"

"Great enough to buy me my life back?"

"Ach! Zo you are scared! I didn't tink dat you—"

A high, thin voice interrupted Lord Bertulf. "Jacob can fight it."

We all turned in the direction of the voice. It was Jeanne's.

"Vat did you say?"

"Jacob can fight it," the little girl said again.

"Wait... what?" Jacob demanded.

"You can."

"I can *what*?"

"You can defeat the dragon."

"That's ludicrous!" Lady Galbert-Bertulf exclaimed.

"Yes it is!" Jacob agreed.

"No it isn't. Just as I see the future, Jacob has powers of his own."

Jacob retracted his hand from Jeanne's.

"His abilities are far greater than mine."

"That's not tru—"

But Jeanne cut him off. "With my help, and the help

of these brave knights"—that description surprised Fabian and his comrades, I can tell you—"Jacob's magic can overcome the dragon."

"I find dis hard to belieff," Bertulf muttered.

"So do I," said Jacob.

"But," Jeanne said, "if we conquer the dragon, you've got to let us go free. We were peacefully on our way to see the abbot of Saint-Denis when we were unlawfully kidnapped by these... well... these brave knights."

Lord Bertulf squinted at Jeanne. "You vere on your vay to Saint-Denis?"

Jeanne nodded. Lord Bertulf's bare brow folded into a dozen furrows. At last, he said, "Fine. You rid us of dis dragon, and Zir Vabian and his knights vill escort you to Saint-Denis under my own banner."

"Wait!" said Jeanne. "Not to Michelangelo di Bologna. To Abbot Hubert, and no one else."

Bertulf studied Jeanne. He had never negotiated with a little girl before, much less a peasant girl. After a moment, he said, "Fine. As you vish."

"You swear?" Jeanne said.

"I svear," Bertulf replied.

"Wait," said Jacob. "*I'm* supposed to kill a *dragon*?"

"Shall I go on?" Gerald the Scot asks.

"YES!" we all cry at once.

"It's not easy to tell this story..."

"Please!" we all say. "Don't stop now!"

"...when I'm so thirsty," Gerald concludes.

We all laugh. And I say, "For God's sake, get him another drink! Now!"

The innkeeper obliges, and Gerald goes on.

HAPTER 12

The Second Part of the Chronicler's Tale

That night, we ate in the great hall of Lord Bertulf and Lady Galbert-Bertulf. It was a classic meal of the French lords. It started with boiled meats, moved on to grilled meats, continued with fried meats, and ended with cheese.

The lord and lady sat with Fabian at the high table. I wanted to learn more about the two children who were, supposedly, miracle workers, so I sat at a table near the front of the hall with them and the other knights.

I noticed right away that Jacob was very picky. The first dish was a boiled swan, head still attached, which he would not touch. Next was a grilled pig. He wouldn't eat that either. That's when I began to suspect that he was not a Christian, but a Jew. When a plate was brought filled with fried meats, he asked what was on it. The server did not know, and so he didn't eat that either.

Finally the cheese was served. It had a bright orange rind, and it came in small, round, flat-bottomed containers

of birch bark. These rounds were placed between every two diners. Jacob eagerly grabbed a rind of bread and went to dip it in the cheese—and then he reared back like he'd been slapped.

"What's wrong?" asked Jeanne.

"Ugh, it's putrid!"

Jeanne smelled it. "Blech! It's rotten!" She looked up, and saw that Marmeluc was about to dip his bread into the cheese. "Sir Marmeluc," she whispered urgently, "don't eat it! It's gone bad!"

Marmeluc cocked an eyebrow at her. Then, with a dash of theatricality, he took the bread, dipped it, and then lifted it, dripping with yellow, soupy cheese, to his mouth. He paused, inhaled the odor of the cheese deeply, and then popped it in his mouth. He closed his eyes and leaned his head back, chewing slowly. Jeanne and Jacob watched the performance in horror. Finally Marmeluc swallowed, and smiled, and leaned toward the children. "It's not rotten. It's Époisses. From Burgundy. The best cheese in the kingdom of France." He paused. His eyes became misty and distant. "Which probably means that it's the best cheese . . . in the world." He kept staring into the distance.

"*Maybe it's poison,*" Jeanne whispered. "*I think he's lost his mind.*"

Marmeluc straightened up and laughed. "*Not* eating that cheese would be insanity." He returned to the pile of bread ends and the goopy, pungent cheese.

Jeanne and Jacob leaned over their own stinking serving of the stuff. Jeanne poked it with her finger. It was soft and sticky, almost like honey. Disgusting, putrid honey. "You're not going to eat it?" Jacob asked her.

Jeanne stared at the cheese balefully. "On the one hand, I'm still hungry. On the other hand, it smells like my cow's butt."

"You could just eat bread. I'm just going to eat bread."

Jeanne looked again at Marmeluc. He and his brother had nearly finished their cheese and were now scraping their wooden container with the stale rinds of bread.

How could they be enjoying it so much? Jeanne wondered. She was curious. And, like she said, still hungry.

So, facing the cheese like a condemned man faces the gallows, Jeanne reached for a crust. She brought it to the goopy surface of the cheese. She touched the bread to the orange rind. A dab of white, surrounded by orange, appeared on the bread.

"Oh, come on!" said Marmeluc, catching sight of her. "Are you *afraid* of *cheese*?"

Jeanne's nostrils flared like a bull's. "No!" she snapped. She drove her bread to the bottom of the container and scooped up a drooping, goopy mound of it. She brought it to her face. Jacob watched in horror. She tore off a huge bite.

Marmeluc and Haye leaned over to see.

As Jeanne chewed, tears formed at the corners of her eyes. Her nose began to run.

"What's it like?" Jacob asked.

Still chewing, Jeanne said, "It tastes like being punched in the face."

Haye laughed. Marmeluc waved a hand at her dismissively.

"Also," she went on, still chewing with her mouth open, "feet." Haye slapped the table, grinning. Jeanne kept chewing. "And—and butter."

Marmeluc raised an eyebrow. Jacob stared.

"Feet and butter . . . and, and grass," Jeanne said, chewing, chewing, chewing. "Now it tastes like a cow pasture . . . a sunny cow pasture."

"Wait . . . really?" said Jacob.

Jeanne was nodding. Tears were now streaming down her face. Then she swallowed.

She looked at Marmeluc.

We awaited her verdict in silence.

Finally she announced, "I have never tasted anything more disgusting in my entire life."

Haye chuckled. Marmeluc rolled his eyes.

"I think I liked it," she added.

Marmeluc's scowl transformed into a smile.

Jacob took a piece of bread and reluctantly reached for the cheese. Jeanne popped the rest of the Époisses-coated crust into her mouth.

As she chewed, she said, "You know what it really tastes like?"

Jacob's hand hovered over the cheese. "What?" he asked.

"It tastes like life."

"What?"

"Rotten and strange and rich and way, way too strong."

Jacob was looking between Jeanne and the soupy cheese. Then he said, "I've had enough life these last three days. I'm sticking to the bread."

Marmeluc was gazing across the table at Jeanne. When he finally looked away, he caught me watching him. He said, "That is some kid."

And you know what? He was right.

The next morning, the six knights and the two children crouched in a circle at the edge of Lord Bertulf's wood. I was there, too—for whether these children conquered the dragon or, as was much more likely, died trying, I would not miss it for all of Christendom. It would make a great chapter for my chronicle.

Sir Baldwin the Bald turned to his leader, Sir Fabian, and said, "So, what's the plan?"

Fabian shrugged his bony shoulders. "This is the girl's show, not mine. We just have to make sure the kids don't run away. Though I would like to know how exactly she plans to fight a dragon."

So we all looked to Jeanne.

But she merely said, "Jacob's going to defeat it."

"Why do you keep saying that?" Jacob demanded.

She smiled slyly. "Remember when I said there was a sickness in the land?"

"You were wrong there, little peasant." Fabian smirked.

"No, I wasn't," Jeanne rejoined. "There is a sickness. It's in the dragon."

Jacob furrowed his brow. His dark curls fell into his eyes.

Jeanne turned to me. "Didn't you say that the farts were a 'diabolical new development' or something?"

"Indeed, they are."

Marmeluc cut in. "You know, Baldwin's *always* had the power of deadly farts."

All the knights laughed except Baldwin, who said, "You've been waiting on that joke all day, haven't you?"

"Couldn't have made it in front of the lord and lady, could I?"

Baldwin threw a fistful of dirt at Marmeluc. The knights laughed harder. Jeanne watched them and, to my surprise, she was grinning, too.

But Jacob was staring into the dirt, his lips pursed. The knights fell quiet. They watched him, half skeptical, half wondering whether this little Jewish boy was as strange and potent as his companion. Finally he said, "I can't cure it until I see it."

Fabian grunted. "Seems plain, then. We gotta attract the dragon, and then make it—well, fart." He hesitated, and then he looked to Jeanne. "Right?"

The little peasant girl forced herself not to smile. Fabian was asking *her*? She just said, "Right."

Fabian began ordering people about. He sent Baldwin

and Haye to go get bait for the dragon. Then he and Georges and Robert scouted out trees to hide in. Jacob went off on his own, looking for I don't know what. Marmeluc watched him. I stayed with Jeanne.

The tree was found, and Jacob returned; Baldwin and Haye came back with an old, lame sheep—half dead already, it seemed to me.

The idea was to scare the beast, because that's when it unleashed its diabolical flatulence. So while everyone climbed up the tree, two knights were to stay hidden near the sheep and, when the dragon came, jump out and startle it. This was by far the most dangerous task. But the dragon had adopted the strategy of running away, leaving its weapon hanging in the air behind it. We figured that if the knights leapt out and startled it, and then immediately dove back into hiding, they would survive unscathed. Probably.

As you might imagine, though, no one wanted that task. So Fabian took six long pieces of dried grass, cut them to the same length with his sword, and then cut two of them shorter. Then he gripped them in his fist so the short ones looked like all the rest. The knights drew. Marmeluc and Haye got the short straws. "The brothers!" cried Sir Fabian.

The other knights looked very relieved. But Jeanne grabbed Marmeluc by his sleeve. He crouched down beside her. She whispered, "Be careful." All the knights were staring. Marmeluc didn't care.

He said, "I will be. Thank you."

And he followed his brother into a thick copse of fern and gorse.

We all clambered up into the chosen tree, straddling the big, damp branches. Beneath us, the old sheep, her wool in dirty clumps, cropped wild herbs.

The day was gray but not cold. Time passed.

And then, Jacob pointed skyward. I followed the line of his finger. There, circling above us, were the scavenging birds. Ravens and vultures. Circling. Circling above our heads.

The hair on my neck stood on end. I whispered, "I think the dragon is near."

Fabian, sitting with his back against the oak's trunk, put two fingers in his mouth and whistled, long and low. After a moment, the whistle came back through the trees.

I saw Jeanne shift her weight, trying to get a better view of the clearing and the old ewe. She put her hand on the wet bark and lifted her leg up over the branch—and lost her balance. I saw her, like an instant frozen in time, her leg in the air, her body angling out away from the branch, her face frozen in surprise—and then she went tumbling right out of the tree.

Jacob shouted. She hit the ground with a thud. Luckily, the earth was soft, for the day was wet.

"Someone go get her!" I cried. "Before—"

But it was too late. Out of the nearby trees came the dragon.

. . .

He's bigger than I'd remembered. His body is a patchwork of black skin like a seal's and green and blue scales like a snake's. His legs jut out from his body at right angles. His eyes are a sickly yellow. And his lips are curled back around teeth as long as carving knives.

He had been coming for the ewe. But the sheep runs around to the other side of the tree, and Jeanne is just sitting there.

The dragon sees her. He stops. He stares.

Jeanne decides to slide backward away from him.

Not smart.

In an instant, the dragon has bounded across the turf. His huge eyes are within a finger's length of hers. He sniffs at her. We can smell him from where we sit. The stench is awful. Unbearable.

The dragon's teeth part, and a long, lavender tongue slithers toward Jeanne. It explores her face, traces her chin, her jaw, to her ear, across her cheek.

I shudder just to see it.

The dragon's mouth opens wider, and Jeanne cannot move back, cannot go left, cannot go right. The dragon has turned his head, and his teeth are on either side of her neck.

"*BLAR!*" someone screams.

Marmeluc and Haye leap out of the foliage. "*BLAR! BLAR! BLAR!*" they shout, brandishing their swords above their heads. "*BLARRRR!*"

The dragon is terrified. He snaps his jaws shut—just

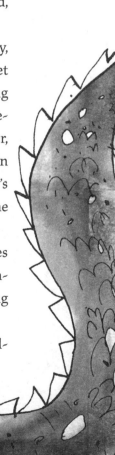

shy of little Jeanne's neck. He flips around, lashing his fleshy tail at the knights, and then darts into the trees from which he's come.

"Watch out!" screams Jacob. Too late. Marmeluc and Jeanne have both dived to the side. But Haye is standing there, brandishing his sword and screaming, *"BLAR!"* Which is when the fart hits him.

For an instant, he smells it. I know, because I see his eyes go wide with shock and his face begin to contort in utter, stomach-wrenching disgust—and then the flames leap to life all over his body.

He lets out a horrible scream and falls to the ground, fire consuming his flesh.

"Roll!" Marmeluc cries. Jeanne is on her feet already, sprinting toward Haye. The knight writhes on the wet earth, the flames enveloping him like a dancing, burning blanket. Jeanne plants her shoulder into his side and begins rolling him over. Marmeluc arrives an instant later, his tunic already half over his head. One end is caught in his belt. He yanks and yanks and finally it's free and he's smothering Haye with it, and he and Jeanne beat at the flames through the damp wool of the tunic.

We're all at Haye's side a moment later. The flames are gone, but now, suffusing the clearing is the sickening smell of the dragon's fart—and the more frightening smell of charred skin, hair, and flesh.

Jacob has leaves in his shirt—that's what he was collecting. He thrusts them at the knights. "Chew this!"

"We're not the wounded!" Fabian barks.

Jacob ignores him. "Chew it and spit it into my hands! Now!"

The knights hesitate. For just a moment. And then Fabian—yes, Fabian—grabs a handful of leaf and shoves it into his mouth. He winces at the taste, but he's working his yellow-bearded jaws until the leaf begins to break down. We all follow his example. Jacob runs to a nearby tree and begins pulling up the moss at its base. "Jeanne, help!" he cries. So she does.

They carry armfuls of mossy soil back to Haye, whose moans are dying now. "Spit it out! Here!" Jacob commands the knights, holding out his hands. So the knights disgorge the bitter leaf, black with saliva, into Jacob's small palms. "Take off the tunic!" Jacob cries. Marmeluc obliges, revealing charred flesh and clothing burnt into Haye's skin. Georges turns away to be sick. But Jacob sets his jaw and begins smearing the wet pulp onto Haye's burns. The moaning starts up again.

"You're hurting him!" Marmeluc cries.

"I have to!" Jacob barks back. He smears the masticated leaf all over Haye's body, and then packs it with mossy soil. He steps back, takes a deep breath, and wipes his brow. Finally he kneels and prays.

The words are strange, but soothing somehow. To all of us.

After a little while, Jacob rises.

We all stare at him.

"Now what?" Marmeluc asks.

"Now we lure the dragon back."

"*What?*" we all say at once.

"Why?" Jeanne wants to know.

And Jacob says, "I know how to cure it."

We moved Haye to a secluded bank by a nearby brook. Marmeluc tended to him, cupping cool water into his unmoving mouth. Jacob searched in the shade of the ferns for something.

Meanwhile, Georges and Robert pulled the old ewe back into the clearing.

Jacob returned from his search, apparently satisfied. He said a prayer over the ewe, a prayer of sacrifice, and then asked Fabian to slaughter it. Once that was done, he told Fabian to poke holes in the sheep's flesh. Finally Jacob revealed what he had been searching for this time: foxglove buds, small and round like purple fists. He poked them into the puncture wounds, like rosemary into a chicken.

We found a new tree to hide in, far away from Marmeluc and his brother. Georges and Robert laid the sheep carcass at the base of the tree.

"No need to ambush it this time," Jacob told us.

We clambered up onto a high, wet branch. The cold had made all our noses red. I turned to Jeanne, but before I could speak she said, "Don't worry. I'm not letting go."

We waited and waited and waited. Georges and Robert,

sitting beside each other on the thick branch, began to thumb-joust. The sun sank in the sky. The wet began to seep into our bones. Fabian put his fingers in his mouth and whistled.

No answer.

I caught my breath.

And then, from a great distance, two whistles came in answer. I exhaled. Marmeluc's sign. All was well.

Until it wasn't. Baldwin pointed to the sky. The vultures and crows were gathering. The birds always know.

Indeed, not long after, the dragon reappeared. He slunk stealthily from the shade, as if he were as afraid as we were. He looked around—though not up, thankfully. When he felt it was safe, the dragon tore at the sheep's flesh with his teeth, leaning his head back and coaxing the meat down his gullet. He tore again and again at the stomach, until the soft innards of the sheep rolled out onto the green earth. The beast buried his head in the ewe's soft underbelly, periodically coming up for air, his black-and-green face drenched in the sheep's blood.

And then, he coughed. He coughed again. Jacob reached out for Jeanne's hand, and she gave it to him. The dragon coughed again. Its gorge started working, back and forth, back and forth, like a cat trying to cough up a hairball. And then, it opened its jaws and unleashed a mass of chewed sheep flesh onto the forest floor. We all covered our noses and mouths as quickly as we could. The smell was horrific.

Jacob was the only one not to cover his face. He just watched.

The dragon raised his head. Toward us.

I made ready to jump from the tree.

But he didn't seem to see us.

His eyelids drooped, his breath became labored. He began limping around the clearing. Suddenly, he convulsed again and let go a long, goopy train of yellow liquid from his throat. The liquid poured and poured onto the green ground. The dragon pulled himself backward along the grass, letting the yellow fluid flow in a long, viscous trail.

I nearly threw up right then. But I held it in as if my life depended on it. Because it very well might have. It's not often your life depends on not throwing up. But this was such a time.

The stench became worse and worse. We cupped our hands over our mouths—even Jacob now—and tried not to pass out.

Finally the dragon was spent. He collapsed to the ground, heaving, surrounded by a long, thick trail of yellow vomit.

"Give him a while," Jacob whispered.

We did. We waited. Baldwin's head was between his legs to prevent himself from throwing up or passing out. Fabian pinched his rat-like nose so hard it turned purple. Georges and Robert had covered their faces with their shirts.

But at last, Jacob said, "On the count of three, scream as loud as you can."

Baldwin said groggily, "That shouldn't be too hard."

Jacob whispered, *"One . . . two . . . three!"*

The scream shook the birds from the trees and chased the scavengers from the sky.

The dragon leapt to his feet, spun around a few times, and then dashed from the clearing. Behind him, a tiny burst of fart squirted out. A twig caught the brunt of it, burst into weak flame, and then the flame died.

The clearing lay quiet and still and completely putrid.

"What just happened?" I asked.

Jacob said, "I cured the dragon. No more deadly farts."

"Why not?"

"See all that yellow goop down there?"

We all nodded—while trying not to actually look at it.

"That's Époisses."

Then we did all look. I was still confused.

"When I first smelled the dragon, I recognized it right away. It smelled like old, digested cheese. And didn't you say the deadly farting began when it passed through Burgundy? After attacking that inn? Cheese creates bile in some people. Makes them spend all night squatting on the dung heap. My mom is like that."

"Does she fart fire, too?" Jeanne asked. We all laughed. Except for Georges and Robert, who actually wanted to know.

"So the dragon was just allergic to cheese?" I said.

Jacob shrugged. "Something like that."

We climbed out of the tree, gingerly avoided the dragon-vomit, and made our way back to Marmeluc and Haye. "Look!" Marmeluc cried as we approached. "Look at him!" Marmeluc had taken off the moss and the leaves and washed his brother in cool water. The burns had healed, leaving faint, spidery scars across Haye's skin. Haye was sleeping peacefully, his eyelids fluttering, his chest rising and falling. Marmeluc rose to his feet and took Jacob's hand. "You cured him! Not a half a day's passed, and he's . . . he's totally cured!"

Jacob stared at Haye, as if he were a little surprised himself. Finally he said, "God cured him. God made the plants and gave them their magic. I just used them."

We all looked at Jacob in silence. After a moment, Marmeluc said, "Do you think God told you about the dragon, Jeanne?"

Jeanne shrugged. "Maybe."

And then Sir Marmeluc did something very surprising indeed. He fell to one knee. He bowed his head and crossed himself. "Bless us," he said.

The other knights looked at one another. Then they looked to Haye, healed of the burns that should have killed him. Baldwin knelt next. "Bless us, please." Georges and Robert did as Baldwin did, crossing themselves. I knelt, too. Finally even Fabian fell to one knee.

"Bless us, Holy Ones," we all said gruffly, earnestly. "Bless us."

Jeanne and Jacob stood in the midst of the kneeling knights. Utterly bewildered.

———————

Suddenly, I am more interested than I have been throughout this entire long, interesting evening. "You asked them to bless you?" I say. "Why would you do that?"

"It's pretty obvious, isn't it? Jacob healed a man who should have burned to death! Jeanne saw the future!"

"And . . . ?"

"Well, if that doesn't make them saints, I don't know what they are!"

I lean back on my stool and cross my arms. "You think they're saints. Touched by God, doing His work on earth through miracles that mere mortals are not capable of?"

"What else could they be?"

I nod. "What else, indeed? What else, indeed . . ."

Gerald is looking at me. He is clearly uncomfortable. I can have that effect on people. When I want to.

"Please," I say very quietly. "Go on."

Gerald clears his throat, looks at me one more time, and then decides that he should do what I say.

"That very night, we were attacked."

CHAPTER 13

The Third Part of the Chronicler's Tale

After the vanquishing of the dragon, there was a feast in the great hall. Jacob and Jeanne and all the knights and I were the guests of honor, and we sat with the lord and lady at the high table.

Over dinner, Bertulf admitted that the children had earned their safe passage to Saint-Denis.

"And we will *not* be turned over to Michelangelo di Bologna?" Jeanne confirmed.

Bertulf looked at us for a while, as if considering. Then he nodded his bald, fat head. "I zvear it."

I swore, too. "I will personally escort you to the good Abbot Hubert, whose piety and wisdom is known even as far as Aberdeen. And the Red, Fat, Wicked Monk shall not touch a hair on your heads!" The children were very grateful.

If only they had known.

The hall was lit with dozens of torches, dancing and

fluttering, casting strange shadows over the hundred feasters, either revealing their true nature or concealing it—one can never tell. A grandmother of a petty knight, an ugly woman with a crooked nose, seemed stately and beautiful in the torches' strange light. A handsome man, a traveling preacher with a wide, white smile, seemed cruel and frightening in the same flickering glow.

Servants appeared and brought rabbit pie, which was delicious. After, though, came out little rounds of cheese. Époisses. We all gagged and pushed it away from us as fast as we could. I was sure Georges was going to be sick, right up there on the dais.

After the cheese was—mercifully—taken away, Lord Bertulf lifted himself to his feet.

"Oyez!" he cried. "Hear ye!"

The hall fell quiet.

"I hope you have eaten vell?" he announced.

The question was answered with a mix of halfhearted cheers and more than a few grumbles. Lord Bertulf was a miser. Only the tables in the front of the hall had gotten rabbit pie. The rest had just pie, with no rabbit inside— despite what the servers were calling it. Lord Bertulf smiled and put his hands on his enormous belly. If his guests had been satisfied, he would have known his cook had been too generous.

"I vill now accept petitions and reqvests. If dere are any grievances, I shall hear dem." A servant brought a long candle and set it beside Lord Bertulf and handed him a flame. "I shall light dis candle. Ven dere is no tallow left, the period for grievances shall end. Then, ve shall have song!" Some scattered cheers for that. But mostly there was a rush to form a long line by one of the wooden walls.

And so began the most boring part of the evening, when landholders accused one another of moving boundary stones, peasants complained of their neighbors stealing their lambs, and knights demanded satisfaction of one another for imagined and exaggerated insults. The children put their arms on the table and their cheeks on their arms and watched the petitioners file by. I wondered if they were falling asleep.

Lord Bertulf rarely let his tenants and vassals finish their claims before announcing his judgment. His wife whispered in his ear and twice forced him to change his verdict when she thought he was being too generous. Her bright eyes shone exactly as brightly, I guessed, as her money box.

Then, as the tallow dwindled and the flame began to gutter in the wet wax of the candle, a hunchback approached the dais. Everyone quieted to see this lump of rags, shuffling forward, his weight leaning on a gnarled stick, his legs bent like bows and caked with mud.

"Vat business do you have in my hall?" Bertulf bellowed. "I don't give alms but on holy days! And never in my hall! Begone, you pile of vilth! Knights! Eject him!"

Sir Fabian and his crew stood up. Baldwin jumped over the table and approached the beggar from behind.

But before he could arrive, the hunchback spoke, his voice strange and high.

"You have something that is not yours," the hunchback intoned. "Return it, and I shall leave your august presence."

The people in the hall grew quiet, tense.

"*I* have something dat belongs to *you*?" Lord Bertulf demanded. "How dare you imply zuch a ting!"

Lady Galbert-Bertulf intervened. "Let him say what it is, my dear." Her eyes were shining cold and hard. "What do you claim is not rightfully ours, beggar?"

Suddenly, the hunchback seemed to erupt. He doubled in height, and from his back sprung a missile of fur and teeth. "JEANNE AND JACOB!" the former hunchback bellowed. And in the time it took for the faces of the lord and lady and all the knights to transform from suspicion to surprise, the boy called William had picked up his walking stick, spun, and smashed Baldwin in the face.

The missile of fur and teeth—once the beggar's hump—was Gwenforte, of course. She had bounded over the knights' table and grabbed Robert by the collar of his shirt.

"Knights!" Lord Bertulf screamed.

"Mercy!" Lady Galbert-Bertulf cried.

"Get him!" Sir Fabian bellowed.

"Stop!" Jeanne and Jacob both shouted.

But since everyone was hollering at the same time, no one heard anything, and Fabian, Haye, and Georges

rushed at William, while Robert struggled with Gwenforte, Baldwin lay unconscious on the ground, and Marmeluc stared, stunned. William picked up a table—yes,
an entire table, I saw it with my own eyes—and began
swinging it over his head. Dirty plates and goblets went
crashing to the floor. So did Lord Bertulf, who fell flat on
his face and tried to scramble to the back of the dais. Lady
Galbert-Bertulf grabbed a knife in each hand, leapt up on
her chair, and let loose a high, savage battle cry. There
were concentric circles of madness radiating out into
the hall. Knights and courtiers charging to the front,
ladies and children either hiding below tables or standing
on them to get a better view, a troupe of jongleurs (the
now-superfluous entertainment for the evening) grabbing as many pewter serving plates as they could carry
and running for the doors.

But up at the front, Jeanne wasted no time. She stood
up, planted her foot on her stool, leapt onto a table, and
launched her entire body at William.

The knights, their swords drawn, saw her and froze.
William, his back to her, the table raised above his head,
felt her before he saw her. She crashed into his back and
wrapped her arms around his neck. William staggered,
trying to spin and strike whatever was on his back with
the table, when he heard Jeanne shouting directly in his
ear. "Stop! They're our friends! Stop!"

William stopped. He looked at the knights, swords
drawn, not moving.

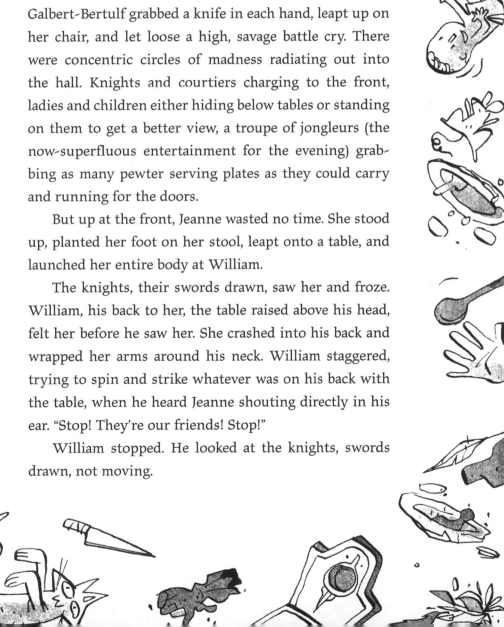

The more distant circles of the hall kept up their con-vulsions, but the central one had altogether frozen. Lord Bertulf (from the floor) and Lady Galbert-Bertulf (from atop the chair) and I (crouching behind the table, I must admit) and Jacob (standing behind the table) and the knights (stock-still) and even Gwenforte (standing above Robert, his collar in her mouth) all looked at William.

"Say you're sorry," Jeanne told him.

So William said, "I'm sorry."

"Put down the table."

William dropped the table. A leg broke, and the table lurched and toppled onto its side.

Jeanne, still clinging to his back, said, "Turn around and kneel." William did so, turning his smaller friend with him like a rucksack.

"Lord Bertulf, Lady Galbert-Bertulf," Jeanne intoned, "may I introduce our friend William. And also Gwenforte the greyhound."

To which there was absolutely nothing to say.

The next day, I accompanied the children and the knights—and Gwenforte the greyhound—on the day's journey to Saint-Denis. William recounted to us how Gwenforte had tracked Jeanne and Jacob all the way to Bertulf's hall—for which the dog got many pats on the back and scratches behind the ears. They told William of the farting dragon, and he laughed so loud the hills echoed. But after the story, I saw how he looked at them. Like he was worried that they had created some sort of bond that he could never break into. I could see it all over his face. And, if I had to guess, I'd say it was an old thought, formed over years of exclusion by the other oblates. I was an oblate once myself. I know how they are.

The mind is like a muddy road. Two ruts run down its center, from all the carts that have passed that way. No matter how many carts try to roll alongside the ruts, to stay out of the mud, sooner or later, a turn here or a jolt there will send them down into the ruts for good. Just so is the mind. As hard as we try to keep our thoughts out of the old ways, the old patterns, the old ruts, any little jog or jerk will send them right back down into the mud. So it was, I imagined, with William.

As we approached the town of Saint-Denis, the road widened, the traffic increased, and I saw Jacob becoming increasingly nervous.

He said, "I'm not going to the abbey. I've got to find my parents. They're probably worried to death about me."

For a moment, neither William nor Jeanne spoke. The road was very quiet.

At last, William said, "Jacob, do you *know* that your parents escaped the fire?"

Jacob's face was tight. His nostrils flared. "They escaped," he said. "They'll be waiting for me at my cousin Yehuda's. My mother said so."

William said, "Yehuda, the rabbi?"

Jacob stopped. He passed his sleeve violently across his eyes as he turned to William. "You know him?"

"*You* know him? Rabbi Yehuda is your *cousin*?" William asked.

"My mom's cousin. I've never met him, actually."

"Who's Rabbi . . . You-hoo-doo?" Jeanne wanted to know.

"Rabbi Yehuda. A famous heathen," William said. "His arguments blind the eyes of good Christians with tricks of the Devil."

Jacob glared up at him. "You mean he's a Jewish writer."

"Correct."

"He's very famous."

"Notorious."

"Wise." Jacob's voice was rising.

"Wicked." So was William's.

Gwenforte started to growl at the boys.

"Learned." Jacob's face was getting red.

"In the ways of the Evil One!" William bellowed. Gwenforte barked at them.

"His writing is beautiful!" Jacob bellowed back.

William paused. "Yes, that's true."

Jacob looked surprised. The big boy shrugged. Then he smiled. "Brother Jerome knows Hebrew. He's translated it. Rabbi Yehuda writes more beautifully than any living author, I think."

Jacob gazed up at the giant oblate. "Well, you might be an idolater," Jacob said at last. "But at least you have good taste."

And Jeanne laughed.

Gwenforte stared between the two boys. She barked, as if to say, *Now cut it out!* Jacob bent down and started rubbing her head.

Jeanne said to him, "Come with us. Let's stay together. You come to the monastery. How long could that take? Then we can go together and find your parents."

Jacob rubbed Gwenforte's head harder.

"We'll be there before supper," William added.

Finally Jacob murmured, "All right. I'll come with you, and then you'll come with me."

"Of course," said Jeanne.

"Of course," agreed William.

"Thank you." Jacob nodded.

Jeanne reached out and took her friend's hand.

I saw William notice it—and wince.

And then Jeanne reached out and took William's hand.

The wince turned into a smile.

Finally William reached out and took hold of one of Gwenforte's ears. We all laughed. But the dog shook her head and gave William a look that said, *Play with me or don't, but leave my ears alone.*

We began to climb a gentle slope. I slowed my pace, so that I might say to the children, "Sir Fabian and his men will escort us as far as the gates of Saint-Denis. Beyond that, armed men may not go." And then, very gravely, I said, "You must stay close to me. Michelangelo may be there. He is the prior of the abbey, after all."

"I don't understand it," said Jeanne. "Why would the good Abbot Hubert have wicked Michelangelo di Bologna as his prior?"

"Don't you know what they say? Keep your friends close—and your enemies closer. Hubert keeps a watchful eye on Michelangelo. Still, do *not* leave my side until we are in the presence of Abbot Hubert."

William said, "Thank you, Brother Gerald."

"And remember, Hubert is a serious man. More pious than anyone I have ever met. Do not joke with him or be flippant. Be straightforward. Be honest. So he will be with you. And there it is."

The children looked up—and there it stood. Saint-Denis. The first and most holy of the new wave of monumental churches. The building that all the great cathedrals—Notre Dame, Chartres, Rouen—are modeled after. The sun glinted off its black roof. Spreading out around it was the town of Saint-Denis, which was larger than any town the children had ever seen. It bustled and yelped and crackled and rumbled. For a moment, the children stood there and marveled. And then, they took off running down the hill. The knights and I had to jog after them, laughing all the way.

We came into the town, among the two-story wooden buildings lining the narrow muddy lanes. Jeanne and Jacob kept commenting on how they had built one house on *top* of another. William had seen

two-story buildings made of stone in his monastery. But two stories of wood and mud? That impressed him, too.

Merchants and craftsmen leaned out of their windows or strolled by with their fat, pretty wives, clad in richly dyed wool.

"Are these lords and ladies?" Jeanne whispered.

"No," I said. "Just burghers. They live in towns and give their goods and labor to anyone who will pay them."

"Where are their yards? Their farms? And do they work the fields dressed like that?"

"They don't have farms, and they don't work the fields."

"Where do they get their food?"

"They buy it."

"All of it?"

"Yes."

"How rich do you have to be," murmured Jeanne, "to be able to afford to buy *all* your food?"

Jacob, meanwhile, was scouring the tiny alleys that ran between the tall wooden houses.

William noticed. "Any Jews at all?"

"They must be somewhere," Jacob replied, his voice tight.

And then, we were at the gates—and it was time to say good-bye to the knights.

Marmeluc reached out his hand to Jacob, and they grasped wrists. It was sign of great respect. He did the same for William. Finally Jeanne approached Marmeluc and curtsied. He pulled her in for an embrace—which surprised us all.

"Be careful, little one," he said.

Jeanne looked up at him. "Don't worry. We'll see each other again."

Marmeluc's eyes went wide. "Did you have another vision?"

She laughed. "No. I just have a feeling."

"Well, I won't doubt you. Never again."

The children turned and bowed to the rest of the knights. Jeanne said, "Thank you for not killing us." We all laughed.

And then we passed into the grounds of the Abbey Church of Saint-Denis, the domain of Abbot Hubert, and his prior, Michelangelo di Bologna.

We passed under the iron teeth of the gate. The children marveled at the great, wide bailey, where horses were being led to stables. Then they saw the facade of the huge church, and their mouths dropped open even farther. It is one of the great sights of Christendom— hundreds of thousands of stones, perfectly hewn and fit together, shimmering in the sun like a waterfall on a cliff face. But we had no time to gape, for I did not know where our enemy was—and indeed, I was right to worry.

"Follow me," I said, "keep the dog close, and go as quickly as you can."

I hurried them forward, past the refectory, the in-
firmary, the stairwell to the crypt. Into the small cloister, through a hallway to the large cloister. Faster and
faster we walked. Every brother I saw coming from a
doorway or walking up a stair I thought, at first, was
Michelangelo.

The children, too, were peering at the black-robed,
hooded men praying or carrying books—hoping that if
the wicked monk himself were here, at least we would
see him before he saw us.

I felt a tug on my sleeve. I turned. Jeanne was pointing.

Across the great cloister, a mountain of flesh, with
red hair and bristling whiskers and reddish eyes, strode
along with an air of lazy importance, his head thrown
back, his whiskers twitching, his eyes roving over the
faces of the praying monks as if he owned them. As if
they were praying to *him*.

We all stopped. I don't know why. There is something about that man's power that makes one stop and
stare.

And as we stared, his gaze crossed the cloister. His
great body came to a halt. He squinted past the bare trees
in the cloister garden, trying to penetrate the shadows of
the columns where we stood.

And then he stepped from the covered walkway onto
the grass. His walk was no longer lazy. It was vigorous.
And fast. Very fast.

We stood as still as the columns that had not hidden us.

When Michelangelo was halfway across the cloister, I came to my senses. "Run, children! RUN!"

They took off. Michelangelo di Bologna looked surprised, as if he could not believe someone would *dare* run from *him*. Then he began to run, too, and I would not be lying to tell you that the ground actually shook with each footfall.

I turned and sprinted after the children, and an instant later I was pushing ahead of them, to lead the way. We turned off the cloister and ran down a long hallway. A monk was coming down the dormitory stairs, and God forgive me, I shoved him to one side. Gwenforte ran out ahead of me, then fell behind so I could lead, then got out ahead again. Hallway, staircase, cloister, hallway, stair— I was getting dizzy and fearfully afraid that I was lost. I kept glancing over my shoulder. Sometimes I could see Michelangelo, puffing after us in the distance. Other times, he was too far back.

Finally we came to a dark, empty corridor, where the stone is particularly old and shadowed. I ran to the great wooden door at the center of the doorway and banged on it with all my might.

And I heard the sweet voice that I so longed to hear.

"Enter," said Abbot Hubert.

I pushed the door open and shoved the children through. "Tell him I sent you!" I hissed at them. "Tell him everything!"

"Where are you going?" Jeanne demanded.

"To head off Michelangelo!" And with that, I ran back the way I had come to meet the enemy.

The door slammed behind me.

"And that is my part in the great journey of Jeanne, Jacob, William, and Gwenforte," the Scottish chronicler concludes.

Everyone around the table begins shouting at once— "What? What happens next? What happened with Michelangelo? Did he punish you? Did he *attack* you? What about Hubert? And the children? And the dog? What *happens*!?!"

The only person not shouting is the little nun. I am not surprised.

"Please, Sister," I say, "tell us what happened behind Abbot Hubert's closed door."

Her mouth forms into a question mark. "However would I know that?" she says. But her eyes are glinting with pleasure.

"You seem," I say, "to know all sorts of secrets. Please, Sister, share them with us."

She looks at me like I'm being very impertinent. And then she says, "Very well."

CHAPTER 14

The Fourth Part of the Nun's Tale

The children found themselves standing in a dark room.

At the center of the room was a great wooden table. A dozen candles stood on it—the only light. Wax dripped down the sticks, gathering in craggy hills at their bases.

Behind the candles stood a man.

He was short, with thin hair and small, blinking, gray, honest eyes. They had no ability to deceive. That was clear, right away. The children instantly knew that this was the most honest man they would ever meet.

"What *is* this?" he demanded. "Who *are* you? And what are you *doing* in here?"

"I am sorry, Father," William said, kneeling, and the other children followed his example. Even Gwenforte sat down. "We were brought here by Brother Geraldus Scotus."

"You were?" Abbot Hubert blinked his gray eyes. "Where is he?"

"He had to go...uh...deal with something," William said. The oblate felt awful hiding even an iota of truth from this honest man. "We have never had the honor of meeting, Father Hubert, but I am William, son of Lord Richard d'Orange."

The abbot blinked. "Are you? You're so...big!"

William nodded, a little taken aback by the banality of the comment. He had expected something different, a little more penetrating, from the great abbot Hubert.

"And who are you little people?" the abbot asked.

Jeanne bowed her head. "I am Jeanne, of Ville Sainte-Geneviève."

Jacob bowed his head as well. "And I am Jacob, son of Moisé and Bathsheba."

The abbot leaned over his heavy desk, blinking past all the candles. "A Jew?"

"Yes, Father," Jacob said. He wasn't sure whether, as a Jew, he was allowed to refer to the abbot as "father"—either in his religion or theirs—but he figured it was safest to do whatever William did.

"And is that a dog—in the *abbey*?" Hubert asked, incredulous.

William was rather put out by this level of questioning. "It is, Father. You see, Gerald told us to bring this dog before you. The story is—"

BANG!

The children jumped a foot. Someone had knocked on the door. Rather loudly.

BANG! BANG! BANG!

William leapt to his feet, spun around, and spied a wooden bar standing by the door. "May I, Father?" he asked, and without waiting for permission, he placed the wood in its braces, barring the door behind them.

"Just *what* is going on?" the poor, honest abbot demanded, utterly befuddled now.

BANG! BANG! BANG!

Jeanne stared at him desperately. How could such a weak fool have risen to the highest post in the French church?

"Father," William began again, speaking more quickly now, as the knocking grew louder. "This dog is Gwenforte, of Ville Sainte-Geneviève. She has been venerated there as a saint ever since her martyrdom ten years ago."

BANG!

BANG!

BANG!

Jeanne glanced over her shoulder at the door.

A light kindled in the abbot's eyes. A light of recognition.

"Someone," William barreled on, "we believe Prior Michelangelo, sent men to Ville Sainte-Geneviève to desecrate the holy dog's grave. This girl, Jeanne, had a vision it would happen."

BANG! BANG! BANG! The knocking was growing louder. More insistent.

"She went to the grove where the dog was buried, and

when she arrived, she found Gwenforte, the dead dog, resurrected like Lazarus, standing on her own grave."

The abbot's eyes had grown wider and wider. His thin, gray eyebrows began to climb up his forehead.

The banging was deafening now. *BANG! BANG! BANG! BANG!*

"The men sent to desecrate the grave took it upon themselves to murder this saintly dog." William was warming up, his words ebbing and flowing like the sermon of a wandering preacher. "And this little girl risked her own life, over and over again, to save it." Jeanne put her arm around Gwenforte's neck.

BANG!

BANG!

The abbot's eyebrows now nearly mingled with his thinning hair. He shook his head in wonder. They could barely hear William now over the banging. The door rattled on its hinges.

The abbot came around the great table and knelt next to the dog. Jeanne released Gwenforte. Hubert put his hand on Gwenforte's head. She stared up from her black eyes into his gray ones. "I'm so confused," he said.

Jeanne sighed. Jacob looked awkwardly at the floor. William prepared to explain it all again.

The abbot went on. "Why are you telling me this?"

BANG! BANG! BANG! BANG!

"And why bring me this dog?" he said, stroking Gwenforte's head, his brows knitted with befuddlement.

BANG! BANG! BANG! BANG!

"When I was the one that ordered her killed?"

The children did not move. Abbot Hubert stared into Gwenforte's eyes, still stroking her head. The banging continued, unheeded.

"We cannot have peasants worshipping false saints, can we?" he asked. "Especially not *dogs!*" He laughed and reached behind him for something on the table, still stroking Gwenforte's head. "I have heard of you, too, children. They claim you are performing miracles. Healing? Soothsaying? Acts of strength beyond all credibility?"

The children did not respond. They saw that with one hand, the abbot still stroked Gwenforte's head. With the other, he had taken from the table a sharp instrument like a knife. The banging continued.

"Let me tell you a story," the abbot said. "It's a private story. Almost like a secret, between myself, my confessor Prior Michelangelo, and God. I can tell you, can't I? You won't tell anyone?"

The children's faces were frozen, staring at the sharp object—a tool for removing waxen seals—that was now touching the soft underside of Gwenforte's throat.

"When I was a lad," the abbot began, his voice low beneath the ceaseless banging, his eyes as honest and clear as ever, "I had a friend. A best friend—and yet a rival, too, as best friends often are. We attended university in Paris, and it was impossible to tell who was more brilliant, he or I. We wanted to know *everything*. To plumb the depths of the divine plan, to understand all creation, from the Garden of Eden until today." Still, Hubert stroked Gwenforte's head. "One day, we made a vow, this friend and I. We vowed that whoever died first should return after the space of one week and tell the other whether the afterlife is indeed real, as the church teaches us, or whether Epicurus is right, and we are nothing but particles, millions of atoms, bouncing off one another. To keep this promise, we began to explore the black arts, magic, spells, and sacrifices that would give us freedom, so it was said, to return from that dark, final country."

The candle flames stood straight and tall in the dark room, quivering only when the banging shook the chamber. Hubert's gray eyes flicked to the thick wooden door and back to the children. Still, with one hand, he stroked Gwenforte, and with the other he held the knife to her soft white throat.

"Well, my friend died very young—far before I expected to lose him. I was much grieved, but also I was afraid. I was no longer certain I wanted him to return from the grave. A week went by, and he did not. I was relieved and only a little disappointed. Clearly, the ancient philosophers had been right. We are but atoms, and there is no life hereafter."

The banging had become frantic again. Jeanne was gazing at the candlelight reflecting off Hubert's blade.

"A year went by. Two," the pale, gray-eyed abbot went on. "And then, one night, as I lay in bed, he appeared before me."

"Who? Your friend?" William could not help but ask.

"Indeed, young oblate. My friend."

"Truly?"

"Do not doubt, as I did," the abbot said, his voice gentle, his eyes honest as ever. They could all see it. He was not lying. "My friend appeared before me, and so horrible a sight you have *never, ever* seen. His flesh was white and rent in strips, his innards hung from his body, his teeth had been shattered like glass. But his eyes were the worst. His eyes were deep and sleepless and so, so desperate." The abbot's voice cracked. "He called to me and said he was sorry. Sorry that he had not come sooner. Sorry that he had led me to practice the ways of the Devil. Sorry that he had led me to the brink of Hell. I begged him to explain. He said he had been tortured and tormented in the Inferno since the day he died and only now had he been granted the right to come and see me, and to warn me, but soon he would be plunged back into that endless despair, never to emerge again. 'Turn from error,' he said to me. 'Turn from arrogance. Commit yourself to God, become a monk, be as pure as you can be. Every day of your life fight the evil of the Devil.' Then he flicked his hand at me, and blood flew from an open wound and struck me here, on the chest."

With the hand that held the blade, Abbot Hubert pulled down his habit just far enough to reveal three deep, pitted scars, as if droplets of acid had fallen on his chest.

BANG! BANG! BANG! BANG! BANG!

The knocking was more frantic than ever.

But Hubert was not disturbed. "And so I have never forgotten the torment of my dearest friend. And whenever the Devil leads poor sinners astray with black magic and false saints, I rescue them from their error." He stared at the children with his frank gray eyes, willing them to understand. More banging. His voice trembled. "That is why I ordered your grove destroyed. And that is why I must kill your dog, sweet as she seems." He stroked Gwenforte's head, and she stared up at him, apparently hypnotized, immobilized by his words and his soothing hand—save for a faint tremor in her legs. "Once she is dead, I will have you three burned as well, as false saints and practitioners of the arts of the Devil." He said it as though it were the only possible option among many very sad ones. "Some will say you were saints, martyred for your beliefs. But we will know the truth." The hand that held the blade pressed into Gwenforte's throat. A bead of blood emerged from the white fur and ran down the smooth steel. Gwenforte whined and tried to shy away, but small, honest Hubert tightened his grip and pressed harder.

BANG!

This bang was different. It was louder and was accompanied by the sound of tearing metal, and a great *BOOM* followed it. Everyone, Gwenforte included, looked to the doorway.

There, as large and red and furious as the Devil himself, stood Michelangelo di Bologna. He strode onto the door—which had been ripped from its hinges, had broken through the door braces, and lay on the ground. It appeared to be smoking.

"HUBERT!" Michelangelo bellowed, his voice deep and rich, with just a hint of Italian in it. "Put down that knife! Stand up! Release the dog!"

To the children's amazement, Hubert did exactly as Michelangelo instructed. He rose to his feet, letting the blade fall to the stone floor. Gwenforte bounded over to Jeanne. A small red line ran across her throat, but the cut was not deep.

"You are a sinner, Hubert," Michelangelo said. "You know it, I know it, God knows it. Do not compound your sin on the flesh of innocents! It shall not cleanse!"

"They are worshippers of the Devil!" Hubert objected earnestly. "Practitioners of black magic!"

"Who? These children? The *dog*? Don't be an idiot!" Michelangelo's eyes were blazing like the fires of Hell itself. Or maybe, Jeanne suddenly thought, like the fires of Heaven. "Children, come with me! Hubert, do not test my patience again!"

Jeanne, with Gwenforte at her side, hurried to the smoking, broken door. Jacob and William followed as quickly as they could.

As they stepped over the door—it was hot—and into the hallway, they saw Gerald, cowering against the opposite wall.

"Michelangelo!" he cried, rising to his feet. "What have you done? What are you doing with these children?"

Michelangelo peered down from his massive, ruddy, whiskered face onto the pale Scotsman. "Gerald," he said, "you are a good man. You mean well. But you are a fool. Stay out of the way, before you do harm that cannot be undone." With that, Michelangelo continued down the hallway. Jeanne looked at the cowering Gerald, and then after the great prior of Saint-Denis.

She had a decision to make and she had just a moment to make it. Follow the red monk who had saved them—but had terrified her dreams for years? Or ask Gerald, their sworn protector, to take them somewhere far away from this confusing and frightening place?

And then, Gwenforte made the decision for her.

The white greyhound darted after the great red monk and trotted happily at his heels. Jeanne stared for a moment. Then she and the other children hurried to catch up.

Sometimes, it turns out, the most important decisions in life are made by your dog.

They followed Michelangelo di Bologna through the corridors of Saint-Denis, one after another, too quickly to have any idea where they were or where they were going. Finally they passed through a thick wooden door, which Michelangelo used a long iron key to bolt behind them, and out into a narrow alley. They were outside the abbey walls. Michelangelo led them down the muddy lane and veered off into another.

There, he came to a green door. Jacob noticed that on the doorframe there was a small, oblong box. He pulled up short. "Is that a mezuzah?" he asked.

Michelangelo ignored him, knocking with his enormous fist—it was nearly the size of Jeanne's head—on the flimsy door.

After a moment, they heard the sound of a woman's voice. "Coming! Coming!"

As they waited, hearts pounding from their flight from the monastery and the strange, terrifying encounter they had had there, Jeanne looked at Michelangelo. With red whiskers and fiery eyes and a fierce, fat face that had haunted her her entire life. Now, maybe, rescuing them. Maybe.

William, beside her, gazed at the great man, too. Despite all that he had heard of him—the tales of his wickedness—he suddenly felt a strange affinity for the giant cleric. Like he had at last met someone of his own species.

Jacob, meanwhile, stared in wonder at the mezuzah— the tiny prayer scroll that hangs on the doorframe of a Jewish home. Why were they here?

The green door opened. Standing in the doorway was a plump, older woman, with gray hair pulled back in a messy bun behind her head. From within the house, the unmistakable smell of boiling chicken broth flooded the alley. "Michelangelo!" she cried. "I'm making dumpling soup! You always know! Come in! Come in! And who are these?"

Michelangelo pushed the children inside. "Close the door, if you would, William." The big boy complied. The plump woman stood before them expectantly. "Children," Michelangelo intoned, "may I introduce Miriam, wife of the great rabbi?" At that moment, they heard the thud of a cane on the thin wooden floorboards, and an old man hobbled around the corner. He was bent over his walking stick, and his long white beard hung almost to his waist. But his eyes were bright and lively.

"And this," Michelangelo announced, "is her very lucky husband—Rabbi Yehuda."

Jacob's legs went wobbly beneath him.

"These," Michelangelo continued, now speaking to Yehuda and his wife and indicating the children with a sweep of his hand, "are the saints."

I practically jump from my stool. "He called them saints? You're sure?"

The little nun smiles placidly at me.

"Why does that matter to you so much?" Jerome asks, turning on me. "You seem rather preoccupied by that fact."

I return his gaze. After a moment, I look back to the nun. "Do you know more?" I ask her.

"Indeed I do."

HAPTER 15

The Fifth Part of the Nun's Tale

They sat on stools in the warm, aromatic kitchen. The place was strange to the children. The floor was made of wooden planks. There was a flat wood ceiling above them. And there was a small hearth in the house, like a miniature version of what one would find in a castle's keep. In the hearth, a fire blazed under a pot of soup.

Michelangelo was noisily slurping broth from a carved wooden spoon. Gwenforte was wrapped around his big feet. Jeanne was gazing over the rim of her rough bowl at the giant red monk and her dog. Why did Gwenforte seem so comfortable with Red, Fat, and Wicked?

William had emptied three bowls of soup and was working on his fourth. Jacob, on the other hand, was not eating at all. He was leaning forward on his stool, peering around the house of Yehuda as if something might be hiding in it.

Miriam hovered over the children to ensure that their bowls were never empty. She saw that William had cleared his, and she quickly ladled some more of the steaming broth into the rough clay vessel.

Michelangelo paused at his soup and raised his head.

"I have been looking for you," he said to the children. "Four days now, nonstop, practically no food, absolutely no sleep."

"To kill us?" Jeanne asked.

Michelangelo peered at the little girl on her wooden stool. "Why would I want to kill you, exactly?"

"You killed Theresa, from my village." Jeanne spat out her words like the pits of bitter plums.

Michelangelo di Bologna's great red eyebrows contracted over his strawberry of a nose. "Theresa... Theresa... Theresa of Ville Sainte-Geneviève?"

Jeanne nodded as if this were obvious.

Michelangelo laughed. "Kill her? I did not kill her! I do not believe she has died at all! She is doing God's work in Burgundy as we speak!"

"You took her away! To be put on trial and killed!"

Michelangelo shrugged a great Italian shrug, which he performed both with his shoulders and his lips. "Perhaps that is what you were told. Indeed, I have let many believe things like this. But never have I done that. And never would I. Theresa is a woman of God. Your bailiff—Charles was his name?—he had denounced her as a witch. What could I do but take her elsewhere?"

Jeanne fell silent. She stared at the broad boards of the floor. Inside her, grand castles of comprehension, models of the world as she had understood it, shivered. She could not decide whether to let them crumble or to try desperately to save them.

Jacob had now buried his head deep in his soup. He ate slowly, listlessly, stealing occasional glances at the old man sitting in the corner. Yehuda, too, kept his eyes in his broth, struggling to get dumplings to stay on his spoon.

"Brother Michelangelo," William said, "why did Hubert obey when you commanded him like that, as if you were his master, and not vice versa?"

Michelangelo raised himself up on his little stool. Even seated, he towered over everyone else in the room. Even William. His red whiskers bristled like combs off his face. "There is worldly power, given by man to man," he said, his voice rumbling. His r's, instead of purring in the back of his throat in the French manner, rolled off his tongue in the Italian. "In that, Hubert outranks me. But there is also sacred power, given by God to man. In that, I outrank Hubert. By a very great deal. He knows this."

Jacob again glanced furtively at Yehuda. Miriam, who had been watching the little boy with interest since he'd come through the door, said, "What is it, my little dumpling? What do you want to ask the rabbi?"

Jacob raised his head slowly. Yehuda's sparkling eyes reluctantly abandoned his unruly dumpling and found Jacob across the room.

Jacob whispered, "You are *the* Rabbi Yehuda? Of Saint-Denis?"

Jeanne looked at the floor. She knew what was coming.

"I am," said the old man, his eyes soft and probing. He stroked his beard with a hand as blue and delicate as a bird.

"Do you know my parents? Moisé and Bathsheba, of Nogent-sur-Oise?"

The old man's eyelids fluttered closed. Then they opened, a bit brighter than before. "Bathsheba, daughter of Jacob Solomon?"

"Jacob Solomon was my grandfather. I never knew him."

"Of course you didn't," Rabbi Yehuda agreed. "But I haven't seen Bathsheba since she was a little girl! Is she well?"

Jacob's chin was quivering violently. He tried to form words, but failed. Miriam was immediately at his side. She put her arms around him. He was shivering. She rubbed his thin shoulders.

Jeanne spoke for Jacob, saying what he needed to say but could not. "She hasn't come here? There was a fire in Jacob's town. Set by some stupid boys. Jacob was separated from his parents. They told him they would meet him here."

The rabbi's face fell. William bit his lip and stared at Jacob.

The little room was quiet. At last, Yehuda said, "Did you see them escape?"

Jacob's face was now hidden in Miriam's sleeve. He shook his head.

"How many days ago was this?"

Michelangelo answered. "Nogent-sur-Oise burned six days ago. It was ... not good."

A great lump was forming in Jeanne's throat. William's face was drawn and bloodless. Miriam, stroking Jacob's small back, looked from her husband to Michelangelo. Michelangelo grimaced and shook his head.

Jeanne saw this and then—in a surprise even to herself—burst into tears. William stared into his lap. Gwenforte rose, looked back and forth between Jeanne and Jacob, and came and sat down between Jacob's legs.

"Okay! Get up!" Miriam announced. "Follow me!" She led the children through an open doorway and into the second room of the house. There sat a large bed of straw and blankets in the corner. She made the children lie down on it. Gwenforte crawled in among them.

"That dog better not have fleas," the rabbi's wife said as she returned to the front room.

"They likely *all* have fleas," Michelangelo replied.

The children were more tired than they knew. Within moments, they were asleep. At dinnertime, they woke again but could not raise themselves from the soft straw and woolen blankets. William, who had been snoring like a mill wheel grinding grain, rolled over and threw his long arm over Jeanne and Jacob and Gwenforte. Jeanne

tried to move it, but it was like trying to move a fallen tree. She left it. They fell asleep again.

The next morning, when the children awoke, Miriam was already gone to do her marketing. A steaming pot of porridge hung over the fire.

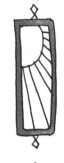

The children took cracked clay bowls from a pile on the worn wooden table and sat down on stools. Morning light, mote filled and yellow, streamed in through the narrow glassless window. Jeanne and William shoveled the porridge into their mouths with silent vigor. Jacob, meanwhile, pushed his breakfast around in his bowl.

"You're going to eat us out of house and home."

The children were startled.

Rabbi Yehuda had been sitting on his stool in his habitual corner, and the children hadn't even noticed him.

Jeanne hurriedly put her bowl down on the table. William and Jacob paused, their spoons aloft, and looked uncertainly at the old man.

"Eat! Eat!" He laughed. "God will provide more food. Money, probably not. But maybe food."

The children still waited, eyeing the old rabbi.

"Eat! Eat! I'm just teasing. Eat!" His eyes danced, and a smile cracked his old, wrinkled face like an egg.

Slowly, the children began to eat again. Soon, William had finished his porridge. He eyed the pot over the fire.

"Seconds?" the rabbi said. "You want *seconds*?"

William quickly shook his head.

YEHUDA

RASHI

BACON

"Don't listen to that old invalid!" Michelangelo's voice boomed from the doorway. "He's a liar and a satan and you should never believe him." Michelangelo left the flimsy door standing open, so the fresh morning air swirled into the little house. "Trust him, but never believe him. Have seconds. Thirds. Miriam would insist." The great man stood in the center of the room, his head nearly grazing the ceiling. William got up and ladled more porridge into his bowl.

Michelangelo stomped his foot on the floorboards. "Have you ever seen these?" he asked, looking at Jacob.

Jacob shook his head. His eyes were heavy and rimmed with shadows.

"A new thing they've done," Yehuda said. "To reduce disease, they tell us. Only in the most advanced cities. We live in a new Rome, my friend. An enlightened age!"

Michelangelo frowned at the old rabbi. "He's lying," he said to the children. "As usual. Don't believe him."

"Lying?" Yehuda said, with heat. "How, lying? With Crusades and murder, heretics and executions? And every penny going to that fortress of stone in the name of God—when not a man inside knows what, or who, God is? Surely the Messiah is come, and the Kingdom of Heaven has arrived!"

"The Messiah IS come, you satan!" Michelangelo suddenly bellowed. Jeanne nearly fell off her chair. "And the Kingdom of Heaven is near indeed! The Cistercians have carved wood and bent iron into a pump of perpetual movement! In Chartres, they have erected a cathedral that literally touches the belly of Heaven! And wise men like you and Roger Bacon and Rashi show the benighted the error of their ways!"

"And peasants," the old rabbi replied, straightening his crooked back, his beard quivering, "pretend they are going to the Holy Land and descend on Jewish villages and loot and murder and burn! Surely, God is smiling!"

"That makes God weep and you know it!" Michelangelo began, his voice swelling. But then he stopped. He glanced at William. "Our young brother, though, finds something funny." They all looked at the young monk. Indeed, William was grinning.

"What? Are you laughing at us?" Yehuda demanded.

William shook his head, but he could not stop grinning. He said, "How are you two friends? A rabbi and a prior? Shouting at each other and calling each other satan?"

"You call this *friends*?" Yehuda said, throwing his hands in the air. But then he laughed. "No, it's true. You should be so lucky to have a friend like this."

And then Jeanne said, "He does. Two."

William took in his breath sharply. One corner of his left eye was suddenly damp.

Jeanne turned to Michelangelo. "Why do you call him Satan?" If someone among the present company looked like Satan, Jeanne thought, surely it was Michelangelo. Jeanne saw that Gwenforte was curled around his feet again, while Jeanne's bare feet were cold.

Michelangelo replied, "He *is* satan! Or rather, *a* satan. In Hebrew, *satan* means an advocate of the alternative, the one who makes the arguments you don't know how to refute." Michelangelo looked to the old Jew, still grinning wickedly in the corner. "That *satan* is my best friend."

The room fell silent. The children's gaze drifted between the two men, one huge, red, and robust, the other shriveled, bent, and so gray he was almost blue. Red whiskers and white. A crazy head of hair and almost none. It was a very strange pair.

Michelangelo looked to Jacob. He was hunched over, leaning on his knees, staring out the open front door. In fact, it appeared that he hadn't been listening at all. He had been peering through the doorway, the shadows under his eyes darkening, twisting and tugging on his curly hair.

And then, before they could rouse him from his apparent stupor, he leapt to his feet and banged out the little house's entryway and into the muddy alley.

Jeanne and William were instantly after him.

They found Jacob, standing in the narrow, muddy lane, staring toward the main street of Saint-Denis. Tears were coursing down his face. "Where are they?" he said. "Why aren't they here yet?"

William stepped down from the doorway, put a great arm around his friend's small shoulders, and let him weep in the morning sunshine.

"Why?" Jacob cried. "Why aren't they here?"

. . .

Jacob sat on a low stool. Across the warm little room, his friends gazed sheepishly at him. There is something embarrassing about someone else's grief. It is hard to know what to do around it. The right answer, always, is *hugs*. But Jeanne and William were sitting all the way across the room, and their arms weren't long enough to reach Jacob. Besides, they didn't know that *hugs* is always the answer. *Listening* is also a good response to grief. But unfortunately, Jacob wasn't speaking.

Michelangelo di Bologna was leaning against a wall. Yehuda's eyes were closed, and his head was tilted back.

Jeanne broke the silence. She had more questions for Michelangelo. Many more questions. She started with this one: "Michelangelo, when we came in, you called us *saints*. Why?"

Michelangelo pursed his lips. Then he pushed off the thin wooden wall—making the house tremble slightly—and closed the front door. He came to the center of the room and looked down at little Jeanne.

"What do you think?" he replied. She shrugged diffidently and eyed him from under her brown brows.

"When you have a fit, Jeanne, what do you see?"

"Things that ... that will happen?"

"Yes. You see the future." He turned to William. "And have you ever met anyone who could break a stone bench with his fist? Or dispatch a dozen fiends using nothing but flesh and bone?"

"You heard about that?" asked William.

"Indeed. Your fame is spreading, children. And Jacob, you heal mortal wounds with just your hands, some plants, and a prayer. Is this not unique?"

Jacob's hollow eyes gazed up at Michelangelo, but he did not reply.

"To review: We have a dog that's been resurrected, a peasant girl who sees the future, a supernaturally strong oblate, and a Jewish boy with the power of miraculous healing."

The children almost laughed in the silence that followed. When you put it that way, it sounded rather insane.

"So yes, I believe you are saints."

Yehuda said, "Even Jacob? A Jew?"

"Of course there are Jewish saints!" Michelangelo replied. "And Muslim saints, and saints in lands where they worship God in all sorts of ways."

The children sat in stunned silence.

"Well," said Yehuda at last. "I hope you're mistaken."

"Why?" Jeanne wanted to know.

"Being a saint is not a nice thing. The abilities may be useful, yes. But they aren't worth what happens at the end."

"The end?"

"Or course! You should know that, my Christian friend! Saints are martyred!"

Gwenforte opened her eyes and raised her head.

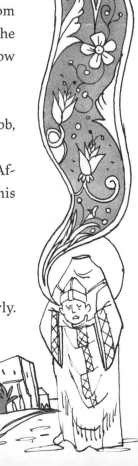

"Just think about Saint Denis!"

"What happened to him?" said Jacob.

"You don't know the story of Saint Denis?" Jeanne asked.

"How would *I* know the story?"

William said, "He was the bishop of Paris in the time of the Romans. He converted many pagans to the True Faith."

"Judaism?" Jacob said.

"Don't try to be funny," William retorted.

But Yehuda chuckled. "I thought it was funny."

"Denis, Bishop of Paris," William went on, always happy to share, "was decapitated by the Roman authorities for spreading Christianity. But after the Romans cut off Saint Denis's head, he picked it up and *walked* from Paris all the way to where Saint-Denis is now. And the whole way his disembodied head *preached a sermon*. Now *that's* a saint!"

Jacob laughed. "That did *not* happen."

William raised his eyebrows. Jeanne exclaimed, "Jacob, that's heresy!" Even Gwenforte barked.

Jacob looked to Yehuda. The old rabbi merely said, "After all the miraculous things you have seen and done, this you cannot believe?"

Jacob didn't know what to say to that.

"Tell him about Lawrence," said Michelangelo.

"Who's he?" Jacob asked.

"He's one of my favorites," said William eagerly.

St. Lucy

St. Vitus

"He was the deacon of a church in Rome, also under the Roman Empire. His church served only the poor and had no funds, until one day a rich woman died and left the church a great deal of money. When the Roman emperor heard this, he sent his soldiers to get the treasure to add to the empire's coffers. But before they arrived, Lawrence distributed it all to the poor. Then he brought beggars and lepers and orphans into his church. When the Roman soldiers arrived to collect the money, Lawrence brought them all before the poor people and said, 'Here it is! For the downtrodden are our greatest treasure!'"

"So what happened?" Jacob asked.

"What do you think happened? He's a saint. He got martyred."

"They took a gridiron," said Jeanne, "and they placed it over hot coals until it started to glow. Then they put Lawrence on the gridiron and roasted him, until his flesh sizzled and blackened and peeled from his bones. After a while, he turned to his tormentors and said, 'This side's cooked. Flip me over.'"

Jacob began to laugh—and then did not. Jeanne, when she realized that she'd just described someone burning to death, covered her mouth.

"I'm sorry," she murmured. "I didn't think . . ."

Jacob looked at the floorboards. After a moment, he said, "So will we be martyred, too?"

"That depends," Michelangelo replied. "You may flee

your fate. Ignore your gifts. Maybe stay alive. Jeanne, you could go back to your village with that lovely dog of yours. William, we could find a new monastery for you, I am sure. And Jacob . . ." He hesitated.

"We're staying together," Jeanne cut in. She looked at the two boys. "Right?"

William grinned. "Right."

Jacob looked up at them. His face was pale. But he managed to smile. "Right."

Michelangelo's eyes met Yehuda's. Something silent passed between them. "In that case," said the big monk, "there is something that I am trying to do. I could use your . . . your special skills." Michelangelo paused. "There is to be a burning. A great conflagration. Of books. They are to be stacked like logs, or thrown on a pyre, in the center of Paris," Michelangelo explained. "And they will be burned."

St. Giles

"What are they?" Jeanne asked. "Which books?"

"What does it matter? They're books!" William said. "Do you know how much work it takes to make a book? Years and years of a monk's life, to make just one! How many books are they burning?"

"Dozens and dozens, I hear," Michelangelo replied.

"Dozens and dozens of volumes of Talmud," added Yehuda. "Though, really, they'll burn anything written in Hebrew. For how should they know Talmud from Bible from the commentary of Rashi?"

St. Christopher

William said, "Wait—just Jewish books?"

Michelangelo raised his eyebrows at the young monk. "What does it matter, William?"

Everyone in the small room turned to the oblate.

William's face flushed with shame. "It doesn't," he said. "That's not what I meant."

"Why would they do that?" Jeanne asked.

"The bitter fruit of a poisoned tree," Yehuda murmured. "Once, we Jews were seen as the People of the Book. Useful to Christian society as an example of the Old Way. Augustine himself described us like this. But then, Jews who converted to Christianity, and were looking to climb in the ranks of power, went to the pope and told him that we actually have *two* books: the Bible and the Talmud. The Talmud is the collected wisdom of the rabbis—a discussion of the Bible. But apparently, since we are the People of *the* Book, we only get one. The Bible. The rest are to be consigned to the flames."

William's disgust had returned to its original proportions. "But *your* writings, great sage? Will they burn the books of Yehuda, too?"

"Of course," the rabbi replied. "Mine and those far greater than mine."

Jacob's eyes shone. Another burning. Again, aimed at his people and what they treasure. "But what can we do?" he asked.

Yehuda, almost imperceptibly, smiled.

"Well," said Michelangelo, "you could come with me as I try to stop the book burning. In so doing, you would face enemies. Persecution. Maybe death. But you would be fighting for goodness, wisdom, and what is right. You would walk boldly into your fate, whatever it is. Or, you could go back to your old lives—what is left of them."

The children found one another's eyes. There was, really, nothing to discuss.

Jeanne sat up a little straighter on her wooden stool. "We will walk boldly. We will be saints."

"You can't just decide to be a saint!" I cry, unable to control myself any longer.

"They haven't *just decided*!" Jerome retorts. "They are! Look at their acts! Their miracles!"

"Yes, a miracle *can* be performed by a saint," I say. "But it can also be performed by a charlatan! A trickster! I bet that jongleur sleeping out in the barn could dazzle our eyes if we let him."

Aron the butcher stands up and leans across the table. "Could he have saved my life? Healed my wounds with yarrow and a prayer?"

"Demons have magic, too, do they not?" I go on. "Magic alone does not a saint make. A saint must do God's work. A saint must be the embodiment of God's goodness on earth. Saint Lawrence gave great wealth to the poor. Besides healing your head, what have these children done?"

The innkeeper counts on his fingers, "Rescue a dog, kill a dozen fiends, heal Aron's head, rescue each other from bloodthirsty knights—"

"And then," I interrupt, "they *befriended* those *same* bloodthirsty knights!"

"They also defeated a dragon, like Saint George."

"Saint George killed the dragon. They just made it puke." The folks around the table are glaring at me. I throw up my hands. "Why are you all so committed to these children being saints?"

"Why are you so dead set against it, I wonder?" Jerome replies.

I do not answer.

The handsome man leans forward. His voice is quiet and rich, his French perfectly exact. "When I first met them, I also doubted their sanctity. And now, I am more conflicted than ever."

"You've met them, too?" I ask. "What is this? A we-met-the-kids reunion?"

The handsome man sits back on his stool. "Do you doubt me?"

"No," I say. "I suppose I don't. Go ahead. Tell us your story."

CHAPTER 16

The Companion's Tale

Jeanne, Jacob, William, and Gwenforte left the town of Saint-Denis, following the famous prior Michelangelo di Bologna.

"So," William said, once they had left the town. "Where are those books?" The wind was cool and fresh on their faces. Others traveled down the road, but none close enough to overhear them. At least, so they all thought. After these children became outlaws, I pieced together their conversation from snatches gathered by those who remembered seeing this strange band.

"I do not know," Michelangelo replied. "But we do know that the Talmuds have been collected by the various abbeys and then sent to Paris. So our first stop is an abbey just to the west of Paris, in the wood of Vincennes. The abbot there is a friend of mine. I will ask him what he knows of this conflagration: where it is to be and when.

And also, of course, if he knows where the books are. He may. He is, after all, a confidant of the king."

"Why would the king know?" asked Jacob.

"It is the king who is burning the books, is it not? Well, his mother, Blanche of Castile, is the prime mover, I am sure. But I gather that the king is collaborating enthusiastically."

The blood drained from the faces of all three children. "The king?" said Jeanne.

"I thought we were going to steal some books from an abbey or something," said William.

"You would rather steal from the church than from the king?" Michelangelo replied.

William hesitated, and then he said, emphatically, "Yes!" He added, as if Michelangelo should know better, "Stealing from the king is *treason!*"

"Lower your voice!" Michelangelo whispered. And then he added, "I told you it would be dangerous." And then, as if that had ended the conversation, he strode out ahead of the children. Gwenforte trotted along beside him.

William, Jeanne, and Jacob looked at one another. William pointed at Jeanne. "*You* volunteered for this."

Jeanne said, almost to herself, "We're going to steal from the king?"

"And die," Jacob added. "I'm pretty sure we're going to die, too."

The wood of Vincennes is a deep wood, full of grand old trees and runs of sparkling water. The sunlight shone through the bare branches in slanting golden rays as they approached the abbey. The monks there—Grandmontines, they are called—are silent. Always. Only the abbot may speak, and then only to distinguished guests.

The abbey door was small and modest. Just a rounded wooden affair set into porous, honeyed stone. A black bell hung beside the door, with a leather thong dangling from its center. Michelangelo whipped the leather thong against the metal, and the bell hummed quietly in reply. Michelangelo turned to the children and put a finger against his lips.

The wooden door opened, and a thin man in a gray monk's habit appeared. When he saw Michelangelo, he bowed, and the great red monk inclined his head in response. Then the Grandmontine looked at the rest of them. His eyes went wider and wider as they passed from Jacob, who was dressed like a peasant, to William, who looked like no monk the Grandmontine had ever seen, to Jeanne, who was not just a peasant, but a *girl,* and finally to Gwenforte, who was, it will be remembered, a *dog.* But the small gray monk sighed and looked to Heaven, as if to say, *What else would I expect from Michelangelo di Bologna?* And he waved them inside.

He led them up a stony path to an orchard. Pear trees stood in rows. A robin sang from a nearby branch into the disapproving silence of the abbey. Jeanne had the urge to shush it. That's how quiet the place was.

While Michelangelo walked with the monk to the

low-slung buildings of the abbey, the children were set to wander—silently—through the orchard.

William put his arm around Jacob's shoulder. Jacob leaned his head against William's ribs. The big boy's warmth was calming. He sighed. Jeanne led Gwenforte by the scruff of her neck to prevent her from chasing the robin.

At the far end of the orchard, a group of monks were tending to one of the abbey's exterior walls. Sprawling vines of ivy had grown across it. The vines were beautiful, deep green against the glowing sun-kissed stone, like the illuminated marginalia in a manuscript. But these marginalia contradicted the text, because the ivy was silently eating away at the mortar between the stones and would one day bring the walls down. So the monks were tearing the beautiful lines of ivy away.

But were they monks? As the children came closer, they heard whispering and—could it be?—laughing. Jacob was prepared to turn away, but Jeanne was drawn to the group.

The whispering and chuckling grew louder. These young monks hadn't noticed the children and were laughing about whatever young men laugh about when they think they are alone.

Suddenly, one of them shushed the others, and they became silent. They looked chastened. They went back to ripping the ivy from the walls.

While the other monks tore ivy from stone, one busied

himself collecting the fallen vines and heaping them in a pile. Like all the monks, his head was covered with the gray cowl of the order. He was doubled over and grunting when he noticed the children. He stood up, and as he did, his cowl fell back from his face.

He was a handsome man. Clean-shaven, with a square jaw, dark ringlets for hair, and smiling eyes. The children gasped. But not for his physical beauty, striking though it was. They gasped at the thin golden crown that settled in his black curls like eggs in a thrush's nest.

William was the first on one knee. It was shocking, really, how quickly the big boy got there. His head was bowed and with his hands he steadied himself against the cool, wet grass of the orchard.

Jacob was just a moment behind him. He, too, fell to one knee and bowed his head.

"God protect His Majesty!" William said, entirely forgetting the vow of silence. Meeting a king tends to induce a temporary but powerful amnesia. Trust me. I know.

William's voice made the other young monks spin around. It was clear, though, that they were not monks. Their gray robes hung like cloaks from their shoulders, and under the robes shone the richest, finest garments the children had ever seen. Not festive clothes, mind you. No furs or silks. Just the finest traveling clothes in the kingdom of France. Each of the king's men had the bearing of someone who expects to be respected and accepts that respect gracefully. But none was so regal, so striking, nor so handsome as the man who wore the crown.

Which is why William was nearly frantic when he whispered, "Jeanne! Bow!"

But Jeanne did not appear to hear him, for she did not move at all. Terror roared like a tiger in William's chest. *She's having a fit*, he thought. *In front of the king. How in God's name will we explain that to him? Will he have her killed? Drawn and quartered? Decapitated, with her head on a stake?* All of these flashes of future miseries occurred to William in the time it took him to turn his head to see *what* Jeanne was doing.

When he finally clapped his eyes on her, his heart sank even further. She was *not* having a fit. She was just *not* bowing to the king. The punishment for refusing to bow to the king was worse than the punishment for witchcraft. William didn't know what it was, but he was sure that it was much, much worse.

Jeanne took a step toward the king. And then another.

Jacob turned to William and hissed, "*What is she doing?*" William shook his head in despair. Jacob whispered, "Should we tackle her before she reaches him?" William shrugged as if to say, *Maybe.*

By this point, Jeanne had crossed the distance between the boys and the king. She had turned, just a few degrees, as she approached the lord of all France. And then, at last, she knelt and bowed her head. But, to the utter horror of William and Jacob, *she was not bowing to the king.* And then, as if the situation was not horrifying enough, Gwenforte trotted up and sat down beside Jeanne, as if she, too, were refusing to pay obeisance to King Louis IX of France.

Little Jeanne was bowing to one of the king's compan-ions. A young man, about the king's age, with a thin, pale face, a nose like an eagle's beak, lank, dark hair, and a weak chin. If anyone was more obviously *not* the king, he was not present in the group.

Jeanne said, "Bless me, Your Majesty."

The pale young man replied, "Bless you, my child."

The king's men, including the one wearing the crown—that is, me—looked on with mild wonder.

William and Jacob, on the other hand, stared with their mouths as wide-open as cathedral doors on Easter Sunday.

"And that is how we met the children. And their dog," the handsome man concludes.

"Wait, *you* were wearing the crown?" Marie the brewster says.

"Yes."

"But you're not the king."

"How astute of you. I am Jean de Joinville, one of the king's companions. When the king goes out, one of us often dons an imitation crown, for the king's protection."

Marie sweeps us all with her eyes and then says to the king's companion, "You ain't all that humble about your appearance, are you?"

Jean de Joinville smiles. "False humility is no humility at all."

"And you don't seem to think King Louis is all that good-looking either."

"King Louis is the most beautiful man I have ever seen, but his beauty radiates from his wisdom, his piety, and his kindness. Not the dust and flesh that cling to his bones."

"Fair enough."

I sit quietly, examining the courtier. "You are really Jean de Joinville? Companion of the king? Seneschal of Champagne?"

The handsome man smiles. "I see my reputation precedes me."

"And do you," I ask, "know more of this tale? How did these children, who seem to have done no harm to anyone, become the most wanted people in all of France? Why has the king declared war on them?"

He arches his black eyebrows and smiles. "That is an excellent question, my friend. And I am just the man to answer it."

CHAPTER 17

The Second Part of the Companion's Tale

The refectory of a Grandmontine abbey is as spare as the monks' lives. In the Abbey Vincennes, wooden tables and wooden benches stood in rows. No tapestries hung on the honey-stone walls. The few windows were glassless, and the air blew in like the chilly breath of a silent and distant God. There was not even a dais for the abbot and his distinguished guests, as there would have been at a Benedictine abbey, for the Grandmontines don't hold with the pride of status. I think that's why the king visits them so often.

The children sat opposite the king, staring at his milky face and weak chin and lank, wet-looking hair. In stark contrast to the darkness of his hair, though, his eyes are limpid and blue.

"How did you know?" King Louis asked the little girl. I should tell you that our king is both gentle and firm, self-possessed and sympathetic. These apparent

203

contradictions express themselves in everything that he does, down to his elocution. It is exact and perfect in every way—and yet it is not ostentatious. Like his clothes. The richest in France—and yet simple, almost forgettable. "You say you have never seen me before—and yet, you recognized me. How?"

Jeanne opened her mouth—and then shut it again. She was appraising the king. As if she had a secret and could not decide whether it was safe to share it or not.

I lost patience. "My lord, isn't it obvious?"

"Is it, Joinville?"

"But of course. She's seen a *drawing*, Your Majesty. A *picture*. Your royal seal, emblazoned with your *face*."

"Where on earth would she have seen my seal, Joinville? She's a peasant!" the king retorted. He asked Jeanne, "Have you ever seen my seal?"

She shook her head.

"Have you seen a picture of me?"

Again, Jeanne shook her head.

"A manuscript? An image of any kind?"

Jeanne continued to shake her head.

"Then you gave it away!" I said. "Your kingly bearing, your imperious gaze. Your royal regard!"

The king's long face grew longer. "Did I give it away, my child?"

Jeanne shook her head.

My impatience boiled over. "Well? Does she speak?

Will she shake her tongue and unlock the mystery of your identification?"

The little peasant had trapped her lips between her teeth.

I leaned across the table. "It is not wise to play *games* with *the king*."

She seemed to consider that. Her mousy hair all a-tangle on her head, her small eyes focusing first on the king, then on the table, then on the king again. She was afraid. I could see that. Afraid of letting something go that she had long guarded.

Finally she opened her mouth to speak—and the heavy hand of Michelangelo di Bologna fell on her shoulder.

"May I, Jeanne?" he said.

The little girl's eyes traveled up to the great monk's red face. She closed her mouth and let him speak.

"What I am about to tell you, Your Majesty, will surprise you." He looked to me and added, "Your highly skeptical friend may not believe me at all. That notwithstanding, it is true."

The king moved forward on the plain wooden bench. I shifted uncomfortably.

"These children are each capable of extraordinary acts. The boy here"—he indicated Jacob—"can heal a wound as fast as Saint Luke himself. The oblate, William, can perform feats of strength that would make Samson tremble. And this girl, this peasant girl, is taken by miraculous fits. She falls, she shakes, she cannot see nor hear, and yet she has visions of the future. True visions, Your Majesty. If I had to guess, I would hazard that she saw you in one of her fits. Is it true, Jeanne?"

The refectory was totally silent as we waited for the little girl to speak.

She still seemed to be wrestling with something, for though she stared at the king, she said not a word.

Pious Louis leaned across the table, until his hair swung back and forth across his cheeks. "Did you see me in a vision, little girl?"

Silence.

And then, "Yes, Your Majesty. I saw you."

"And what else did you see?"

Jeanne became very still. She studied the grooves in the wooden table.

"My little friend, please, tell me—what did you see?"

"I . . . I don't want to say."

I barked with laughter. "You *don't want to say*? I'm sorry, little peasant! You don't exactly have a choice!"

But the king rebuked me. "Don't threaten her. Please, little girl. Your king is asking you to share your gift with him."

I didn't mind the rebuke—it is an honor to be rebuked by the king. But I did not like him trusting her so soon, and so far.

But, as has happened many times before, the king proved himself wiser than me. His goodness is contagious, for he gave Jeanne trust—and she felt it. And so, reluctantly at first, she gave her trust to him.

"I had this vision long ago," she said. "It is the strangest, most confusing vision I have ever had."

King Louis did not speak, but he nodded his head gently, encouragingly.

"I saw Christ on the cross," Jeanne said. Instantly, we crossed ourselves—thumbs inward, shoulder to shoulder, forehead to sternum. Everyone, that is, save Jacob, who saw it happen too late to try to imitate us. At the time, I noticed and wondered, just for an instant, if this boy was not of our faith. But the thought quickly escaped my mind, as greater things presented themselves for my attention.

"Christ was on the cross," Jeanne went on, "but it must have been by magic, because there were no nails in his hands or his feet. But they were still bleeding . . ." She halted.

"And?" the king asked. "Is there more? Was I there?"

"You were at the foot of the cross. You were crying."

"How crying? Crying aloud? Weeping?"

"I am sorry, Your Majesty. You were . . . you were kind of . . . throwing a tantrum."

The king sat straight up, stung. I laid a hand on his shoulder. "It is becoming to weep at the sight of Our Lord's crucifixion," I assured him.

"Yes," he replied, "but tantrums are less becoming in the presence of God, I would think."

"Don't be too proud, my lord," I said.

My beloved king turned to me and said, "*You're* telling

me not to be proud?" His other companions laughed. I was pleased to be the butt of his joke. And then he asked, "Is there more, little girl?"

"No . . . well, there was a huge bird—an eagle or a vulture, I guess—flying overhead, in circles around the cross. It was crying, like it was hungry. Like I said, it was the strangest vision I ever—"

Jeanne stopped speaking. The abbot had entered the refectory. His face was so dark, I was certain he brought news of someone's death. He walked to the king's side, and then gestured for Michelangelo to join him. They knelt together, the three of them, and the abbot began to whisper. A feeling of great darkness and foreboding entered my heart.

I was right to worry.

For just then, a scream ripped through the stillness of the abbey. It was my beloved king. "By the scallop of Saint James!" he wailed. "By Saint Hilda's hair, it cannot be!" The king launched himself onto the floor and began tearing at his clothes. The greyhound scrambled out from under the table. "It cannot be!" the king was shrieking. "It cannot be! Why, Lord, oh, why? I would rather the best city of my kingdom ruined! Razed to the ground by the infidel!"

"My lord," I cried, beseeching him, "My lord, what's happened?"

But he could not string two coherent words together. I thought at first, of course, of his mother. He is closer to no one on earth. Surely, she had suddenly died? The king

writhed on the floor like he was being stung by a swarm of wasps.

So I turned, desperately now, to Michelangelo di Bologna. The prior looked like he had been struck in the face. "What is it?" I pleaded with him. "What's happened?"

Michelangelo's voice was like the pealing of a funeral bell. "The Holy Nail, at Saint-Denis, has been stolen."

I nearly fell off the bench on which I sat. The other companions to the king covered their faces with their hands or cried aloud in horror.

Amidst the commotion, Jacob turned to William and whispered, "What's the Holy Nail?"

William turned on him like he was a two-headed cat. "What do you mean 'What's the Holy Nail?'"

"I don't know what that is!"

The commotion continued. Crying and shouting and literal hand-wringing.

William hissed at Jacob, "The Holy Nail! *The* Holy Nail!"

"That's not helping me," Jacob informed him.

"From the *hand* of *Christ* on the *cross*! The nail that held the Lord God in place during his crucifixion!" William practically shouted.

"Oh!" Jacob said. "Oh ... I guess that's pretty important."

William replied, "You think so?"

The king was moaning and squirming on the cold stones of the refectory. "The Holy Nail ...," he whimpered. "The Holy Nail ..."

Which is when I fixed my gaze on Jeanne. It could not have been more than a murmur when I said it, but it silenced the whole refectory: "There were no nails in his hands or his feet."

My dear king was still weeping. We had collected him off the ground and made him sit on a bench. He sat with his shoulders slumped, his hands pressed between his knees, his tears streaming steadily down his pale, soft cheeks. If someone had told him to "sit up like a big boy," it would not have felt out of place. The greyhound had stationed herself between the king's legs and was periodically reaching up and licking his face. He did not resist.

While my beloved king recovered from the shock of losing the most precious relic in France, I turned on the children and their guide, Michelangelo.

"As I see it," I said, standing before them, my legs set apart, my hands on my hips, "there are two possible explanations of what has just occurred. One is highly unlikely. The other is *very* disturbing.

"The first: that you are a group of modern saints. One of you just *happens* to have a vision predicting the disappearance of France's greatest treasure. Then, you stumble upon the king—just moments before he learns of the loss of the Nail. It should be noted that this 'saint' claims never to have seen the king before, and yet she recognizes him from her highly convenient 'vision.'

"The second explanation, both more likely and more

disturbing: This was all a plot. You stole the Holy Nail. You knew where the king would be, perhaps through friends of Michelangelo's here in the abbey. You present yourselves as miracle workers—without the *faintest* evidence, I might add—in an attempt to gain the king's trust. I don't know what you did with the Nail. Sell it? Or maybe you'll return it, having 'found the cul-prit' and pinned your crime on some poor fool? Either way, you'll have ingratiated yourselves with the king. Which, I imagine, would have been the prime purpose of the plot."

After letting my accusation hang in the quiet air of the refectory for a moment, I added:

"If this second explanation is the case, I must note, you are *incredibly* good actors, because right now you all look completely flabbergasted."

It was true. They did. All four of them stared at me with their brows knitted and their mouths hanging open.

The king had, thankfully, stopped weeping by now. Occasionally a tear would slide down his royal nose and dangle from its curved tip, but at least the loud sobbing had ceased. He was paying attention to my trial. Interest-ingly, the dog was, too. She came and sat between myself and the children, and her head moved back and forth be-tween us, like a spectator at a university debate.

After a moment of stunned silence, Michelangelo replied, "Do we even know that the Nail was stolen? The abbot here tells us it was lost while it was passed around for pilgrims to venerate. Might it not have just fallen from its jar?"

"You keep the Holy Nail in a jar?" Jacob said.

"Well, a vase, really. It is passed around in its vase for the pilgrims to kiss. The vase and the Nail are kept in a great golden reliquary, adorned with gems and precious metals and the great eagles of Charlemagne, who had the reliquary made."

"Great eagles?" said William.

"Yes," I said, "Charlemagne's coat of arms was an eagle—" I stopped speaking, for I suddenly knew what William had meant. He was referring to Jeanne's vision.

Louis understood, too. He stood up and turned to the abbot. "Do you have horses?"

"Of course, my liege."

"Fast ones?"

"Yes, of course . . ."

"Saddle them now!" He turned to Michelangelo and the children. "You will not leave here till the Nail is found." The greyhound barked at the king. He looked at the dog. "Nor you neither."

Before I left the abbey with the king, I instructed one of the monks to listen behind a door at the side of the refectory, in case Michelangelo and the children revealed some treachery. This is what he witnessed:

As soon as they were alone, William announced, "Either they find the Nail, or they hang us from our thumbs until we tell them where we've hidden it."

"Indeed," Michelangelo said, sighing. "Our mission may be over before it has begun."

"Our *lives* may be over before *they've* begun," Jacob added, cradling his head in his hands.

"Why did you tell the king about my visions?" Jeanne snapped at Michelangelo. "After he's done hanging us by our thumbs he's likely to burn us as heretics and magicians."

Michelangelo frowned and stared at the floor.

"Well?" Jeanne demanded.

Michelangelo shrugged. "I thought it would help."

"It's more likely to get us killed."

Michelangelo tugged at the fat under his chin. Then he said, "I do hope he finds the Nail."

Jacob groaned. Jeanne put her head on a table and covered it with her arms.

Rain was falling outside the small, high windows, tiptoeing on the black branches and cold soil when we returned to the refectory. The earth smelled of thaw, and the smell, which is both hopeful and sad, seeped into the room, riding the wetness of the air.

We entered like a funeral procession.

First the abbot. Then I, and the other companions, and finally the king.

Or perhaps it was more like an execution.

The king walked directly to Jeanne. He stood over the little girl.

"Stand up!" I shouted.

Jeanne stood. Jacob and William and Michelangelo did, too. The dog began to whine.

The king said, "We have searched the church."

Jeanne closed her eyes. The rain was falling harder now, beating the roof of the refectory like the drums of war, running down the sluices in torrents.

And then the little girl was lifted into the air. She opened her eyes. She was suspended *above* the king. *By* the king.

"We found it!" the king cried. *"We found it!"*

Michelangelo bellowed, "God be praised!" We started laughing, clapping the children on the back and rubbing their heads. William turned and threw his arms around Jacob, who was nearly crushed to death.

And still the king carried Jeanne around the room, beaming up into her face, singing, "We found it! We found it!" Gwenforte danced at the king's feet.

Jeanne managed to say, "Where?"

The king stopped dancing. He kept Jeanne suspended above his head. He looked into her eyes. "It had fallen into the mouth of one of the eagles. All the way down its throat and into its hollow belly. A hungry eagle indeed!" He laughed and started dancing again. "We found it! We found it!"

I watched Jeanne, hoisted up and down in the air by the king. She glanced at the other children. Their lips were lined with sweat, their faces drawn. But they were smiling at her.

As the king thrust her over and over again into the air, she tried to return her friends' smiles. But as she was going up and down, up and down, she was mostly focusing on not being sick all over the king's head.

———————————

Outside the inn, a rooster crows.

Joinville stops speaking and looks up, as if woken from a dream. "Was that the cock?" he demands.

"Just the first," I say. "Calm yourself. It is long before dawn."

"But I don't have until dawn!" he says. "I have to be back in Paris tonight! We set out in the morning. I just stopped in to have some food, and I got caught up in your tales . . ." He stands and quickly bows. "My apologies for leaving my tale half told. But I hope to be by the king's side when he brings these outlaws to justice. He and his hundred knights."

"When did they become outlaws? And why?" I cry. But Joinville is already banging his way through the crowded inn and out the door, into the fallen darkness. I look around, at a loss. "Does *anyone* know?"

And then, my eyes swivel to the little nun. She has not moved from her stool. During Joinville's tale, she seemed to have grown smaller, more thoughtful. Now she looks up. She doesn't say a word. But of course she knows.

"Please," I say, "Sister, tell me. What crime did these children commit that they have fallen so far, so fast?"

"A crime most terrible," says the nun.

CHAPTER 18

The Sixth Part of the Nun's Tale

The king asked if he might take the travelers back to Paris, and Michelangelo eagerly agreed. They traveled in caravan—two carts, each pulled by strong horses. The king and Joinville sat in the back of the first cart, and the king insisted that Michelangelo and the children ride with him. The rest of his companions rode in the second cart.

The rain was still falling, so the cart drivers suspended woolen blankets between four stakes that stuck up from the corners of the carts. Though the king and his companions were still wrapped in their cloaks of gray, no one would mistake them for monks, for, as William noted silently, what monk would ruin a perfectly good blanket just to keep the rain off his back?

As they rode toward Paris, Louis peppered the children with questions. About their gifts and about their histories. Jacob was careful to keep clear of any hints of his religion and therefore obscured his own story as much as possible. William, on the other hand, was happy to share details of his exploits with the king and his companion Joinville. The big oblate could barely contain his enthusiasm, and he recounted his history very amusingly. The king seemed utterly taken with the children. Can you imagine how the most pious king in the history of France would feel about sharing a cart with living, breathing *saints*?

On the other hand, can you imagine how Michelangelo and the children felt sharing a cart with a living, breathing *king of France*? They could not have been more nervous and awestruck if the Archangel Gabriel himself had descended to earth.

As the carts rumbled along, Paris began to grow around them. At first it was scattered villages, surrounded by the tendrils of the wood of Vincennes. Then the density became more like the town of Saint-Denis—tall wooden houses packed side by side. And still it grew.

The humanity multiplied. And multiplied. Like turning over a log in a wood and finding the underside teaming with life, and then realizing that the entire forest floor teems, too, and that this log, pulsing with creatures, is only one sliver of the great seething masses of life spreading out in every direction all around one's feet—just so, as the royal oxcarts rolled on, each street of Paris appeared to the children like its own world, its own universe of life, teeming with more humans than they had

ever seen. And then they would be reminded, by some skittering side alley or diagonally crossing lane, that this stretch of street was but an infinitesimally small slice of Paris, and that the city multiplied out and out and out. Trying to comprehend its enormity was like trying to imagine the enormity of God. The human mind is simply not up to the task.

There was every kind of person the children could imagine on the streets of Paris. There were wealthy trades- men, wearing the emblems of their guilds on their finely woven, rain-soaked sleeves. There were peddlers, who were like the tradesmen but poorer, that carried their goods on their backs. One was selling broomsticks, and he shuffled over the muddy roads like a walking stack of kindling. There were lepers, moaning for alms. There were proud young knights, pushing past the wet rabble, their sheathed swords swinging like ship booms, occasionally smacking in the face the children who ran behind them, begging for bread. There were merchants, whose sons had set off on ships up the Seine to England or on horses down to Italy or even the Holy Land, their fathers left at home to pull the skin below their chins and worry loudly over their balance books—as they worried silently about their sons. There were students, students, and more students. One day, they would be the gray counselors of the world. But now they were just black-clad boys, some depressed, some drunk, shouting at one another across the lanes about philosophy and that butcher's beautiful redheaded daughter.

They passed streets full of bakers, streets full of butchers, streets lined with the stalls of seamstresses, and another with the shops of tanners, and then another of furriers, and finally a street of only hatmakers—which the children had not even realized was a job.

A sudden thumping on the side of the cart made everyone turn their heads. A student, dressed in black, with freckles, black hair, and a chipped tooth, grinned at them all. "Sorry to bother you, friends. But there's an event tonight you won't want to miss down the university way. The English house debates the Flemish—a *sic et non* argument on whether God or free will is the cause of evil in the world. Just after vespers, at the Learned Scholar Tavern." His smile widened. "We English'll swab the floor with them. You'll see."

The student was about to start off, but Joinville's round, refined voice called him back. "Student! Which side are the English arguing? God or free will?"

The student suddenly looked at a loss. "Well, you see, *I'm* not actually arguing, sir. So I don't really know. But I'll be there!" The student smacked the side of the cart, grinned at them with his chipped-tooth smile, and crossed the road, shouting, "Debate tonight! English to trounce the Flemish!"

"He'll be there, all right." Joinville laughed. "Soused to the gills."

"Can we go?" William asked.

"You wouldn't want to do that," Joinville replied. "It'll

just turn into a fistfight before the night's out. Always did in my day."

William sat up straighter. "That sounds all right with me."

Even the king laughed.

Just then, they passed one man shouting at two others. The shouting man was tall and blond and clad in a rich robe. His accent was somewhere between Italian and German, which likely meant he came from Lombardy. His face was red with fury, and he spat as he spoke.

"It was *my* account! Mine! How dare you undercut my price!"

He was shouting at two Jews. One was old, with a long beard, streaked with gray. The other was younger, and nearly as tall as the blond man. His beard was short cropped and handsome. He was holding the Lombard back and shouting, "You offer a usurious rate! Forty percent! Forty! My uncle offered thirty. Thirty is reasonable! Thirty is standard! But thirty is undercutting now?"

"Ah," sighed Joinville. "The disputes of the moneylenders. The Lombards only recently brought their usury to Paris, you see, where the money-lending trade has always been Jewish. The Lombards are not used to the competition. I don't think they like it."

"They moved here," King Louis sniffed, "because I disallowed my Jews from lending with interest. And yet still they do it! Oh, my wicked, wicked Jews! Paris is packed with them. I look out my window and the bridges around the isle are *thronging* with Jews. A good Christian can barely pass. It's an infestation. They say there are ten thousand in Paris alone. Ten *thousand*! How I *hate* them!"

Jacob stopped breathing. He should have known. He did know, but he had made himself forget it. He had begun to like King Louis—if it makes any sense to say you *like* the *king*. But he should have kept forefront in his mind that he was a Jew, and Louis was bound by law and religion to hate him and all his kind. Had he remembered that, maybe this moment, this inevitable moment, wouldn't have been quite so shocking and painful. Jeanne glanced at Jacob, saw the thoughts that were passing behind his frozen, glassy eyes, and wished that they were anywhere, *anywhere* else.

The Lombard had raised a big, pale hand. The young Jew pushed his uncle back against a timber-framed wall. He would not raise his fist against the Lombard, for it would be a serious crime for a Jew to strike a Christian. The cart was past them now and slowly moving away. Jacob wondered whether striking a Jew was a crime at all.

"They are worse than peasants, the Jews are," Louis went on. Jeanne started like she'd been slapped. Jacob saw her face and nearly laughed, jerked out of his misery by someone else's. "Both are filthy," Louis went on. "Both unruly. Both ignorant." William gaped at the king. Jeanne was sitting *right beside* him—surely he hadn't forgotten? "But the Jews lead the peasants away from Christ, and for this, they are worse."

And then, there was the sound like an axe hitting a tree. Everyone in the cart turned. The Lombard had reached around the nephew and struck the elder Jew, knocking him to the ground. The nephew was crouching beside his uncle now, trying to protect him from further onslaughts—without risking his life by hitting the Lombard back.

It was all William could do not to leap from the cart and tackle the Lombard. He felt Michelangelo grab his sleeve to stop him. Jacob was gripping the side of the cart and his nails dug into the wet wood. The sound of the slap had woken Gwenforte, and she barked and barked at the Lombard, not sure what was going on but knowing she did not like it.

And then Louis was out of the cart. It was too fast for Joinville to prevent. He saw it happen, made a grab for the king to hold him back, and missed.

"God's body!" he swore. Then he turned to the cart driver. "De Villiers!" he barked. "Go help the king!"

The driver was down in an instant, and the driver of the other cart, seeing what was happening, was running to the king, too, his sword drawn. The children watched as the king strode toward the Lombard and the Jews. "What is going on?" muttered William. The king had untied the cord at his throat. The gray cloak slid to the mud. Rain pelted his fine clothes.

"Stay your hand!" the king bellowed.

The Lombard spun.

"Kneel before the king!" the driver, de Villiers, barked. The Lombard was so surprised and disoriented that he likely would have kneeled to a pig farmer. He fell to both knees in the muddy road.

The young Jew assumed a knee, too. His uncle tried to struggle out of the mud.

"For disturbing the king's peace," the king announced, "the fine is five silver *livres*. All three of you will pay this fine. Do you understand?"

The three moneylenders nodded, bowing their heads, their eyes averted.

"For assaulting one of the king's Jews," Louis went on, "the fine is fifteen *livres*." The Lombard looked up at the furious king, and raindrops splashed off his freckled cheeks. He looked shocked. "Can you pay twenty *livres*?" the king demanded. "Or will you go to prison?"

"I can pay!" the Lombard said. "I can pay!"

"What is your name?"

"Johann Montefiore, of Lombardy!" the man said, groveling.

"Johann Montefiore, of Lombardy, if you do not report to the Hall of Justice tonight, you will be found and thrown into prison."

"Yes, my king! Thank you, my lord!"

Louis stepped around the groveling Lombard. "And you!" he said, addressing the Jewish men, their cloaks covered in mud.

He pointed a finger in their faces. "You will report to

the Hall of Justice as well, and you will render every *livre* of every usurious loan you've made to the chancellor. If you did not persist in your wicked usury and your incomprehensible refusal to acknowledge the Gospel of Christ, good Christians would not strike you in the streets! You have no one to blame but yourselves!"

With that, Louis marched back to the cart and climbed in. Joinville grabbed his elbow and his underarm and helped him up.

"Well," sighed Joinville, once the king was aboard, "so much for going incognito."

As they rumbled along the muddy roads of Paris, an uncomfortable silence settled on the group. Jacob's feelings raged so hot and confusing that they stopped up his throat. But a thousand questions buzzed behind his eyes. Jeanne saw this, knew Jacob dared not speak, and knew just what he would ask if he dared to—for she had the same question.

"Your Majesty, why did you do that?" she said.

"Why did I do what?"

"Prevent that Lombard from beating those men. Why do that, if you hate Jews so much?"

The king looked genuinely surprised by the question. "We are not barbarians! Let them attack the Jews in the Rhineland, with their Peasants' Crusades. Not here. The Jews are my children. Wayward, wicked children. But my children nonetheless. I hate them, but I will protect them."

Jacob tried to keep his face under control, but his jaw was quivering, and his eyes were like cups of water. Brimming, but not spilling. Yet.

"Your Majesty," Jeanne said, in her gentlest voice. "What about the town of Nogent-sur-Oise? It burned this week. A fire started by Christians in the Jewish quarter. People died."

Michelangelo cleared his throat and said, "That is nothing to do with us. It is none of our business, Jeanne."

But King Louis said, "I heard about that. It is a *disgrace*." He looked as if he'd bitten into a rotten pear. "A stain on all of France. It makes me sick."

Jacob stared at the king, his limp hair dripping with raindrops. How could he hate the Jews and yet feel sick when they were attacked? Louis hated peasants, too, apparently, and yet he had no problem sitting beside Jeanne—hoisting her in the air and dancing, even. Jacob tried to turn this over in his head, around and around, like the cartwheels beneath him. But after a while, he gave up. People were too strange to understand, he decided. They were like life. And also that cheese. Too many things at once.

The carts rumbled through the streets, and now they came into the quarter of the Jews. They shouted and gestured in their lanes like any Christian would in any other alley of the city. Save for a few more beards, they looked no different from any other Parisian. But the children realized that each one's life depended on the king and his

good will. A change in his disposition, and each one could be driven from their homes by fire or thrown by angry Lombards or rowdy knights into the river Seine. It was an existence that hung by a thread. Louis held the thread.

And the children, led by Michelangelo, were going to pluck it. They would try to save the entire written wisdom of the Jews of France. They might very well fail. Worse, though, in either failing *or* succeeding, they might anger the king—and thus cause him to let the thread go.

Jeanne, Jacob, and William were becoming aware of the consequences of the task they had undertaken.

And they were afraid.

———————

The nun has stopped speaking.

"Is there more?" I say. "There is more, isn't there?"

"There is, but I have run into a problem."

"What? For God's sake, tell us!"

She lifts her mug. It is empty.

"More ale!" the innkeeper cries. Ale is brought, and the nun goes on.

CHAPTER 19

The Seventh Part of the Nun's Tale

Suddenly, the sound of the horses' hooves changed—from dull clopping on wet dirt to sharp ringing. The children sat up. Gwenforte began to whine. Jeanne and William looked over the edge of the cart. "What's happening?" Jacob asked.

"Stones!" said Jeanne. "The ground is all stones! Like in a church!"

"It's paved," Joinville laughed. "Have you never seen paving stones before?"

They shook their heads. They had not.

And then the cart was inclining, and they were climbing up onto a bridge, clattering over it and then down onto the other side. Here, the road was paved, too. What power, what riches, the children wondered, could cover the entire earth with finely hewed stone?

Then they saw, lurking in the haze of the Paris rain, a monster. Like some giant crab, all spines and legs, but

larger than a castle. A monstrous, mountainous, stone crustacean.

"Look!" Michelangelo di Bologna said to the children. "Notre Dame!"

Indeed it was. The greatest cathedral in the world, perched miraculously at the narrowest edge of an island in the middle of the river Seine. Perhaps it was not a crab, but a spider, and Paris was the spider's web, each road a strand of silk leading back to the great stone beast at its center. Straight ahead of the cart, emerging from the gray mist, were walls as gray and imposing as Notre Dame herself. Fine spires poked up above them into the rain. The entire western half of the isle at the center of Paris was trapped inside those walls.

"Is that . . . ?" William asked.

"The palace," Joinville replied.

"Welcome to my home," said the king. "Well, one of them."

The cart rattled on toward the palace's gatehouse.

"Are we going . . . in?" Jeanne asked.

"You sound as if I've taken you prisoner!" the king said with a laugh. "I was hoping, my little miracle workers, that you would stay with me awhile. I would be honored."

At this, even Michelangelo choked on his spittle. They were all too stunned to reply.

As the carts passed through the huge gatehouse, royal-blue-clad guards stepped to one side and moved to kneel to the king—until they saw who the king was riding with. One guard stopped mid-knee-bend and stared. Another dropped his spear and had to go diving after it as it clattered on the stones.

The king and Joinville exchanged small smiles.

They rumbled into a huge grassy courtyard. As they rolled to a stop, a dozen men streamed out of a nearby door and surrounded the cart. They wore red cloaks with rich blue lining and hoods that spilled over their shoulders and down their backs. Their faces were perfectly composed—but their eyes kept drifting to the children in the cart and then snapping off into the middle distance again as they recovered their discipline.

"These are my valets," Louis explained, as the cloaked men took him by his forearms and lowered him gently to the grass. "They are the sons of the finest families in France and are more loyal than anyone in the kingdom."

"Except for d'Avignon over there," Joinville said. "He's a real pain in the buttocks."

D'Avignon smiled but did not reply.

The valets helped each of the children down to the grass, which was soft and wet under their feet. Michelangelo was the last to slide down from the cart, and he refused the valets' help. "I'd crush you," he said simply, easing his legs over the side one by one, and lifting his belly over the wood with his hands.

Jeanne had kneeled beside Gwenforte to prevent her

from running off to explore the castle grounds. Or peeing in front of the king. That would be mortifying.

"Eric," the king said to the youngest valet. "These are my honored guests. Find them a room and give them new clothes." Eric looked at William and Michelangelo, and his eyes bulged. "Do your best," the king said, laughing. Then, to the children, he said, "I'll see you at dinner. You can meet my mother. She'll be thrilled to make your acquaintance."

The king led the way toward a great stone building. One of the valets ran out ahead of him, opened the door, and put his back against it, as if it might attack the king as he passed through. The king's companions followed, and then the valets went after them. Once they were out of sight, Eric the valet turned to Jeanne.

"You can let her pee now," he said.

So Jeanne let Gwenforte go. The greyhound shook herself indignantly, trotted out into the middle of the green lawn, and peed directly onto the royal grass.

The ceilings were low and the walls were close inside the Palace of the City, and everything was made of stone. Tapestries clung to the walls, which were supposed to keep the corridors warm, but also made everything smell vaguely of damp silk. As Eric led the group through the warren-like halls, the children's skin tingled, and their hair stood on end. Their senses were doubly sharp, noticing every detail. They were in the palace of the king of France. *The* palace. And why? To *commit a crime.* Jacob thought he might faint.

They came to a wooden door. Eric lifted the iron latch and pushed the door open. "Come in," he said.

The children entered a room the size of Jeanne's entire house. In the center stood an enormous bed, decked with brightly dyed blankets. Suspended from the ceiling was a cresset, and from the cresset hung curtains of silk around the bed. In the corner, five pallets—with thin mattresses and undyed blankets on each—stood in a tall stack.

"There are enough beds for all of you," Eric said. He was a young man with eager, bright blue eyes and an accent as correct as the king's. His father must be someone very important—a bishop or a lord. No doubt one day this valet would be commanding an army or managing a prince's domain somewhere, for only the most promising boys become valets for the king. "I'll set them up for you in a moment. For now, make yourselves comfortable. I'll be back with dry clothes. And firewood." Indeed, built into one wall was an enormous fireplace, cold and blackened with soot. The valet bowed as he retreated from the room.

The children gazed around them. Jacob started laughing. It was giddy, nervous laughter. William grinned and wiped the rain from his forehead—and it was replaced by sweat.

"We're in *the palace* ...," Jacob murmured.

"I cannot believe it," Michelangelo marveled. "Never did I think ..."

Jeanne said, "Are we *friends* with the *king*?" She was laughing.

William said, "Of course we are. A giant monk, a Saracen oblate, a Jew, and a peasant girl. Aren't all the king's friends like that?"

They all started laughing now. But they were laughing like travelers crossing a great river on a tattered rope bridge, finding that the rotted boards beneath their feet were, for the moment, holding.

"And a dog!" Jeanne added. "Don't forget—GWEN-FORTE!"

Everyone spun around. Gwenforte was pooping in the fireplace.

Eric had the fire going, which made the room fragrant and warm. He had also found Gwenforte's turd and somehow managed to dispose of it gracefully. He would indeed be a talented administrator one day.

"We must discuss our strategy," Michelangelo said. He sat on the great bed, and the children sat on the pallets that Eric had spread over the floor. Michelangelo still wore his Benedictine robes, for Eric could find nothing large enough to fit him. He had offered Jeanne the kind of dress a lady's daughter might wear, but Jeanne said it would make her feel stupid. Also, Eric had no idea how to help her put it on; he was relieved not to have to try. So the children, even William, wore red silk stockings and blue tunics, like royal squires. Once Eric had left again, they could not help but look at one another and laugh.

"Our luck has been outstanding," Michelangelo continued. "Never could I have predicted this." He pulled at his red whiskers and ran a hand through his thinning hair, which made it stand up like flames rising behind his head. "But we have come to the crux of our campaign. Tonight, at dinner, we will be introduced to Blanche of Castile—the king's mother." Michelangelo ran an enormous hand down Gwenforte's back, for she lay curled beside him on the great bed. "Blanche and Louis could not be closer. So this is our chance. Tonight, during the meal, I will bring up the burning of the Talmuds. I will pretend to have no opinion on the subject."

"And then?" said William.

Michelangelo exhaled heavily through his nose. He turned to Jeanne. "I did not want to ask you this, my young friend. I have considered many alternatives. But after all that we have learned of the king today, I believe this is the best way. So, I must ask: Can you fake a fit? Can you pretend you are having a vision?"

"Oh!" William exclaimed. "That's a good idea!"

But Jeanne was wrong-footed. "I don't...I don't know."

"If you could, and say that you saw the burning of the books, but the flames were the fires of Hell, and you saw that the Devil was laughing and all of France was burning, too—that might convince them to abandon their plans, don't you think?"

Jacob and William were now nodding enthusiastically. But Jeanne said, "I don't know if I can." She shifted on her mattress, and the pallet beneath her creaked. "I feel weird about it."

Michelangelo nodded slowly. "Why would that be?"

"If my visions really are messages from God, I don't want to pretend God is speaking to me when He isn't."

Michelangelo sighed. "I understand. I would expect nothing less, my earnest and good young friend." Jacob and William looked crestfallen. But Michelangelo went on. "Allow me, though, to make a counterargument. Do you believe that the books of the Jews should be burned?"

"No. I think it's awful."

"And this revulsion you feel—where does this come from?" Michelangelo had placed his enormous hands on his mountainous belly. Gwenforte raised her head to ascertain the reason that he had stopped stroking her back. She could find none and pushed his elbow with her black nose. He ignored her.

"I'm . . . not sure. I just feel it. Like a sickness in my chest," Jeanne said. "Destroying someone's books, someone's preserved wisdom, is . . . wrong. A sin."

"Yes," said Michelangelo. "I agree. But how do you know that?"

"I'm not sure."

"I know how," said Jacob. "It is the voice of God that tells you."

"This is what I believe," Michelangelo agreed. "When I see you and William and Jacob laughing together—a peasant girl, an oblate, and a Jewish boy—I think, *This is good.* When I see petals fall from a pear tree at the end of spring, spinning like dancers to the ground, I think, *This, too, is good.* But what have they in common? And when a Jew is struck by a Lombard in the street, I think, *This is very bad.* And when a book is destroyed, I think the same thing. But what have those in common? What does a Jew have in common with a book? Children with petals spinning to the earth?"

A log cracked and fell in the fireplace. The smell of roasting wood wafted out into the room.

"I don't know," Michelangelo said. "But I believe that it is the voice of God, telling me what to love and what to hate."

William saw the end of the argument and lunged for it. "So you wouldn't be faking it, Jeanne. God has told you He hates the burning of the Talmuds. Just not with a vision. He's told you with that sick feeling in your chest."

Slowly, imperceptibly at first, Jeanne began to nod. "Yes. I think that's true."

But Jacob, suddenly, had doubts. "King Louis hates Jews," he said. "He probably feels *that* in his gut as well. And peasants, too. Is that God, telling him to hate me and Jeanne?"

Michelangelo sighed. "God is mysterious and works in mysterious ways. But Louis held Jeanne aloft and carried her around a room. He sat beside you both on our trip to Paris. I do not think he hates you. I think he has been taught to hate the *idea* of Jews and peasants. By his mother, by the church, by his lords— who benefit from exploiting their peasants and con- fiscating the Jews' money on the flimsiest pretenses. Distinguishing the voice of God and the voices of those around us is no easy task. What makes you spe- cial, children, beyond your miracles, is that you hear God's voice clearly, and when you hear it, you act upon it." He fixed Jeanne with his beady red-brown eyes. "So, will you act now?"

Jeanne sucked in her breath. She looked to William and Jacob. They were watching her with a mix of hope and apprehension. She exhaled. "I'll do it."

"Good." Michelangelo smiled. "Very good. Now, listen carefully. Besides Jeanne's performance, you will all be models of politeness. You will *not* express opinions about the burning or about Jews or, really, about anything. We do not want them to think we have come with an agenda. Give them no cause for suspicion. Yes?"

"Yes," William and Jacob said at once.

After a moment, Jeanne said, "Yes," too.

Even Gwenforte barked, but it probably just meant *Why is no one petting me?*

"Hopefully, Jeanne's performance will convince the king of the wickedness of his plans. But if it does not, if we fail tonight," Michelangelo concluded, "we must take . . . rasher action."

"What action?" Jacob asked.

Michelangelo stared at the flames consuming the dry wood.

All he said was, "For the safety of us all, let us hope we do not fail."

————————

"Please forgive me," Gerald says, rising to his feet.

"You don't want to hear this?" I shout.

"I want to hear this *very* much. But I also have to pee really, really badly."

"Water break!" the innkeeper bellows. I rise to my feet. Aron and Marie stand up, too. We'll all go find some bushes outside the inn.

I look to the nun. "You don't have to go?"

She smiles at me. "Oh no, I'm fine."

"You've had quite a lot to drink."

She just smiles placidly at me. We get our water break over as fast we can, so we can return to the story.

CHAPTER 20

The Eighth Part of the Nun's Tale

The torches sputtered and spoke in their sconces on the walls of the corridor. Eric led the way. Michelangelo walked behind him, and after him, the children padded along in single file, their leather soles scuffing against the stones. Gwenforte trotted beside Jeanne, her head erect and her nose working the air, taking in the scents of the coming feast.

Jeanne was sweating. She was walking as in a dark dream. She was trying to remember what she did during her fits—or rather, trying to imagine—for during them she wasn't conscious of herself or her body. She threw her mind back to what others had told her about them. *Do I fall down first? Do I cry? Grit my teeth? Be still? Tremble?* Mostly, she could not quiet the nagging voice that said, *No one will believe you.*

Jacob, walking behind Jeanne, was lost in his own thoughts—about his parents and Lombards and fires—

until William reached over him and put a hand on Jeanne's shoulder. "Are you all right?" William whispered.

"I don't know."

Jacob let his other worries slide away. He said, "You'll do great, Jeanne."

Jeanne shook her head as if she knew that he was wrong. Jacob hoped he wasn't. For their sakes and for the sake of the Talmuds and all the Jews of France.

They came to a T in the corridor and went left. Eric had explained that those dining at the high table, as the children and Michelangelo had been invited to do, waited in the corridor outside the great hall until the king was ready to enter. They would, for the evening, be part of his entourage. Even Gwenforte. William, peering past Michelangelo's shoulder, could make out a single file of men, already waiting ahead of them. The one at the end of the queue turned. It was Joinville.

"Ah!" He smiled, his teeth unnervingly white, his dimple unnervingly handsome. "Children! Come! Come! I want to introduce you to a friend." Eric stepped out of the way, and Michelangelo pressed himself against the wall so the children could squeeze by.

As they passed him, Jeanne felt Michelangelo's hot breath. "Good luck," he whispered. Her stomach felt like a dog making its bed—turning around in circles and then flopping onto its side.

Joinville was holding the arm of one of the king's other companions. The man had a heavy brow, with dark lines

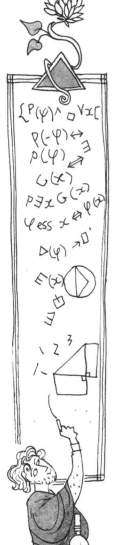

of hair like caterpillars above his eyes. "This is Robert de Sorbonne. Besides being a great man of the church, he has founded a college for poor scholars at the university." Jeanne and Jacob nodded politely, their minds very much elsewhere. But William had suddenly forgotten their task for the evening. He straightened his long back and smiled at Robert de Sorbonne. "Robert, this rather large oblate was expressing interest in the university."

"Indeed?" Robert said, wrinkling his chin and sending his caterpillars crawling toward each other. It wasn't clear whether he was more taken aback by William's size or the unexpected hue of his skin.

Joinville smiled slyly at William and then said to Sorbonne, "Maybe you would consider enrolling him in your college?"

William's mouth fell open. It literally fell, as if he'd lost the use of his lower jaw. Meanwhile, the caterpillars continued to crawl toward each other and upward on Robert de Sorbonne's forehead.

William saw where this was going. *Here it comes*, he thought. *He's going to ask if I'm a Saracen. Or maybe a demon. No, no, he's learned. A Saracen.*

"It depends," Robert de Sorbonne said at last, eyeing William skeptically, "on what he thinks of Master Albertus's proof of the existence of God."

That was *not* what William was expecting.

Jacob craned his neck to see the big boy's face. To Jacob's dismay, William looked utterly lost. They stood in silence, William's mouth working, but no sound coming out. He was being given an entrance exam to the University of Paris. And he wasn't saying a word.

After a moment, Robert de Sorbonne murmured, "Not sure? That's all right. Don't worry about it." He sounded slightly disappointed, but not surprised.

At which point William said, "I'm sorry—"

"It's quite all right."

"—but which proof do you mean?"

"What?" Sorbonne said, slightly taken aback. "Albertus Magnus, of the—"

"Yes, Master Albertus, late of Cologne, now of the University of Paris. Of course. But he has two proofs of God, one in the *Summa de Creaturis* and the other in *De Praedicabilibus*. I'm not sure which you're referring to."

It was Robert de Sorbonne's turn to stammer. "Uh . . . either one."

"Well, if I have to choose between the two, the *Summa* proof is stronger. The other's a bit slippery for my taste. Rather convenient." William shrugged apologetically.

Sorbonne threw back his head and laughed from deep down in his belly. "And I thought I'd stumped you!" He turned to Joinville. "I daresay we could find a place for him."

When he heard that, William tried not to smile so broadly that you could see straight down his throat.

"Now, now! The revelry is supposed to happen over dinner! No fair starting without me!" It was a woman's voice, reedy and low in the darkness of the corridor. It

stilled Robert de Sorbonne at once. Joinville's smile froze
on his face. He stepped to one side. "My lady," he said
stiffly, "allow me to introduce—"

"I *know* who they are," said the Queen Mother, Blanche
of Castile. "My *son* has told me *all* about them."

Standing in the dark corridor, illuminated by the
torchlight dancing in the sconces, was a short woman
in a simple white dress, which was fastened around her
waist with a simple blue cord. Her hair was dark brown
and worn in braids upon her head. Perched upon that nest
of braids was a simple ring of gold, very much like the one
Joinville had worn earlier that day. On her left hand she
wore a ring that was as simple as it was ostentatious—a
single sapphire, bright and blue and round like an egg. She
smelled strange to Jeanne, Jacob, and William. Musky and
sweet at the same time. They did not realize it, but she was
the first person they'd ever met who wore perfume.

"Greetings, my children," she said. "Though some of
you hardly *look* like children," she added, nodding at William. "You are very welcome in my—"

She stopped speaking. Gwenforte had begun to growl.
The growl had started so low in her throat that it had, at
first, been inaudible. But it rose in volume and pitch. The
hair on Gwenforte's back stood up. "Gwenforte!" Jeanne
hissed.

"It's all right," Blanche of Castile assured them, edging
away. "Just skittish around strangers, I'm sure."

Gwenforte barked. Viciously. The rasping, warning

bark of an angry dog. She pulled her lips back from her teeth, which glowed yellow amid her gums in the dim light of the torch fires. She barked again.

"Gwenforte!" Jeanne reprimanded her. But Gwen-forte would not quiet. She growled and barked, growled and barked some more. Her intensity was frightening. She was no longer a greyhound. She looked like a wolf. Blanche of Castile recoiled. Everyone in the corridor had turned to look.

"Jeanne!" Michelangelo whispered. "For God's sake, get her out of here!"

Jeanne tried to grab Gwenforte by the neck, but the greyhound shimmied away and barked again at Blanche.

"What's wrong with her?" Jeanne muttered.

"The king!" William exclaimed. "He's coming!"

Indeed he was, striding down the dark corridor to-ward them, followed by his wife and her retinue. In one swift motion, William scooped Gwenforte off the ground and carried her down the hall toward their room. The greyhound barked and snarled over his shoulder.

Jeanne and Jacob and Michelangelo watched them go, shaking, sweating, spent already. And dinner had not even begun.

"What was that about?" King Louis asked, approach-ing the group.

"Nothing to worry over, my dear," his mother cooed, turning to her son and patting his face with a small, plump, perfumed hand. "Just a stupid animal. Shall we go

in to dinner?" She took her son by the arm and led him away from the children.

Michelangelo peeled himself from the wall and leaned down to Jeanne and Jacob.

"So far, I think the plan is going beautifully."

The doors to the great hall were thrown open, and a sextet of natural trumpets blared as the king walked out upon the dais. Once the trumpet fanfare faded away, a chorus of men began to sing, their voices blending like threads of silk on a loom.

The retinue entered the hall after the king—first Blanche of Castile, followed by Queen Marguerite, King Louis's wife, with their infant daughter in her arms. Next came the king's companions and a few companions of Marguerite's. Finally Michelangelo and the children, with William catching up with them just in time.

"I shut her in the room," William whispered. Jeanne nodded. She thought she was going to be ill. The hall was the grandest space she had ever been in—higher roofed than any church, wider than most fields, filled with hundreds of diners at scores of long tables. And these were not the rough wooden tables of Lord Bertulf's hall—no, each table shimmered with silver. Above their heads, the double-barrel-vaulted ceiling was painted deep blue, with golden stars aping the real heavens just beyond.

As Jeanne took all this in, her step faltered.

"If you're going to have a real fit," William whispered in her ear, "that'll work, too."

She made her way, half in a trance, to the high table, where she found, to her horror, that she was sitting directly opposite Blanche of Castile. Jacob was to her right, and William was next to Jacob. Joinville, Michelangelo, Robert de Sorbonne, and the king were seated around them. Jeanne felt like she was going to throw up all over the silk tablecloth.

Servants began to bring forth food. Massive, elaborate dishes. An enormous boiled peacock, its head and tail feathers intact, was placed between Jeanne and Blanche. Now Jeanne was pretty sure she *would* throw up.

"So, children," Blanche of Castile began. "You are a strange and piebald crew!"

The children didn't know what to say to that, so they sat mutely and waited. Blanche's face had the plumpness of adolescence, but in the flickering firelight of the great hall, wrinkles collected at her eyes and lips. Her youthful beauty was betrayed by the shadows.

"And this is your brave leader, I take it? Michelangelo di Bologna, of Saint-Denis?"

"At your service, madame."

"Are you?" Blanche replied, cocking her head. "I've heard such *strange* things about you, Brother Michelangelo. Red, fat, and wicked. Don't they say that?"

"Well, yes, I suppose—"

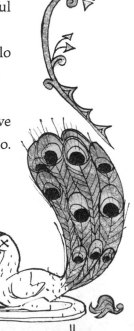

"They got the *fat* part right, didn't they?" Blanche laughed a high, arching laugh—like notes on a flute. Sweat began to sting the back of Jeanne's neck. Joinville looked at the table. The king said, "Mother, *please*."

"Oh, it's just a joke, my darling! No need to be so pious *all* the time! God knows I don't *blame* the poor man for wobbling like venison jelly!" She laughed again. Michelangelo smiled graciously and wiped his forehead with his sleeve.

"And you, my little peasant girl," Blanche said to Jeanne. She had a way of claiming possession of everyone and everything: *my darling, my child, my little peasant.* Now Jeanne's stomach had curled up like a caterpillar in the shadow of a bird. "I see we don't like girl's clothes, do we? Used to wearing breeches out in the fields?"

"I-I suppose so . . . ," Jeanne stammered.

"That's all right!" Blanche smiled. "You're not very pretty, so dressing as a boy rather suits you!"

"Mother!" Louis exclaimed.

"The truth will set you free, my love," she cooed. "And you—" She turned to William, pointing with the hand that wore the ovoid sapphire. William clenched his fists under the table. Striking the queen mother dead with his bare hands would *not* advance their cause. "Your father was supposed to be on Crusade, and instead he fell for a Saracen girl, hm?"

William felt the veins in his head throb. *Don't kill her,* he thought. *Don't kill her.*

"Then he shipped you off to a monastery, so his wife wouldn't find out? You probably don't see him much. How sad." William suddenly didn't know if he wanted to scream or to cry. Joinville put his face in his hands. Robert de Sorbonne smiled distantly, as if he were listening to an entirely different conversation.

"And you," Blanche said, turning to Jacob. Suddenly Jeanne's worries about herself and her playacted fit evaporated. She realized that a much greater charade, with even more serious consequences, was being played by her Jewish friend. How had she forgotten that? How selfish had she been? William and Michelangelo seemed to realize it, too. William leaned forward over his untouched food. Michelangelo pretended to drink his wine, but his eyes bulged over the rim of his cup. "I was told by a little bird," Blanche went on, "that your village burned down. What a tragedy. However did it happen?"

Through lips as white and brittle as a swallow's egg, Jacob said, "I suppose someone was careless with their cooking fire."

"Is that all?" Blanche murmured, raising her thin eyebrows. "Just like a peasant, to burn his own village from sheer stupidity!"

"*Mother . . .*" Louis sighed.

But at the same moment, Jacob said, "Better than burning books from sheer stupidity."

Michelangelo dropped his pewter cup onto his silver plate. The crash echoed through the hall. Nonetheless, no one at the table was looking at him. They were all staring at Jacob. Which, in one sense, was good, because Michelangelo's mouth was still open, as if he'd expected his cup to be pouring wine into it, while in fact the wine ran over the tablecloth and into his lap.

"What was that?" Blanche asked very quietly.

"I said at least we don't burn books out of sheer stupidity, like you do." Jacob's hands were trembling, but his voice was strong.

The king sat up a little straighter in his wooden chair.

"And what books would those be?" Blanche asked, innocent as a flower.

"Jewish books. The work of centuries. The wisdom of the ages," Jacob said.

Blanche leaned in. "What a strange peasant you are. Not many peasant boys defending the Jews, are there?"

"Listen," the king cut in. He was clearly as uncomfortable as everyone else. "These books that we're burning. They're not wisdom."

"Yes," said Blanche. "And I wonder who told you they were." Her gaze moved to Michelangelo. His red eyes caught hers and dove for the table, where wine was still pouring into his lap.

"They're not Bibles," Louis went on. "They're Talmuds. New laws. Not God's. They are misreadings of the Good Book, perpetrated by rabbis to lead the Jews away from God's word."

"It's for the Jews' own good," Blanche agreed.

William could not contain himself any longer. His large rear end had been wriggling in his chair as he tried to keep his mouth shut, as if the energy of his lips needed to be transferred somewhere. But the butt-wiggling solution proved temporary and insufficient. "But think of the work alone!" William practically shouted. "One book can take a lifetime to compose, copy, illuminate, gloss, and annotate! A lifetime in each book. You'll be confining *dozens* of life-times to the flames!"

"Dozens?" said Blanche. "Who told you dozens?"

"I—" William stammered. "I assumed it was at least—"

"Thousands," Blanche said proudly. "We've collected thousands of Jewish books from all over the kingdom. The abbots collected them for us, actually. They asked to 'borrow' them, for 'copying' purposes, from their local Jews. Lots of flattery was involved, I'm sure. The Jews are so proud. Probably a few threats, too, truth be told. But it's all for the good of their souls!"

"Sometimes we must harm in order to help," the king agreed.

"Yes, yes. They were counted at Saint-Denis, and they'll be coming to Paris tomorrow for the burning!"

"Tomorrow?" Michelangelo exclaimed.

"Why, yes! Right on the old bridge, where the mon-eylenders are. Send the Jews quite a message, right, my sweet?" Blanche said to her son.

The king nodded, his lank hair swaying beside his

pale cheeks. "If it will save a single soul of my Jews, it will have been worthwhile."

Jacob stole a glance at Jeanne. Would she perform? Her head hung listlessly over her untouched food.

"Tomorrow," Michelangelo muttered. "Tomorrow."

"Shall I . . . ?" the nun says, looking at the avid faces of her audience.

"Yes!" we all cry at once.

So she continues.

CHAPTER 21

The Ninth Part of the Nun's Tale

That night, Michelangelo lay in the large bed in their room and the children lay on their pallets all around him on the floor. William was using two. Gwenforte lay beside Jacob, curled between his ribs and his arm.

"I'm sorry," Jacob said to the darkness. The pallet beneath him creaked. "I'm sorry I mentioned the burning. I couldn't help it."

No one could blame him. No one could forgive him.

"I hate her," he said. "I *hate* her."

"You and Gwenforte both," William answered.

"We all hate her," said Jeanne. Her hands rested on her belly, and she gazed up at the ceiling. Candlelight from the cresset over the great bed threw the faintest flicker of brown light over the stones.

"Why didn't you have the fit, Jeanne?" Jacob asked. "Because I brought up the burning?"

"She couldn't very well have done it after, could she?" William said. "No one would have believed it."

Gwenforte whined and kicked Jacob in her sleep.

"Try to close your eyes, children," Michelangelo said. "Tomorrow, martyrdom may call."

A choking silence squeezed the room.

Finally William said, "Oh, I'll fall *right* to sleep now."

Jeanne and Jacob laughed.

Except it sounded more like crying.

Jeanne had no idea what time it was when Michelangelo's fat hand grabbed her shoulder and shook her awake. The candle in the cresset still burned dimly, but the lack of windows in the stone walls made it impossible to tell whether it was dawn or the middle of the night. She lay still and listened for a moment as Michelangelo moved to wake up the other children. There was no sound in the corridor. If it was morning, Jeanne guessed it was very early yet. Jacob sat on his pallet, rubbing his face with his hands. William snored on. Michelangelo grabbed a shoulder and shook him. He shook him again.

"You have to get Gwenforte to do it," Jeanne said. Jacob smiled wanly.

Gwenforte was led—reluctantly, for she was still sleepy—from Jacob's pallet up to William's face. She dutifully began to lick him. William winced, tried to push her away, and then rolled over onto the floor.

"Does your wickedness know no bounds?" he muttered.

Jeanne smiled. But her stomach felt hollow and sour, and she couldn't tell whether it was the early hour and her empty belly, or dread of the day to come.

Michelangelo opened the door to their chamber. Eric was lying on a pallet in the corridor. He raised his head sleepily.

"We have an early morning rendezvous," Michelangelo whispered. "You might show us out."

Eric led them through the darkened corridors—where every other torch had been extinguished and the tapestries looked woven from black silk—and back to the courtyard they'd come through. The Parisian sky was gray and low. The sun would not rise for a little while yet. Gwenforte ran out onto the grass and squatted. No one stopped her.

They left the palace through a small door by the main gate—the guard nodded them through sleepily—and walked on the paving stones to the great square in front of Notre Dame. Her two towers seemed to touch the belly of the clouds. Her great rose window looked down like a dark and malevolent eye.

"The street of the bakers is this way. We shall forage for breakfast," Michelangelo said, his voice hushed in the quiet hour. It was strange to see the great city, home to the whole world, so asleep. A few beggars lay under the great tympanum of Notre Dame's doorway. Along one side of the church, a priest clad in black stole from an alley and into a side door.

"I wonder where he's been," William smirked. No one replied.

The street of the bakers was just a short walk north of the Isle of the City. The streets were dirt again here on the north bank. This was the territory of merchants, of tradesmen, of butchers and tanners and brewsters. To the south of the isle, Paris was mostly farms and university buildings.

The houses here had candles blazing in all their windows, and men and women and children hurried back and forth, up and down the street, bringing flour from the market stalls a few streets away, trading with a neighbor some salt for some yeast. Some windows were open and from them wafted the intoxicating smell of fresh bread. Michelangelo approached one of these and leaned his large elbow on the sill. A woman's head appeared. One of her cheeks was pasty with flour.

"Three loaves," Michelangelo told her. "If you please. And if you have some scraps for our dog, she would thank you."

Three long, thin loaves of bread appeared on the sill, plus a misshapen lump of burned dough. Money was exchanged. Michelangelo gave one loaf to William, split another between Jeanne and Jacob, and threw the lump to Gwenforte. She began to attack it ferociously, gnawing on it with the side of her mouth, dancing around it as if it were an animal she had successfully brought down in a hunt. When she saw Michelangelo and the children begin to walk away down the street, she picked it up in her mouth and trotted proudly after them, carrying her kill high for all to see.

Michelangelo led them down an alley of dim residences, much like Yehuda's alley in Saint-Denis. It spilled directly out onto the Seine. They found a grassy patch and sat and ate their warm, fresh bread. The children tore at the hot firm crust with their teeth and dug out the soft, yeasty white center with dirty fingers.

They watched the gray river wind between the tall banks. The palace loomed on the island in front of them. Seagulls turned on the damp and cool morning air. Jacob rubbed sleep from his eyes.

"I want to save those books," Jeanne said. Gwenforte sat between her legs. She stroked the greyhound's coat, from the copper blaze on her nose all the way down to the middle of her back. Long, soothing strokes. Soothing for them both.

"Yes," said Michelangelo. "It is very admirable of you."

"But," continued Jeanne, "I'm not sure I want to *die* for them."

Silence. The Seine churned below.

"I see," Michelangelo said at last.

"No matter how much wisdom is in a book, is it right to trade your life for it?" Jeanne looked to William and then to Jacob. Both stared across the river. If she knew

them at all by now, she knew that they, too, were doubt-
ing the trade of life, of *lives*, for books.

Michelangelo, after a great space of cawing gulls, said,
"I agree with you, Jeanne. A life is worth infinitely more
than a book."

Jacob, still staring at the Isle of the City, said, "You
told us to prepare for martyrdom."

"Sometimes," said Michelangelo, "martyrdom takes
you unaware, when you least expect it. I certainly do not
plan for you children to die."

Through a jaw clenched like a fist, William said, "Well,
that's a relief."

Some time passed. The sky brightened. The sounds
of the north bank grew behind them—clattering and
shouting and children squealing at one another. Jeanne
remembered when she might have done the same thing.
Her childhood felt very long ago indeed.

"The plan is simple," Michelangelo said at last. "If this
burning is like any other burning—of books or people—
there will be a pyre at the center of the bridge. To the north
of the pyre, the officials will stand. Also nobles and, perhaps, royals will be there. Behind them, there will be some
spectators. Since many Jews live to the north of the isle,
they'll likely be on that side. I will stand with them or, if
I am allowed, with the officials and the nobles. The entire
south side of the bridge will be packed with the rest of
the spectators. You children will stand there. Just before
the burning begins, I will create a distraction. Jeanne, you

will grab a book. Jacob, you will grab a book. William, you must keep your hands free. You will run south, away from the pyre and the palace and the officials. You will lose your pursuers in the university quarter and then find a way out of Paris. Once you are outside the city, go north."

"We're only saving *two* books?" Jacob exclaimed.

"Why can't I take some?" William objected. "I could carry a lot more than two!"

"You, my strong friend, will need your hands free to defend Jeanne and Jacob. There will be the king's guards and men-at-arms. They will not like you taking the books. They may try to make you a martyr, whether you want it or no."

"There isn't a better way to do this?" Jeanne objected. "To save more books? To stop the burning altogether?"

"There was another plan last night. It failed, you will recall," said Michelangelo. Jacob exhaled loudly. "But if you can think of something better, I will listen."

The children stared across the river. Like ripples on the water, half-formed plans rose and died in the currents of their thoughts. William considered fighting—but, as Michelangelo said, there would be guards and men-at-arms. Would William really kill them all?

Jeanne thought of Joinville. Could he be enlisted to help? But what could he do? And besides, he seemed half in love with Louis. Surely he could not be trusted.

Jacob dreamt of raising the Jews of Paris in a great rebellion, washing over the bridge in waves of righteous anger like the Maccabees washed over the Romans. But the Jews of today were not warriors—how could they be in their cramped alleyways, surrounded and outnumbered by Christian soldiers and Christian knights?

"Once you are free from the city, do not go to Yehuda's. If they suspect us at all, they may search for you there. Go as far north as you can, to Normandy. It will take you many days. At the monastery of Mont-Saint-Michel, on the coast, I have a friend. Brother Odo. He is in charge of the greatest scriptorium in France. Give him the books. He will copy them, and copy them again. Thus, the wisdom of the Talmud will be saved. At least, as much of it as you can carry."

They sat in silence. The sun began to warm the day. The thin grass between their feet glowed with rays of the slanting sun.

"Well," said Jacob, at last, "if this is the best plan we've got, I'm taking more than one book."

The day had become warm, and it was made warmer by the crush of bodies on the south side of the old bridge. They had streamed across from the south bank—mostly university students, as well as their masters. There was also a large group of friars—Dominican monks in brown robes.

Jeanne, Jacob, William, and Gwenforte pushed through the throng until they were nearly at the front. The brown wool of the friars' robes was scratchy, and the sun shone brightly on the children's faces. They peered around the backs of the other spectators. Except for William, who peered over their heads.

In the middle of the bridge stood the pyre—a huge pile of logs, kindling, and hay. It was aching for a flame, like an unlit candle at dusk. No more than a spark would be needed to set it roaring to life. On the far side of the pyre, the children saw a clutch of nobles standing amid the merchants and Jews who had come from their homes on the north bank.

"Do you see him?" Jeanne whispered. William leaned down to bring his head beside Jeanne's and Jacob's and pointed around the brown sleeve of a friar. Standing head and shoulders above the crowd to the north was Michel-angelo di Bologna. In the morning sunlight, his eyes were tiny red points of fire.

Jeanne took William's big palm in her right hand, and Jacob's small one in her left. Both were damp with sweat. The children peered at one another. "I think we should pray," Jacob whispered.

"A Jewish prayer or a Christian one?" William asked.

"I don't think it matters," Jacob replied.

Jeanne looked surprised—and then she didn't. She smiled.

So they closed their eyes—and Gwenforte, nestled between Jeanne's legs, sat down—and William said, "O Lord God, we have tried to hear Your voice above the din of other voices. Above the heresy—and even above the orthodoxy. Above the abbots and the masters. Above the knights and even the kings. And though this world is confusing and strange, we believe we have heard Your voice and followed it—followed it here, to this place. Now please, God, hear us. Help us, watch over us, and protect us as we face the flames of hate. Please, God. Please."

And they all said, "Amen."

A single trumpet blared through the warm afternoon. It was followed by a platoon of horns, blasting a fanfare above the bridge and out over the glassy Seine. The friars and students around the children shifted eagerly and tried to peer over one another to see who was coming. On the north side of the bridge, the crowd was parted by palace guards. More guards followed, carrying a litter behind them—the sort of thing an ancient king might be carried around on. But instead of a king, this litter carried books. They were stacked high on the litter—half a dozen wide, a dozen deep, a dozen long. And then, behind the litter, there came another one. And another. And another. And another. And another. And another. And another. And still, they kept coming.

Twenty-four litters in all.

Jeanne thought she might throw up.

Even from a distance, one could tell the books were beautiful. Some were richly decorated, their hammered-gold covers encrusted with pearls and emeralds. Others were bound in the finest leather, tanned to a deep mahogany, shining and oily in the

sunlight. Others were worn, tattered, practically
falling apart. To Jacob, these tattered ones were the
most beautiful of all. They were not the property of
some wealthy community, with money to bind their
books in gold. But they were loved all the more, the
only possession of a poor section of Jewish houses
on the outskirts of some French town, passed down
delicately from generation to generation, losing tiny
scraps of leather and corners of parchment each
year. Jeanne, too, noticed those first. They reminded
her of Rabbi Yehuda's thin bluish hands. Both Jeanne
and Jacob silently resolved to grab as many of those
old, tattered volumes as they could carry as soon as
Michelangelo's diversion began.

The books were dumped, like animal refuse out of
a wheelbarrow, onto the pyre. William winced as each
book landed, as if each were a sleeping infant being
dropped. He tried to look away from the books, to the
guards that were arraying themselves around the pyre.
He wondered whether he could fight them all off with
one hand, while he cradled half a dozen books or so with
his free arm.

Another blast of trumpets. King Louis appeared
on the far side of the pyre. Blanche of Castile took her
place to his right, Jean de Joinville to his left. Joinville's
expression was mournful. Blanche, on the other hand,
glowed with the certainty of a zealot. Jeanne indicated
the queen mother with a finger and whispered to

Jacob, "She scares me." Jacob couldn't even nod. His whole body felt frozen.

"Oyez! Oyez!" a fat man called, clad entirely in the blue of the palace. He looked like a berry. "Oyez! Oyez! Witness the cleansing of the books of the Jews! Their error will rise on the wind like ashes! Let them see their folly and give themselves over to the mercy of Christ!"

There were some scattered calls of support. "We hear! We hear!" and "Burn the heresy!" But the Jews on the north side of the bridge shifted silently, like buoys in a bay.

"Oyez!" cried the crier again. "The king would have it known that any Jew who converts to the True Faith on this day, here on the Old Bridge, shall receive from him a sum of forty gold ecus! Behold the king's generosity!"

An explosion of murmurs on both sides of the bridge. The king would *pay* Jews to convert? "That's preposterous!" a friar behind the children bellowed. A student leaned to his friends and said, "I'll convert. You think I can pass for Jewish?"

The crowd quieted. Everyone strained their necks to see if a Jew would come forward to take the king's offer.

Just a few days ago, William and Jeanne would have begged Jacob to follow Christ, and save his soul from damnation. Now the idea of it seemed ludicrous. If God would save their souls, surely, *surely* He would save Jacob's, too. What difference was there between them, except the language in which he prayed? And the idea of converting here, on this bridge, for money? It would be as degrading as being publicly whipped. What was a Jew, that his faith could be *bought*?

And indeed, no one came forward. The crowd waited, hushed. A warm breeze swept over the Seine. And no one came.

Finally Louis waved a hand at the crier.

"Oyez! The error of the Jews shall be consigned to cleansing flames, that the kingdom of France shall—"

"STOP!"

The voice was loud and round like a cathedral bell.

"STOP!" It came again. Michelangelo di Bologna was pushing his way through the crowd on the north side of the bridge, past the nobles and then past the guards. He clambered in his black robes, his fat legs crawling over logs and books, up onto the pyre. "STOP!" he bellowed a third time.

Whispers whipped and cracked through the crowd.

"Michelangelo!" Joinville shouted. "Get down! Don't be a fool!"

"These books shall not burn!" Michelangelo intoned. "They are the wisdom of God!"

The tension in the crowd built. The silence grew. It hung over the bridge like a cresting wave.

And then it broke.

Nobles threatened Michelangelo. The Dominicans shouted curses at the blasphemous Benedictine. Students laughed and pointed, reveling in the spectacle, the drama.

Jeanne, Jacob, and William had lost all use of their

hearts and lungs. They stood, dumb, bloodless, and breathless.

"They will burn!" Blanche of Castile shouted, her voice shrill and thin. "And you will burn with them!"

"Mother!" the king exclaimed.

She pointed at the books, her sapphire ring flashing in the morning sun, and screamed, "Light it!"

It was not clear who obeyed her order. It may have been a soldier. It may have been a spectator, wrestling the fire from one of the palace guards. But a torch was thrown onto the pile of books and tinder. Michelangelo's small eyes grew wide.

"No!" William cried. He lunged forward, past the Dominican friars. Two guards drew their swords to stop him. The flames crackled and roared to life.

"Now!" Michelangelo was bellowing. Or was he saying no?

Jeanne and Jacob were frozen. Staring. William was, too, the soldiers' swords leveled at his neck.

But Gwenforte bolted forward, past the palace guards, and into the smoke and the flames.

Jeanne screamed, "Gwenforte!" She ran after her dog. Jacob ran after her.

Gwenforte had bounded up among the burning books to Michelangelo and was trying to grab his already-flaming robes. As Jeanne tried to leap onto the pyre after Gwenforte, a soldier caught her by the shoulder and turned her around. And then the soldier was stumbling sideways, his helmet crushed by William's fist. Jeanne charged into the flames. Another soldier swung his sword at William. William raised his hand to protect himself—and the blade bit into his forearm. He bellowed in pain. Jacob, meanwhile, was collecting as many books as he could hold.

An instant later, Jeanne was carrying Gwenforte, singed and whining, out of the flames and toward the south bank. Jacob was running after her, his arms full of books, and William was behind them both, one huge fist raised in warning, while his bloody arm was cradled across his stomach. Everyone was shouting and pointing at them. One voice, high and shrill, rose above the tumult. "The children! Stop the children!" Soldiers began shoving people out of the way. William did not even see them. He was staring at Michelangelo. The great monk had fallen to his knees. The king looked on, horrified. Joinville was covering his face. Michelangelo's robes were on fire. The soldiers were gaining. Blood had soaked William's fine shirt. He turned and ran after Jeanne and Jacob.

Jacob swam through the crowd, his arms overflowing with books, trying not to trip, trying to see. "Hey! You!" a Dominican friar cried. And he grabbed at the books in Jacob's arms.

"No!" Jacob shouted, wrenching them back. But another friar grabbed at them and tore them from the small boy's grip. They tumbled to the paving stones at the foot of the bridge, the ancient leather splitting, pages of parchment flying. Jacob bent down to retrieve them. But

William, fleeing the soldiers, stumbled into Jacob and shoved him forward.

"I dropped the books!" Jacob cried.

"No time!" William shouted. The soldiers were a yard away, shoving friars and students from their path. William pushed Jacob again, and they came down off the bridge into the muddy road on the south bank. Jeanne had already ducked down a narrow lane, and William guided Jacob after her. The big boy stole a last glance behind him; Jacob and Jeanne looked, too. A soldier stood at the end of the bridge, brandishing his sword, looking left and right. Another was collecting what was left of the tattered books from the ground, with the friars' help, to bring them back to the pyre. And on the pyre, his legs trapped among books and flaming logs, his torso slumped over at a gruesome angle, the body of Michelangelo di Bologna burned.

"He's dead?" I say. "Brother Michelangelo is dead?"

"Burned with the books of the Jews," the nun replies.

Around the table, we are cradling our heads in our hands or rubbing our tired brows with shaking fingers.

"When was the burning?" I ask.

"Yesterday," says Aron. "It was a day of great mourning for all Jews."

"For all France," says Jerome. "And now my William and his friends are hunted. Hunted by the king, his knights, and the queen mother. All for trying, and failing, to save a few books."

"All for trying to save a few books," Aron echoes.

"That's the last the kids were heard from?" Marie asks the nun.

The sister gnaws on a fingernail and nods.

Brother Jerome stands up. He stretches his thin arms above his head, and his whole body, especially his white beard, quivers. Then he rubs his bald tonsure and says, "Well, I am expected tonight at the Abbey Maubuisson. I fear they will lock the doors on me if I don't show soon." He turns to Marie. "They have an almshouse, you know. They would let you sleep there, if you haven't the money to afford these lodgings."

Marie stands up. "Beats the bushes, which is where I figured I'd be sleeping."

The brewster and the monk thank the innkeeper for his hospitality, bid the assembled company farewell, and head out into the night.

"I'll retire as well," says Gerald, pushing back his stool. "In the morning, perhaps we will see the king march by. I'll record it for my chronicle."

Aron the butcher stands up, too. His eyes are full and wet. "Twenty-four cartloads . . ." he's muttering. "Twenty-four *cartloads* . . . What is that, twenty thousand books?" His voice is breaking.

I've done the math in my head. Twenty thousand sounds about right.

"I doubt there's a single Talmud left in all of France."

"I wouldn't think that there is," the nun agrees.

Aron closes his eyes and mutters, "My God . . . my God . . . why have you forsaken us?" Then he sighs and slouches off to one of the inn's small bedrooms, to collapse on a pile of straw. Gerald the Scot does the same.

Now it's just me and the nun sitting together. The innkeeper is collecting empty cups and swabbing the tables. There are a couple of men sitting off in a corner of the inn, and one drunk Franciscan friar, asleep on a table. That's it.

"So that was their crime?" I ask. "Attempted larceny? Trying to steal some books, and failing?"

The little sister's lips are ironic. "It was indeed a crime most terrible—in the eyes of the king and the queen mother."

"And what happens next?" I say.

"Why would you want to know so badly?" Her eyes glitter over clasped hands.

I do not answer. After a moment, I say, "Do I really need to tell you? Or do you already know that, too?"

Her laughter is like bells. "Maybe I do," she says.

"And you know what happened to the children after the burning."

"Maybe I know that, too."

"Tell me."

She smiles at me coyly.

CHAPTER 22

The Tenth Part of the Nun's Tale

The sunlight was offensive. It made the infant green buds glow. It glimmered through branches and turned bare sod gold. It had no business shining so gloriously on such a miserable day as this.

Jeanne, Jacob, and William sat on the earth in the wood of Vincennes, their backs against the smooth bark of young trees. Gwenforte's head was in Jeanne's lap because Jeanne was crying the hardest. But even Gwenforte seemed to be crying. Yellow streaks ran from the corners of her eyes. It was not clear what could have caused them but tears.

After a while, Jeanne said, "I never got to say I was sorry."

William wiped his face with a big hand. His arm was wrapped in yarrow and mud, thanks to Jacob's quick work. "For what?" William asked.

"Calling him fat."

"When did you call him fat?" said William.

"When I was four."

William sniffed hard. "You also called him wicked, as I recall."

"He deserved that."

William snorted, half laugh, half sob.

"It wouldn't have been worth it," Jacob muttered.

"What wouldn't?"

"Michelangelo dying. Even if we saved every Talmud. It's not worth it." He started crying harder. He shed tears for the red, fat, wicked monk and tears that he had yet to shed for his parents, like one river flowing into another. Gwenforte got up, walked over to him, and tried to nuzzle her head under his chin. He let her, holding her soft white face close to his.

"Why?" Jacob whispered. The trees creaked in the mocking sunlight of the late afternoon. "Why would God let it happen?"

They slept that night against the honeyed walls of the Grandmontine abbey. They did not dare go inside, for while they had failed—utterly failed—to save a single book, still they had tried. For that, they were likely outlaws. False saints or pagan sorcerers. What had been their divine gift was now their mortal sin.

So they slept with their backs propped against the wall at the farthest point from the abbey door, and when dawn came golden and warm, they were up with the thrush and pushing north as fast as they could go.

But there was discord.

"We should go back to Saint-Denis," Jacob announced, the thin branches creaking over their heads.

"We can't go back there," Jeanne said. "It's where Michelangelo lives . . . lived." Pause. After a moment, Jeanne said, "My village is safer."

"They know where you're from. Abbot Hubert knows for sure."

"But they won't ask him!"

"I want to see Rabbi Yehuda," Jacob murmured.

"It's not safe!" Jeanne insisted.

"But it's safe to see *your parents*?"

Gwenforte acted as their scout, ghostly and white, leading them through the trees. They soon found the road but they avoided it, preferring instead the obscurity of the wood. Each child looked haggard, haunted by the image of Michelangelo, surrounded by books, burning alive.

"Maybe we should split up," Jacob said. They sat among a grove of smooth-barked beech trees, a day's walk north of Paris.

Gwenforte raised her head. She was the only one. Both William and Jeanne were desperately hungry and very angry and they could barely make eye contact without shouting at each other.

"Jeanne could go home. I could go to Yehuda's."

"And where would I go?" William said. "Just a big Saracen wearing the king's colors, wandering around France?
You two go hide in nice, safe houses. I'll wait until they
find me and set me on fire."

Jacob stared at the sky, fading from royal blue to indigo
above the black buds of an ash.

"I could go find a leper community to live with,"
William went on. His fingers had found the outline of the
golden belt that ran through the loops of his underwear.
"That'd be easier for you both, wouldn't it?"

Jacob muttered, "I didn't mean that."

"My ass you didn't."

"What did you just say?" Jeanne snapped. She leapt to
her feet. She looked wild, furious.

"Sit down, peasant girl," William growled. "Don't
make me mad."

"No!" Jeanne shouted. "What did you just say?"

He looked up at her, angry and bemused. "I said, 'My
ass you didn't!' So what? Do you want to fight me?"

"No, you idiot!" Jeanne exclaimed, grabbing his
shoulders.

William pushed her off him. She went stumbling
backward. He jumped to his feet. "Touch me again!" he
bellowed. "Touch me again, I dare you!"

"Your ass!" Jeanne was shouting. "Your ass!"

William looked at her like she was going crazy. He
glanced at Jacob, who looked just as confused. "I think she
wants me to knock her out," William said.

"Please don't," Jacob muttered.

"No, you dummies! William's ass! It's at the inn! We never got it!"

William's face unclouded, like the night sky after a summer storm. "My ass! That's true!" But then he shook his head. "So what?"

Jacob had gotten to his knees. Gwenforte stood beside them and barked once, as if to say, *Yeah! So what?* Or, more likely, *Is it time to play with me?*

Jeanne's face glowed like a coal in a fire. "Weren't you delivering books from your abbey to Saint-Denis? Where all the Talmuds were collected?"

William's eyes started to grow and shine. "Good God ...," he said slowly. "But—they weren't in Hebrew."

Jeanne's face went gray.

"Did you read them all?" Jacob demanded.

"No ... just a couple ... and now that you mention it, I did see a strange one. I suppose it could have been ... Perhaps ..."

"For God's sake!" Jacob shouted. "Let's find out!"

They ran. Gwenforte sprinted out ahead, lost them, turned around and came pelting back, and, when she found them, sprinted off ahead again. They soon came to a road. Jacob was sent out to ask a peasant passing by if she knew the Holy Cross-Roads Inn. She did. It was on this road, to the east of where they stood. Jacob was much obliged.

They ran as hard as they could.

At this point, the nun stops speaking.

There are voices in the yard.

I get up from the table. The hair on my neck is standing on end.

The innkeeper has gone to the door and opened it, spilling the buttery light of the inn out onto the ground. "Who's out there?" he shouts.

I have gooseflesh up and down my arms. All over my body. I am tingling. I stand behind the innkeeper.

The yellow light of the inn is being cast on three figures. A huge boy and two smaller children—a boy and a girl. Well, four figures. There is also a white greyhound, with a copper blaze down her snout. The children are still wearing the royal-blue garments from the palace.

I cannot breathe.

"I am looking for my ass," says the big boy—William. "My donkey." He is breathing hard—they all are. Even Gwenforte is panting. I am surprised by how high William's voice is. A great big boy like that, I guess I expected him to have a voice like a man's. But he sounds like a child. A big, pudgy child—who can shatter a stone bench with a bare fist.

"You're looking for your donkey?" replies the innkeeper. "That's good, because I'm looking for payment for lodging him and feeding him for going on a week now."

The smaller boy—Jacob—says, "So you still have it?"

"Sure."

The kids turn and break for the stable. I push past the innkeeper and follow them into the darkness.

William pulls the sliding door to one side. It does not budge. He pulls it harder. Nothing. "God's bones!" he swears. And then he says, "Oh, wait." He pulls it in the other direction. It slides open easily. They spill into the stable. I slide in after them.

There is a donkey in the far corner. William sees it, spins around, and nearly tramples Jeanne and Jacob— and me. I am not a large man, and when William pushes past me, thrusting me into the boards of the barn wall, I worry he's cracked all my ribs. He's bellowing, "Where are the satchels? Where in God's name are the satchels?" Gwenforte is barking in the darkness of the yard.

The innkeeper, framed by the light of the inn, says, "Calm yourself! They're inside! I brought 'em in for safekeeping."

William allows himself a moment to bend over and put his big hands on his knees. "Thank God," he pants. "Thank God."

"Come on," the innkeeper tells them. "I'll show you."

The children follow him inside. I peel myself from the wall of the barn, decide that maybe my ribs aren't broken after all, and hurry after the miraculous children and their miraculous dog.

The innkeeper leads the children to a back room, Gwenforte padding along beside them. I cannot believe what I am witnessing. William, Jeanne, and Jacob in the flesh. If William is more childlike than I had imagined, Jeanne is smaller, fiercer. Jacob is just a hair shorter than Jeanne, and his freckled face is alight with passion. There is something about these children that makes it hard to look away from them.

"They're back here," the innkeeper is saying.

The back room is small and lit by a single candle. A table, an iron strongbox, and a stool sit in the center of the room. Slumped against a wall are two leather sacks, speckled with the dried blood of the fiends of Malesherbes.

The children stop suddenly. I nearly crash into Jacob from behind.

They stand in the doorway as if they're afraid to advance. Afraid to open the bags. Afraid to discover whether there is a single Talmud left in all of France.

Then Gwenforte barks once, and the spell is broken. William launches himself to the dirt floor beside the satchels. He throws one open, withdraws a book, and opens the cover. "Latin," he mutters, and hands it to the innkeeper. My guess is the innkeeper has never held a book before, because he's holding it gingerly, away from his body, like a first-time father holding a baby girl. William picks up another. "Latin," he says, and it sounds like a curse this time, and he hands this book to the innkeeper, too. Jacob's shoulders slump. Jeanne falls to her knees beside the oblate. William picks up another. "Latin!" He shoves this one at the innkeeper like it's done something to him. He picks up another. "Latin!" And another. "Latin! . . .

Latin! ... God's wounds!" He throws another and another at the innkeeper, who is now staggering under the weight of them. But he's not going to protest. I don't blame him. William looks ready to break something. Like a neck. The oblate opens another. "Latin!" he shouts, thrusting it away from him. William picks up one of the last in the sack. He flips the cover open.

Everything in the room becomes still. Jeanne and Jacob are craning their necks over William's shoulder. Gwenforte is staring up at his face. The innkeeper is balancing a dozen books in his arms. Even the flames of the candles seem unnaturally still.

And then Jacob murmurs, "My God ..."

"Hebrew," says William. "This one's in Hebrew."

I can just see the strange letters, inscribed on the page in pale brown ink.

Jeanne is already picking up the next book. She opens it. "Look!"

"Hebrew!" William shouts. They tear open the other bag. Latin books on top. But again, at the bottom, there are books in Hebrew. Mostly simple, leather-bound books. Some new-looking. Others ancient and delicate as a dried flower. There are five Hebrew books in all.

"Thank you, God," Jacob murmurs, his throat thick, his nose running. He starts to laugh. He says it again. "Thank you, God."

CHAPTER 23

The Friar's Tale and the Troubadour's Tale

Jeanne, Jacob, and William are sitting at a table by a shuttered window. I'm across the room, watching.

They've eaten their fill. Gwenforte lies at their feet, gnawing on a mutton bone, her strong yellow teeth scraping away the last scraps of meat and gristle. The innkeeper agreed to give them room and board and to forgive the rent on the stable space in exchange for the donkey. The children thought the trade was more than fair. William told them he'd carry the sacks himself.

They now sit on the bench beside the children.

The sacks. With the books. The only Talmuds in all of France.

They balance in the children's minds as on one end of a seesaw. I can see it in their faces. And on the other end, Michelangelo's burned body. At some moments, the books are lifted into the air, and the children feel grateful and proud. And then, for no apparent reason, the balance shifts, and Michelangelo rises in their thoughts, his slumped body, the dancing flames, his burning flesh. And the books go plummeting to earth.

"It's too much," Jeanne says, pushing the last of her brown stew around with a spoon.

"What is?" William asks.

"Life is. How can you have such pain and such . . . such triumph . . . all mixed together? It's like . . . it's like that cheese."

"What? It's like cheese?" says William.

"Doesn't matter," Jeanne mutters.

But I know what she means.

"Why," Jacob says, "does God allow it?"

Suddenly, a drunken voice rises from the far corner of the inn. "Ish that feology I hear?" The Franciscan, who was asleep on the table, has raised his tonsured head.

I can see the children exchange glances with one another. The glances say, *Don't answer him. Maybe he'll go back to sleep.*

"Hey!" the friar shouts, lurching to his feet and gathering his brown robes around him. "I wanna dishcush feology!"

"No one's discussing theology over here," William says, not turning his head.

But the friar says, "You're a liar!" He pushes a stool out of the way and begins to stumble over to the children. His hair makes a curly fringe around his shining pate. He noisily, laboriously drags an entire bench from a neighboring table over to the children's. The kids watch in slightly amused horror. "Sho," he says. "What are we dishcushing?"

"Feology," says Jacob. Jeanne suppresses a smile.

"Ah yesh!" says the friar. Then he puts his arms on the table and lays his head on them, as if he were going to sleep.

The children look at one another, not sure whether to laugh or to change tables.

But then he lifts his wobbly head. "You ashked de tuff—de tuff—de *hardesht* queshtion in all feology. If God ish all good and if God ish all powerful, why doesh God let bad fings happen?"

The children stop smiling. The stragglers in the far corner have put their mugs down on the sticky tabletop and are watching the group of strange children and the drunken friar.

"Yes," Jacob says, after a moment. "That's my question."

"Itsh hard," says the friar. He raises himself from the bench. His two thin hands are gripping the edges of the table as if the floor were pitching beneath him. He fixes Jacob with a dizzy, furious stare. "Who are you!?" he suddenly shouts.

The men in the corner laugh. The innkeeper looks up from where he's swabbing a table. "Master Bacon, if you can't keep civil, I'll throw you out."

But the friar—Master Bacon, apparently—is still staring at Jacob and rocking slightly back and forth. "Who are you?!" he bellows again. I can smell his stale ale breath from two tables away.

"I'm—"

"That ish what God asked Job, when Job asked what you asked: *Who are you?*"

"Huh . . . ," says Jacob. "Fascinating."

William covers a smile with his wide hand.

"Listen. Itsh not funny," Master Bacon says to William, listing forward as if the inn had just crested a wave. "Who are you? God asked. Were you there when I created de *great whale?*" As his argument gains momentum, he begins to regain mastery of his tongue. "When I created the *monsters* of the deep? The fings you don't even *know about?* Were you *there?*" The friar looks down on Jacob as if the point were undebatable.

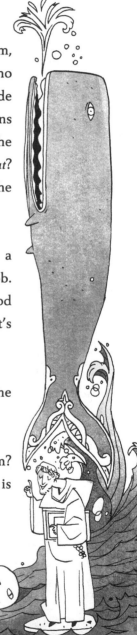

"Uh . . . no," says Jacob. "I wasn't."

"AHA!" the drunken master shouts, pointing a long finger, white and bony and red at the tip, at Jacob. "You weren't there! So how can you know what's good and what's bad? How can you understand God's plan? It's greater than you! Can you see every leaf in the forest?"

"No."

"Do you know where every bird is on the face of the earth?"

Jacob shakes his head.

"Can you track de paths of the fishes as they swim? Every fish? In every river and ocean?" Master Bacon is waving his long finger about like a sword.

"No. I can't."

"So you can't understand God's plan! Only God can! But we must try! We must try! I have devoted my whole life to trying! I study the birds and the bees and the stars and the trees..."

Now Master Bacon appears to be singing.

"The rivers and the streams, the sun and the moonbeams..."

Jeanne starts to laugh, which seems to bring Master Bacon back to reality.

"We weren't there when God created de earth. But we live on the earth now. So we must try to study it as best we can, since it's all a part of God's plan. Then, when bad fings happen, at least we can understand them a little bit. And that helps! God knows, that helps . . ." Master Bacon sighs. And then he lies down on his bench. *"Quod erat demonshtrandum."*

The children stare. After a moment, the friar is snoring noisily.

I watch Jeanne and Jacob and William look at one another. William scratches his head.

"I've got an answer to your question."

This is a different voice, coming from the far corner of the tavern, where the two men have been sitting. One of them stands up, and I see that he's wearing the fancy sleeves of a troubadour, though they're caked with the dirt of the road.

The one who's still sitting—he's got big front teeth like

a rabbit—says, "Aw, no one wants to hear your theories, Chrétien."

Chrétien ignores his companion. "You've gotta hear a song, first, though. Do you want to hear a song?"

Well, there's only one right answer to that question. At least when it's asked by a troubadour. When else do you get to hear real music, outside of church? The children confer with just a glance. Of course they do.

"I'm no cheap jongleur, either, you know. I sing for lords and ladies! One day I'll sing for the king himself!"

"Sure you will," says his companion, his lip curling back around his two prominent teeth.

Chrétien ignores him. He ducks under his table, picks up a gittern—or maybe it's a lute, I can never tell the difference—and plucks a few notes. "This is an old song," he says. "From the time of Charlemagne. 'The Song of Hildebrand.'"

He begins to sing. His voice is pure and round and haunting, like the call of an owl. Gwenforte comes out from under the table and cocks her head. Master Bacon snores on his bench. Outside, it has begun to rain.

The tale of Hildebrand I sing.
Quiet, while I pluck these strings.
Do not, dear children, turn away—
I think you'll like this, if you stay
And hear my song of war and death
And blood and warriors' last breaths.

The minstrel strums some new chords.

In wars of old they spared the lives
Of soldiers young, and weeping wives,
By sending forth a champion
To fight alone, just man to man.
One sunny day, across a dell,
King Dietrich faced Lord Haberfel.
So Dietrich's army first sent out
A warrior who was fierce and stout
but old and creased, like ancient elm.
He stood out front, with sword and helm.
And then from out the other side
famous Hadubrand came striding wide
Into the center of the field
Till the two men stood, shield to shield.
The older man announced, "I will
Know the name of the man I kill.
What is your land? Who is your kin?"
Hadubrand answered, "My sire is him,
Now long dead, called Hildebrand,
Who died a hero in foreign lands."
Staggered, was the older man,
His chain mail shook, he scarce could stand.
His lips did ope, but no sound came.
His ears resound'd with his own name.
"Hildebrand?" he said, at length,

Trying to master his shaken strength.
"And were you born by old Cologne?
If so, I call you now . . . my son."
The battlefield fell deathly still.
No sheep cried o'er the graying hills.
"My son, my son," the old man cried.
"Who told you that your father died?"
He fell upon a greaved knee
And to his long-lost son he reached.
"Take my hand, my darling boy.
Take my hand, my life's last joy."
But Hadubrand stood off and sneered
At the old man shedding old-man tears.
"You expect me to believe such games?
You think I was born yesterday?
This is how you've grown so old.
With cowardly tricks and lies you've told.
My father, Hildebrand, is dead.
You've used his name. Now lose your head!"
"Hadubrand! My darling boy!
This is no game! No trick! No toy!"
The old man wept and swore it true.
But Hadubrand would not be moved.
The ancient bones creaked with pain
as Hildebrand stood up again,
"Thirty years in foreign climes
Always placed in the front lines.
How many times have I fallen? None.

But now I may fall—at the hands of my son.
I could kneel down and forfeit to you.
Perhaps you would then believe the truth.
But thus my soldiers would be taken,
And then I would deprive their children
Of fathers, as were you deprived,
Living an orphan, all of your life.
So Hadubrand, my darling child,
Who laughed and played so pretty and wild,
And bounced and sang upon my lap
And on my shoulder took his nap—
Now you may kill me. Do your worst.
Unless I kill you, my beloved, first."
Then they let sail their ashen spears
And ran at each other, over years
of absence and of childhood missed
And fought one another when they should have kissed.
They split each other's bright oak shields,
Hacking and hewing, refusing to yield.

———————

The troubadour, Chrétien, plays a few more notes, and then lowers himself onto a stool. The inn is cradled in silence. The haunting melody, with its simple drone, still echoes among the rough wooden benches and tables. The only other sound is the snoring of Master Bacon.

William speaks first. "What happens? Who wins? The father or the son?"

Chrétien replies, "We don't know. That's where the song ends."

"That's the saddest song I've ever heard!" says Jacob. "I hated it."

"I love it," murmurs Jeanne. "It's so . . . rich and sad and beautiful. It feels . . . true."

Chrétien points at her. "That's what I meant! That's my answer to your question! You asked why God would make bad things happen? I'll tell you why. God is a troubadour."

The troubadour's rabbit-toothed companion pipes up from the corner, "Not self-important, are we, Chrétien?"

"Listen!" He's deadly serious. He leans forward on his stool, and though half the inn lies between him and the children, he seems to be whispering to them alone. "Life is a song, composed and sung by God. We are but characters in His song. Hildebrand doesn't think his song is beautiful. He's either going to kill his son or die himself. It's not beautiful to him at all. But that's because he can't hear it. He's *in* it. You can't hear a song you're in, right?"

The children are squinting at the troubadour. "Right . . . ," says William reluctantly.

"So! If we could hear our own songs, if we could see God's creation the way God does, we would know it's the most beautiful song there is."

Jacob is frowning. "What kind of God is that, who would write such sad songs? Why would He make us suffer— for a beauty we can't even see?" William and Jeanne nod, their faces illuminated by the flickering firelight. "Why,"

Jacob continued, his voice rising, "would He destroy all the Talmuds in France? And make Michelangelo die? And my . . . my parents . . . ? What's so—what's so damn beautiful about *that*?"

His voice echoes over the silent inn. Even the rain seems to have gone quiet.

"Who's Michelangelo?" Chrétien asks, after a space.

"It doesn't matter. A friend of ours. Our teacher. He's dead."

"I'm sorry," says the troubadour. "That isn't beautiful at all."

"So your theory's stupid."

"Your teacher's death isn't beautiful. And your parents' death certainly isn't," Chrétien continues. "But the song might still be."

No one speaks. The rain begins again.

The innkeeper stands up and raises his arms above his head, arching his back and pushing his round belly out as far as it can go. "Bedtime," he says, sighing. "Look, your dog has joined Roger in the land of dreams." Indeed, Gwenforte is now curled on the floor right under Master Bacon's bench, her flank rising and falling with shallow breath. "And tomorrow?" the innkeeper asks the children, as the troubadours collect their instruments. "Where're you off to?"

William does not wait to consult his friends. "Mont-Saint-Michel," he says. "We have some books to save."

This is my moment. I see it, like a break in the clouds

when the sun shines through. It is an opportunity that may never come again. *Don't screw it up*, I tell myself.

"Do you know how to get there?" I say. "To Mont-Saint-Michel?" I don't want to sound eager. Just an offhand question. "It's pretty far."

The children look at one another. William shrugs. Jeanne and Jacob shake their heads.

"I can lead you, if you want," I say. And then, because the truth is often a better ruse than a lie, I add, "I'm curious to see what happens to you next."

William says, "We'll have to move quietly. Stay hidden. Sleep in ditches and behind walls."

"That's not a problem. I do that all the time."

He fixes me with a quizzical stare and then consults his two smaller companions. "It's better than having to stop and ask for directions at every town," he admits.

Jeanne and Jacob glance at each other. Jacob turns his palms upward.

"You can come," Jeanne tells me.

I am elated.

I try not to show it, though.

The morning is wet and shining, and I am swelled with the idea that I'll be setting forth with the children. The famous children. And their dog. I wish I could tell myself that I had planned it this way.

Sometimes, though, God smiles on the fox and puts the rabbit right in his path.

The innkeeper gives us breakfast, and we set off, among the dripping branches and raindrop-gilded ferns, for Normandy.

"So," William says to me, after I've pointed out the road north, and Gwenforte has sniffed out a path just east of it, in the shadows of the trees, "what is your station in life? Or your trade?"

I am prepared for the question. "My trade is tales," I say. "I collect them."

"Like a chronicler?" William asks.

"Sort of."

"Do you tell them?" Jeanne wants to know. "Like a troubadour?"

"To the right people, and at the right time," I reply.

"Are we," Jacob says, "the right people?" His gaze has become suspicious. I don't blame him. That was too cryptic an answer.

"You don't need to hear the story I'm collecting now," I say. "You know it already. It's your story."

"Why would you collect *our* story?" Jeanne wants to know.

"Don't you think it's interesting? Special?" I ask.

"I don't know. Maybe."

"Of course it is!"

"And who," William asks, "are the right people to hear our story?"

His question is shrewd. Too shrewd. *You walked into that one, Étienne,* I think.

I say, "There's a turning just ahead. Let's not miss it."
I push forward through the brush, trying to catch up with
Gwenforte. I can feel the children's eyes on my back.

The first day passes swiftly. We keep to the woods as long
as we can, clambering over fallen trees and beating our
way through thorn bushes. By sunset, though, the forest
has disappeared, replaced by rolling wheat fields and cow
pastures: Normandy, breadbasket and butter churn of
France.

Jeanne points out that there's no use tramping over
fields instead of on the road, since in the fields we'll be
equally visible—and more conspicuous. Smart kid. So as
the yellow sun falls to its knees on the horizon, we return
to the road.

That night we lie down in a sheepfold, deep in a pasture.
Gwenforte scares off the sheep as we approach, which leaves
the structure vacant—but cold. As we settle in, I wish at least
a couple of sheep had stayed behind. Now I understand why
Jeanne's family sleeps with their cow.

Before the darkness settles completely, William opens
the blood-flecked sacks of books. Jeanne examines a Latin
volume with beautiful illuminations in blue, red, and gold
leaf. I don't think she can read, but her brown hair swings
over the page as her eyes follow the curling vines and
grotesque beasts that run up and down the margins. She
cries out when she finds an illustration of a greyhound.
She shows it to Gwenforte, but Gwenforte just tries to

lick it. William cradles a book by Saint Augustine in his big hands. Grand capitals, in bright red ink, announce the beginning of each new chapter. Jacob opens a slim volume of Hebrew and balances it on his knees. No illuminations in these pages. Just the shaky letters of an amateur scribe.

"How did you learn to read?" I ask Jacob as his fingers scan the letters, right to left.

"We have a *beit midrash* in our village," Jacob says, then catches his breath. "*Had* a *beit midrash*, I mean. All the boys learned to read there. A lot of girls, too."

The children go back to their books. I am not tempted to read one myself. These children are more interesting to me than any book. They look so young, their faces bent over the pages, squinting against the dying light. William looks so much like a child. A very, very big child. Jacob looks a lot like I did when I was his age. Small and thin and wary. And little Jeanne, peering at the illuminations in the book on her lap, is no daughter of Eve, bringer of sin into the world. Looking at her now, pushing her tangled hair from her face, the idea is ludicrous. An insult.

I'd really rather not kill them.

Jacob puts down one book and opens another. "Hey!" he says. "This isn't a Talmud! This is the Bible!"

"It is?" Jeanne leans over, as if looking at the page of Hebrew will help.

"Listen: *Vayakom melech chadash, al mitzrayim asher lo yada et Yosef.*"

Jeanne and William look at him blankly.

Jacob tilts his head back. "'A new king rose over Egypt who did not know Joseph.' It's the beginning of *Sh'mot*—Exodus. The second book of the Bible."

William says, "I don't think my abbot would have sent a Bible to be burned."

"Does he read Hebrew?"

William hesitates. "I think he reads a little . . . Not like Brother Jerome."

"So maybe he didn't know."

William is silent.

Jacob says, "I wonder how many Bibles were burned yesterday."

I wonder, too. I look out into the darkness. But when I look back at the children, I can tell they're not thinking of Bibles burning. They're thinking of Michelangelo.

Out in the fields, a sheep bleats in the pattering rain.

Later, as the children sleep, I take the knife out of its scabbard under my shirt. I rub the edge with my fingers. It is very, very sharp.

I watch the children sleeping, the breath flowing in and out of their innocent bodies.

The morning shimmers with fallen rain, but despite the mud on the road, we make good time. That night, we sneak into a mill that is lying quiet for the evening. The children lean against a wooden wall in the last light of sunset.

I did not sleep last night. Doubt tormented me like a devil's pitchfork. I could have acted as the children lay in dream, and I did not. Why? Why couldn't I?

Now I feel ill. But at least my decision has been made. Tonight.

I grip the knife under my cloak.

Jacob has opened one of the books and is translating—haltingly, but with obvious pleasure. "'And so,'" Jacob reads, "'one day a stranger came to one of the leading Jewish sages, Shammai.'"

"Is this the Bible?" Jeanne says.

"No. Talmud."

"Yes! Read us the Talmud!" William exclaims. "I want to hear what all this has been about! Let's hear the wisdom of the Jews!"

Jacob bends his head over the brown letters. "'And the stranger said to Shammai, "Can you teach me the whole Torah while I stand on one foot?" Do you know what Rabbi Shammai did? He took a stick and beat the stranger with it until the man finally went away.'"

I try to stifle a laugh.

Jacob stops reading. He looks up at his friends.

"*That's* the Talmud?" Jeanne says.

"That's the story . . . ," Jacob mutters, his pale forehead creasing.

William says, "That's the book Michelangelo died for? For *that*?" He looks like he's going to be sick.

Jeanne begins to stroke Gwenforte's back. Hard. The

greyhound wriggles away from her and trots over to a hole in the flimsy wooden wall and sniffs at it.

Jacob examines the page. "Wait, there's more."

"I hope it gets better," says William.

"'Then the stranger went to the great teacher Hillel. The stranger said, "Teach me the whole of the Torah while I stand on one foot." Hillel did not beat him with a rod.'"

William buries his head in his hands.

"'Hillel said, "Fine. Stand on one foot." So the stranger did. And then the rabbi said, "What you would hate to have done to you—do not do to other people. That is the whole of the Torah. The rest is commentary. Now go, and study."'"

William raises his face to Jacob. "What you would hate to have done to you, do not do to other people," he repeats.

"That's what Jesus says in reverse," says Jeanne. "Do unto others as you would have them do to you."

"Which came first?" William asks.

Jacob says, "My rabbi used to say that Hillel was one of Jesus's teachers. I don't know if that's true, though."

"It's true," I say. The children look at me. I feel feverish. I press the cold blade of the knife against my skin. "I learned that at the Cathedral School of Avignon."

"*You* went to a cathedral school?" William asks. He sounds skeptical. I don't blame him. The cathedral schools are for the wealthiest and most promising boys in Christendom. Dressed as I am, in cheap traveling clothes, I seem to have fallen far in the world. And I have. I have.

I say, "Jesus taught that the greatest commandment was to love God with all your heart and all your soul and all your might." Why am I talking? *Keep quiet. You're going to give yourself away.* "And the second greatest commandment was like it: to love your neighbor as you love yourself. I never got that. How is loving God, almighty and perfect and divine, like loving your sinful, crooked neighbor? They're completely different. They couldn't be more different!" Am I shouting? I grip the knife inside my cloak. I feel dizzy.

"You think?" says Jeanne. She leans back against the wood of the old mill and sleepily pulls her royal-blue tunic over her head. "I don't know. They seem the same to me."

Gwenforte goes and lies down beside Jeanne.

But William's eyes are roving over my face.

"Who *are* you?" he says quietly.

Sweat is pouring from my scalp, over my eyebrows, into my eyes. What is wrong with me?

The children are staring at me. Jeanne sits up. They can tell something is wrong. They can tell. I know it.

I feel like I'm standing on the top of a bell tower, staring at the ground forty fathoms below.

"My name is Étienne d'Arles," I say.

I am at the top of a bell tower, and the wind is blowing hard at my back.

My thumb brushes against the blade of the knife. It splits the top layer of my skin.

"Tell us," Jacob says. I have the strange sensation that he is looking *through* me. "Tell us more."

"Yes," says Jeanne. "Please."

The famous children are asking me. *Me.* I cannot . . . I cannot stop myself.

CHAPTER 24

The Inquisitor's Tale

"I am Étienne," I say again. "The seventh son of Guilhem d'Arles. The runt of the litter. The Runt of Arles. My oldest brother will inherit the domain. My other brothers—tall and strong and quick with lance and sword—will be his vassals. But me? I'm useless to them. I always have been, scrambling around their heels, trying to be heard and not kicked. The Runt of Arles. That's me." Sweat is pouring down my back. I am soaked through.

"But then I was sent off to the cathedral school. None of my brothers are clever enough for that. They can't read a line of Latin, much less books and books of it, like me. I was a good student. One of the best."

The children's eyes are on fire. My eyes are on fire. My vision is blurred. *Why am I still talking?*

"And then, a special invitation came. From the pope himself. He was looking for the keenest boys. Those who could speak French and Italian and, of course, Latin.

The more languages the better. Quiet boys, His Holiness wanted. Listeners. Watchers.

"I and a few others were chosen from Avignon, and other boys came from all over Christendom, to Rome, for our training. We learned the ways of investigation, of interview, how to listen, how to persuade, how to threaten. We learned how to be the eyes, ears, and nose of the papacy. And how, on occasion, to be the fist, too. We learned the ways, in short, of the Inquisition."

My eyesight is starting to clear. I see the children's faces. Confusion, mostly. And pity. I think they are pitying me.

They will not pity me soon.

"The Inquisition is how the pope roots out heresy. Sniffs it out and finds it and pulls it up by the roots. For my first assignment, I was sent to Northern Italy, to prosecute a community of heretics. But during my investigations there, I met a young woman of that community. Inquisitors are supposed to be as chaste as monks. But"—*Why am I telling them this? Stop, Étienne! Stop!*—"I fell in love. Our love was discovered, first by the villagers I was prosecuting, and then by my superiors. I was brought back to Rome in shame, whipped like the runt I have always been, and told that another failure would result in my defrocking and expulsion from the ranks of the Holy Inquisitors."

The children are certainly pitying me now. My hand is gripping the knife so hard that my forearm aches.

"I vowed to redeem myself, to regain the status that I had so recently achieved. The next assignment, whatever it was,

would be my glory. I swore it. Then I could return to Arles as one of the greatest men in the church—for the greatest Inquisitors are as powerful as any cardinal in Christendom.

"And then I received my next assignment. There was a village in the north of France where peasants were venerating a dog as a saint. A dog. My next assignment was a dog. How could I redeem myself with a *dog*? I tore at my hair and cursed my fate."

Jeanne pulls Gwenforte closer to her.

"I traveled to the Oise and began collecting evidence. I spoke to peasants at markets and on the road. I talked to the local clergy. I discovered that the story of the dog was not as simple as I had assumed. There were children involved. You children."

They do look so much like children, with cheeks so round and soft. Gwenforte's big black eyes stare at me.

"And so I learned your story. And as I learned, something strange happened to me. I began to believe. The Church was wrong. The Holy Father was wrong. This is no cult, no heresy. I believe in you. You are saints."

I withdraw the knife from my cloak. The children start. Their eyes are now rimmed with fear. There is just moonlight now, in the mill, and the musty smell of rotted grain hangs in the air. The knife is aimed at them. I see William's body quivering. Ready to leap. But I am closer to Jacob than William is to me.

"What can I do?" I say. "Go back to Rome and declare that you are saints? What good would that do me? They will start an inquiry. Cardinals and bishops will descend upon you, shoving me to the back. What use will they have then for the Runt of Arles? And then they will leave, for the canonization process cannot begin until you are dead. Your dead body—your relics, your bones—must perform miracles. That is the new rule for saints. Did you know that? And who will care that I discovered you? No one.

"But if you die . . . if you are martyred . . . then the process of canonizing you as saints can begin! If I am in possession of your bones, I can witness the miracles they perform—and surely, they will perform miracles! And then I can return, triumphant, your relics in my arms, and shepherd you through the canonization process myself! Three new saints! Maybe four, if they accept Gwenforte! All championed by Étienne! The Inquisitor of Arles!"

I am standing up now. I don't remember standing up. The knife is gripped in my hand, undulating in the moonlight. Gwenforte is growling low. Jacob is just an arm's length away. I turn the knife around in my hand, so it is in stabbing position. The muscles in William's legs are flexing. He is ready to strike.

But I am fast. I bring the knife down, hard.

Into the dirt. It stands there, in the earth, quivering with the force of my blow.

"But I cannot do it," I say. "Last night, as you slept, I could have slit your throats. It was my intention. As soon as you arrived in the yard of the inn, the plan leapt into my mind, fully formed. It was perfect. It was easy . . ."

I let the words hang in the silence.

Jeanne speaks. "But?"

"It was wrong," I reply. I feel hot tears welling in my eyes and then running down my cheeks. "It was wrong." My shoulders are shaking. I draw the knife out of the ground. It makes the same scraping sound as a spade cutting the earth. The children recoil. I rise and go to the door of the mill and hurl the knife into the darkness. I fall to my knees. I am weeping.

I feel Jeanne's small hand on my back. I am humiliated. A child is comforting me. "I'm sorry," I sob. "I'm sorry."

"Shhh," she says. "We forgive you."

I press my fists into my eyes and weep.

CHAPTER 25

The Second Part of the Inquisitor's Tale

The next morning is bright and beautiful. All night, I slept with Gwenforte curled beside me, and my sleep was deeper than any I had had since my disaster with the heretics in Italy. I am renewed. We walk briskly along the road. The smell of cows is thick, the wind is just barely warm, and the clouds are white trimmed with gold.

The children seem to have truly and honestly forgiven me. In fact, they trust me now in a way that they did not before. They include me in their conversations and make jokes with me. My heart feels near bursting. There are some people in this world who have magic in them. Whose very presence makes you happier. Some of those people, it turns out, are children.

After some hours of walking, Jacob says, "I read something interesting in the Talmud last night. After you had all fallen asleep."

"Wasn't it too dark to read?" Jeanne asks.

"I sat by the door, and the moon was full."

"What did you read?" says William.

"I read a line that said, 'You are like pomegranates split open. Even the emptiest among you are as full of good as a pomegranate is of seed.'"

I choke on the thickness that rises in my throat. After my humiliation last night, and the forgiveness I received, I can only hope that is true.

"And I read something else," Jacob goes on. "There was this discussion of the story of Cain and Abel, from the Bible. After Cain kills his brother, God says, 'The bloods of your brother call out to me.' Not *blood*. *Bloods*. Weird, right? So the Talmud tries to explain it."

"I can explain it," says William. "The scribe was drunk."

"William!" cries Jeanne. "The Bible is written by God!"

"And copied by scribes," the big boy replies. "Who get drunk. A lot. Trust me."

Jacob is laughing. "The rabbis have a different explanation. The Talmud says it's 'bloods' because Cain didn't only spill Abel's blood. He spilled the blood of Abel and all the descendants he never had."

"Huh!"

"And then it says something like, 'Whoever destroys a single life destroys the whole world. And whoever saves a single life saves the whole world.'"

There are sheep in the meadow beside the road. Gwenforte walks up to the low stone wall, and one

sheep—a ram—doesn't run away. They sniff each other's noses. Her white fur beside the ram's wool—two textures, two colors, both called *white* in our inadequate language.

Jeanne is thinking about something. At last, she shares it. "William, you said that it takes a lifetime to make a book."

"That's right."

"One book? A whole lifetime?"

William nods. "A scribe might copy out a single book for years. An illuminator would then take it and work on it for longer still. Not to mention the tanner who made the parchment, and the bookbinder who stitched the book together, and the librarian who worked to get the book for the library and keep it safe from mold and thieves and clumsy monks with ink pots and dirty hands. And some books have authors, too, like Saint Augustine or Rabbi Yehuda. When you think about it, each book is a lot of lives. Dozens and dozens of them."

"Dozens and dozens of lives," Jeanne says. "And each life a whole world."

"We saved five books," says Jacob. "How many worlds is that?"

William smiles. "I don't know. A lot. A whole lot."

The sun is setting on the third day of our journey. We crest a hill, pockmarked with flashing puddles, and Gwenforte runs out ahead of us, to the top. Then she stops and stands as still as a greyhound in an illumination.

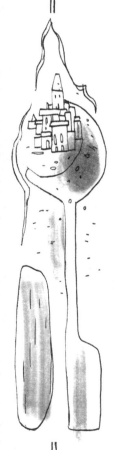

We come up behind her—and all stop breathing at once.

What lies before us is the most beautiful sight I have ever seen in my life.

There is a bay, wide and flat, like a crescent moon laid on its side. The water seems no more than an inch deep in most places, straight across the wide bay, running in shallow currents, crested by delicate foam. The setting sun shimmers off this sheet of water—blue and periwinkle and pink and cobalt and gray and slate and yellow and tangerine— running away from the shifting currents of foam, deepening to black as a current of ripples hurries along the surface, and then eddying, and finally spreading out with a sigh. And rising up from these royal, liquid, silken bedsheets of a holy bay is a mountain, right in the middle. Perched on that mountain is a stone abbey, and perched on the abbey is a tower that points straight up toward the originator of the bay's miraculous swirling colors—the sunset-streaked sky— and higher, to whatever is beyond.

We stand, for a moment, and take in the beauty of Mont-Saint-Michel.

And then Gwenforte bounds forward, down the hill, and the children go flying after her. Their leather shoes splash through the shining puddles on the road, the sacks of books bang against William's broad back, and Jeanne shouts to the heavens. I run after, laughing and trying to keep up.

The road angles down the steep hill and into a tiny town, the last outpost of civilization before the mount. But the children don't stop. They run straight through, toward the bay beyond.

And then, some hundred yards farther on, the road ends. Or rather, the bay begins. Gwenforte doesn't seem to notice, and she goes splashing through the low surf, which is graying now, more lavender and cloud colored, as the sunset fades.

"What happened to the road?" Jacob says, coming to a halt on the last yard of dry land. "It's drowned."

Indeed it has. Where the road should be, the sea swirls, whorls of water twirling by. Gwenforte stands there, looking back at us, wet up to her haunches. We gaze past her, across the bay, at the great abbey on the mountain, surrounded by the sea. The only sound is the whirling waves.

And then a voice breaks the stillness. "You won't get across tonight." It comes from behind us.

A knight stands in the road, his shoulders rising and falling, his sword in its scabbard casting a serpentine shadow on the ground.

I feel a rush of air as Jeanne sweeps past me. She pushes the knight in his stomach and shouts, "Marmeluc!"

Gwenforte barks and barks and comes out of the bay and shakes water all over us. Then she throws her paws up on the knight until he laughs.

"Why are you here?" William demands, dropping the sacks of books onto the road.

"I've been waiting for you in that town there," he says, pointing back at the few poor buildings.

Jeanne steps back from the knight.

Jacob says, "You've been waiting for us? You knew we'd come here?"

"Half of France knows you're coming here. And all of France's knights."

"How?" says Jeanne.

"A troubadour came to the royal court," Marmeluc says. "He told them you were going to Mont-Saint-Michel. And that you had some Jewish books. In exchange for his information, he got to perform for the king."

Jacob knelt and put his head between his legs. I wondered if he was about to throw up.

Jeanne said, "Chrétien?"

"What?"

"Was the troubadour's name Chrétien?"

"No. It was Nicolas something. Nicolas Lapin, I think."

Lapin—the Rabbit.

"The other one," William moans.

"The king and the queen mother are coming here," Marmeluc goes on. "With as many knights as they could muster. To get the books. And to get you."

The last town before Mont-Saint-Michel is barely a town at all. Its only inn is a single room, divided by a woolen blanket to separate where the innkeeper sleeps and where he keeps his one table and two benches.

"I can make some soup for ye," the old innkeeper says, as if it were the greatest hardship he's ever faced. He's bent, with a wild thicket of white hair that looks constantly buffeted by his own personal gale-force winds. His feet are wide splayed, and he swings his right arm more than his left as he walks, as if he were hauling a large and invisible sack of turnips. "The soup'll take a long while," he adds. "I have bread, too. It's stale, though."

"They'll have bread *and* soup, thank you, Clotho," says Marmeluc.

"And I imagine you'll all want *blankets* for the night?" This sounds like an even greater imposition than the soup.

"Yes, we will."

Clotho rolls his eyes and lugs his invisible turnips over to his side of the blanket.

For a moment, there is a heavy silence. Gwenforte is scratching herself. The rest of us are thinking about the army that will soon descend upon these children.

"When do you expect them?" William says.

"They should be here by dawn."

"Then we have to leave now!" William says, standing up. "We must go to the abbey!"

Clotho was hobbling by, gripping five dirty cups by their lips. "Ye won't get across tonight," he sneers. "I can promise ye that. The currents are aswirl right now."

"Tomorrow, though?" Marmeluc says. "The road will be clear tomorrow?"

The innkeeper seems to take a grim satisfaction in being consulted. "Aye, tomorrow it'll be clear. But don't ye stray from the causeway. After a night like tonight, with devils' pools and the cross-eyed currents, the sand will be hungry indeed."

Marmeluc nods at Clotho as if that statement made any sense.

Clotho tosses some stale bread on the table. Jeanne says to him, "Have you lived here your whole life?"

The innkeeper stops and eyes the little girl with something close to hatred. "Ay. Though I didn't use to tend the inn. I took it over from Wulfram, when he died. Why?"

Jeanne shrugs. Clotho glares at her. She smiles at him. He keeps glaring at her. She keeps smiling at him. "God's wounds!" he swears, and pivots on his good leg to go tend the fire.

A short time later, he lugs a great cauldron into the room and begins ladling soup into cracked earthenware bowls.

"That didn't take a long while," Marmeluc murmurs.

Clotho growls.

"Will you eat with us?" Jeanne asks the innkeeper. We are all surprised at the question.

Clotho is, too. After a moment of stunned silence, he mutters, "Keep to myself, I do." And he drags himself back to the other side of the curtain.

We all bend our heads over the bowls. The soup is thick with rue and sweetened with dried apples.

"This is delicious!" Jeanne exclaims. She's right. It is.

We hear *Hmph!* from the other side of the blanket.

Jacob has been spooning the stew slowly into his

mouth and staring into the middle distance. Finally he says to Marmeluc, "You're not going to turn us over to the king, are you?"

The knight frowns. "You saved my brother's life. You three have performed miracles that I thought were the stuff of stories and sermons. I wouldn't turn you in if an angel came out of the sky and told me to."

"You swear?" Jacob says.

"My friend, I swear to you."

CHAPTER 26

The Third Part of the Inquisitor's Tale

We sleep on the damp dirt floor, wrapped in mildewed blankets so rough they could be used to scrape bark off logs. Well, let me be accurate. We *lie* on the damp dirt floor, wrapped in mildewed blankets so rough they could be used to scrape bark off logs. None of us sleep at all, knowing that an army, led by the king himself, will be here by sunrise.

A few hours into the night, there is a strange sound. Like something rattling against the floor. It is coming, I think, from Jeanne's direction. "Jeanne," William whispers, raising himself on one elbow. "Jeanne, are you okay?"

She does not respond. A few of us stir and try to see her in the dark. The rattling continues for a few moments, and then ceases.

William settles down again.

I lie on my back and wonder what that was.

. . .

Some time before dawn, Gwenforte stands and begins to whine. Everyone sits up at once. We listen, but I can't hear anything. Gwenforte barks.

"Shut that dog up!" cries Clotho from the other side of the hanging blanket.

On our side, we are all propped up on our arms in the darkness, totally still.

"I hear it," William whispers.

"What?"

"Shh!"

After a moment, I hear it, too. We all do. I see the children's faces transform. Marmeluc swears under his breath.

Hoofbeats. Slow and steady. Many, many hoofbeats. They sound like war drums. Gwenforte barks again.

"Gwen, quiet!" Jeanne hisses.

But Clotho has had enough, apparently, for he bursts through the blanket, his long brown tunic swinging around his bare knees. "What in Hell is that dog barking at?" He stares at us. None of us move. He is listening now. And then, his face goes slack. He's heard it.

"That'll be the king."

Jeanne nods.

"Ye won't be able to see the causeway in the dark," Clotho sneers. "Even if it *is* dry."

Marmeluc shakes his head.

"It ain't none of my business!" Clotho shouts. "I don't know why I should care!"

"Right," says Jeanne. "You shouldn't."

"I should let the king find ye and do what he likes with ye! Ye and your dog!"

None of us moves. The hoofbeats have grown ever so slightly louder. Gwenforte begins to whine.

Clotho looks miserable.

"Oh, get up, ye layabouts!" the old man snaps. "Come on!" And, without so much as putting his pants on, he leads us outside.

The sky is gloaming, and the waves of the sea are as thin as petals of nightshade as they swirl over the road to Mont-Saint-Michel. The great mountain abbey stands, a sentinel silhouette, in the distance.

"Stay straight behind me!" the innkeeper hisses. In the east, the first sparks of sunlight streak forth from the horizon. "Don't get no independent ideas, ye young fools! To the left or right of me is yer death. Do ye hear?"

"We hear," says Jeanne.

We do indeed. I don't know why straying from the causeway would be deadly. Something about "hungry sands," I gather. But the dark waves slither back and forth like adders, and I am sufficiently afraid that I will do exactly what Clotho says. Jacob is standing very close to me. I reach out and put a hand on his shoulder. He looks up and smiles wanly.

What I did to deserve the kindness of these children, I don't know.

Though following them to my death will, perhaps, be worth something.

We start out on the watery road. Sea foam, gray in the darkness, runs over our shoes. Gwenforte whines and stays close to Jeanne. We splash forward, following the innkeeper's lurching, splayfooted stride.

"The sea is wetting the books," Jacob informs William. So William hoists the sacks above his head, his great arms like the pillars of a church holding up the roof.

Gwenforte stops. Her ears start to twitch as she gazes back the way we've come. Jeanne turns to see what Gwenforte is looking at. I do, too. She seems to be staring at the hill from which we looked down upon the bay yesterday. The sky is pale blue there, dewed with yellow. "What?" says Jeanne. "What do you hear, Gwenforte?"

As if in answer to her question, a figure on horseback crests the hill.

"Look!" I say. Jacob and William and Marmeluc turn and look. Clotho keeps on hauling his invisible sack of turnips through the surf.

Another silhouetted rider on horseback has joined the first on the top of the hill. Then a third trots up beside the first two.

The three figures stop there, taking in the same view we had last night. The bay is beginning to sparkle with the morning's light—black eddies glowing golden in their creases, sea foam blushing chrysanthemum.

There is a call from one of the riders. Small, like a gull's out over the water. I can't make it out. And then a horn blast bursts through the silent dawn. One blast and then another and then one more.

"What did that mean?" Jeanne asks Sir Marmeluc.

The knight exhales slowly. His breath is a cloud of vapor in the cool air. "It means *charge*," he says.

"What?" I say. "Just the three of them?"

"No," says Jacob, pointing. "Not just the three of them."

A line of knights, helms reflecting the sun rising in the east, crest the hill in a clattering silver wave.

"Holy God . . . ," William murmurs.

The knights stand on the hill, like lightning frozen on the horizon. And then the thunder breaks. They course down the hill, their horses' hooves booming. A second wave follows. And then a third. And then a fourth.

"How many are there?" I moan. But really, the question is not relevant. The answer is *enough*. There are enough.

"Run!" cries Jeanne. "Clotho, run!"

Clotho is still waddling along. "T'ain't safe to run in the dark, the tides as they are," the innkeeper calls back, peering casually over his shoulder, as if there were no place to hurry to, and no reason to hurry, ever, anywhere, no matter what. "T'ain't safe at—" And then his eyes grow to the size of apples. And he shouts, "Run! Run!" He sets off, his right arm swinging, his splayed feet flailing in the shallow surf, following the curve of the causeway to the mountain. We don't need any more prompting. We sprint after him, our

ankles splashing in the sea foam. Gwenforte runs out ahead, and the sea sprays up around her like wings.

The horses come pounding down the road, five or six abreast. When they hit the water, they fan out, forming a pincer like a crab's. In some places the water is shallow, and in other places it is nearly gone, leaving sand and seashells glistening in the first rays of the morning. The horses' hooves land like explosions on the water and sand.

Out ahead of us, yellow beams of sunlight hit the stone monastery and shine off the glass windows of the church. Clotho's slow waddle is holding us up, for we can't go out ahead of him, lest we lose the causeway. Though I don't know why we *need* to stick to the causeway when the water is so shallow. "Hurry!" Jacob is beseeching him. "They're coming!"

Indeed they are. The lines keep pouring over the hilltop. Seven, nine, twelve lines of knights, stampeding through the town and out into the bay.

"We can't outrun them!" Jeanne says.

"Will they kill us?" Jacob wonders.

"Yes!" shouts Marmeluc.

"Can't you stop them?" I plead with William.

William, who is trying to hurry Clotho along, says, "I could stop a few of them. Five, maybe ten. Not however many that is."

"A hundred," says Marmeluc. "The king mustered a hundred knights."

"I definitely can't stop a hundred." William adds, "They'll cut us down like summer wheat."

And then, Jeanne has turned around. She has gone completely rigid. "That knight . . . ," she says. "He . . . he disappeared . . ."

Marmeluc swears. "God's bones! Not another fit! Not now!" But I've turned and looked to see what Jeanne could have meant.

And I scream, "Good God!"

For I see it, too. A knight, galloping out front, suddenly disappears. As if he had just—just sunk, instantly, out of sight.

Then another does the same. The horse seems to drop a fathom in a single step. It's up to its chest in water, though the tide is but a few inches high. The horse begins to panic, flailing and bucking. Which only seems to make it sink faster. Faster and faster, until even the knight in his armor is gone beneath the gray and glimmering waves.

"Look!" Jeanne cries. Jacob and William reluctantly slow and turn. The horses on the causeway have closed much of the distance. But just as the boys turn around, two more knights get swallowed by the bay.

"God's nose!" Marmeluc swears again. "What's happening?"

Clotho, still struggling through the shallow waves, peers over his hunched shoulder. Another knight goes down—horse flailing, pitching, and then disappearing beneath the parchment-thin layer of water. Clotho shouts, "Sand's hungry. I told ye to stay on the causeway. Why do you think we call it the causeway? *'Cause it's the only way!*" He cackles—and keeps up his crazy, duck-like running.

But Marmeluc, Jacob, Jeanne, William, and I just stand and stare. Knight after knight, clad in beautiful tunics of green and red and blue, helms shining, swords drawn, are sinking into the sea. A burst of water shoots up around them—and they are gone.

Over on the far shore—and I heard this later, from one who knows—King Louis, Jean de Joinville, and Blanche of Castile are sitting on their mounts. They are the three figures we saw cresting the hill. At Louis's side, on foot, is his page, with the battle horn slung across his chest.

Louis's face is contorted with fear and horror. "What on earth?" he mutters, as the knights are swallowed, one by one. "God be merciful—"

"My lord!" Joinville cries. "Call them back! Call them back before they all drown!"

But Blanche snarls at them both. "Don't be silly!"

"No, it's a sign! It's a sign, my lord!" Joinville is pleading, thinking back, perhaps, to the stories he heard at the inn. "It is a sign from God! This is not His will! Call them back!"

"Don't be a coward!" Blanche snaps. "It's not a sign; it's a test! Only the pure of heart will cross the waters and snatch the books of heresy from the hands of the Devil!"

Another knight disappears beneath the shimmering waves. His horse pitches forward and then cries out. The knight is halfway submerged in the bay. The horse flails, and the knight is up to his cobalt-cloaked chest in water. He tries to plant his hands beside him and push himself upward, but the action only drags him farther down. "Help me!" he screams. "God have mercy, help me!" And then he disappears beneath the waves.

"That was Nicolas de Montagne!" Joinville screeches. "Louis, *sweet* Louis, *good* Louis, *kind* Louis . . . I have never known you to be a fool before. Please—*call back your knights.*"

Before Blanche can say another word, Louis has turned to his page. "Retreat," he murmurs.

"Sorry, my lord. What was that?"

"I said, *retreat . . .*"

The page lifts the horn to his lips. He blows two long blasts, waits, and blows two more. The knights begin to turn.

We cannot believe what we are hearing, what we are seeing. "That's the retreat!" Marmeluc says, his voice aquiver. "They've sounded the retreat!"

Indeed, the knights are turning around. But those who had ridden on the causeway now loop out over the sand. As many as were lost on the way out now sink on the way back to shore. The screams of horses and riders is unbearable.

Like the wailing of children. Gwenforte is whining. Jeanne looks away.

The remaining knights, finally, come back to the king's side, their tunics soaked, their horses frothing at the mouth, eyes of men and horses wild and afraid. A hundred knights had ridden out into the bay. Twenty have come back.

Joinville's words are no more than breath. "It is a sign—"

Blanche spits, "Please! It's a sign that you're a coward. If I'm the only one whose faith is strong enough to trust in the hand of the Almighty, so be it! Knights! Follow me!"

Blanche of Castile kicks her horse and goes galloping out into the bay. A few knights follow her.

"Mother!" cries Louis. "Don't!"

He spurs his horse, but Joinville has already grabbed the reins. Louis turns on him, furious, but the courtier says, "France cannot lose a queen and a king in one day, my lord. We would not survive." So Louis turns to see his mother galloping across the shallow surf. Around him, the rest of the knights watch, their helms under their arms or in their laps, breathing hard, afraid.

We watch her come. It is clearly the queen mother. Her skirts fly out behind her, her leather riding breeches are dyed red, and her thin crown flashes in her dark, braided hair. She rides out ahead of the other knights, faster and faster, framed by the bluing sky and the water flaming

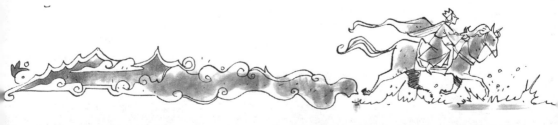

red from the rising sun. Her horse's white hooves pound the surf.

Closer.

Closer.

Closer yet.

We watch her. And I think we all realize, all at once, that we are more afraid for her than we are for ourselves.

The knights behind her begin to sink. One by one their horses crash forward, panicked, crying out pitifully, pulling the knights below the surf, until at last there is only Blanche, riding, riding, riding like Jesus walking on water, the sky ablaze behind her.

And then her horse pitches forward, and Jeanne screams, and the horse disappears into the foam, and the queen is bellowing now, swiftly sinking into the hungry sand.

For one instant, no one moves. We just watch her— Blanche of Castile, Queen Mother of France—flailing and sinking into the crescent bay.

And then Gwenforte lights out, running toward the queen, skimming over the shallow water like an angel. Jeanne and Jacob do not hesitate, do not pause long enough to think. They sprint after Gwenforte. William throws the sacks of books at Marmeluc so hard they almost knock the knight over. Then he follows Jeanne and Jacob as they run, keeping the glistening causeway beneath their sopping leather shoes. I run after them as fast as I can. If their martyrdom is come, I will witness it. A thought strikes me: Perhaps I will return home in glory after all.

The queen is sinking, sinking, sinking, her arms flailing above her head, and she is screaming and pleading with God, but she is sinking, and soon just her head and elbows and her flailing hands are visible. The children have to leave the causeway now, if they are to save her.

I come up behind them.

They are hesitating. Even Gwenforte.

Will they? Will they martyr themselves for Blanche of Castile?

Suddenly, I wonder: Would I want them to?

To my shame, I must admit—I do not know.

And then, I do know.

For Jeanne has started out over the quicksand. And William and Jacob and Gwenforte are following her. I know what I want. I know, at last.

The greyhound, light and fleet, gets ahead of Jeanne and reaches the queen first. I can see, from the safety of the causeway, that Blanche's chin is submerged, and her head is tilted back so that her nose and eyes, along with her wrists and grasping hands, are all that remain above the water. Gwenforte grabs with her teeth the cuff of one of Blanche's sleeves and begins to pull, but Blanche is heavier than the dog, and soon Gwenforte, too, is sinking into the sand. William reaches the queen mother next. His legs are submerged in the bay, and he, too, is sinking, but he reaches out and grabs her hand.

"Lie down! Lie down!" Clotho is hobbling up behind me, with Marmeluc at his side. He is cupping his hands and shouting through them. "Lie down, damn it!"

Jacob, with no idea why he is doing it, throws himself onto his stomach. Jeanne does, too. William, still holding Blanche's hand, lets himself flop forward onto his belly. Now their faces are half submerged in the sucking sand. Jacob spits it from his mouth. Jeanne begins to choke.

I stand on the causeway, frozen with fear.

"Grab each other!" Clotho yells.

William holds both of Blanche's hands. Gwenforte still has her sleeve. Jeanne, coughing and choking, crawls to where she can put her arms around William's chest. Jacob grabs Jeanne's outstretched ankles and turns his head like a swimmer gasping for air.

"Now pull!" Clotho calls. "Crawl back and pull!"

But Jeanne is coughing and choking and Jacob is gasping like a beached fish and William, great William, is sinking. Gwenforte is submerged to her backward-bending knees.

"Pull, ye layabouts!"

The wet sand is all over Jeanne's face. Jacob's mouth is full of it, and his nostrils are closed. When he tries to breathe, he's pulling sand into his nose, his throat, his lungs. And William is going down, down, down.

This is it. Their martyrdom.

"PULL!" Marmeluc pleads.

They try to. They try to drag themselves backward, unable to breathe, coughing and choking and gasping. They drag themselves, unable to see, salty seawater burning their eyes. They drag their heavy bodies, back and back and back, though their brains must be cloudy with lack of air, while the other side of existence, whatever is beyond life, is pulling them down.

They sink into the sand.

And there, I watch them die.

At least, that's what it feels like. But at the last moment, as Jeanne is choking and Jacob is not breathing at all and William is totally submerged in sand, I throw myself forward on my face.

This is no courage on my part. No heroism. It is that—despite all my plans to witness their martyrdom for my own gain—I cannot watch them drown. If they are to die, I will die with them. This is what I want, I know at last. I want to live in a world that possesses these children, or I don't want to live at all.

I grab Jacob's ankles and prepare to sink into the sandy abyss.

And then I feel a pair of hands around my legs. I turn my head, sand clogging my nose and my mouth, and I see Marmeluc, on his knees on the causeway, pulling me toward him. I tighten my grip on Jacob.

He pulls me and I pull Jacob and Jacob pulls Jeanne, who is hanging on to William, who pulls Blanche and, with her, Gwenforte.

One crooked neighbor, pulling another, up from the depths.

Slowly, the queen mother emerges from the quicksand—

first her arms, then her neck, then her shoulders, until even her feet are free, and she is being dragged, sandy and sopping wet, across the surface of the bay.

Finally Blanche, Jeanne, Jacob, William, Gwenforte, and I are lying on the causeway, heaving for breath, snorting up sand, staring at the blue sky streaked with red and gold. Above our heads, gulls wheel and cry, unaware that the queen mother nearly drowned just a dozen yards below.

William pulls himself to his feet. He is soaked through and caked with sand, as are we all. He scoops the queen mother up in his arms—to my surprise she does not protest—and he starts back along the causeway, toward the bank. "Take those books to the abbey," William calls over his shoulder at Marmeluc.

"Yes," says Jeanne. "Give them to Michelangelo. He'll be waiting for them."

William trips. Blanche shrieks. William manages to recover his balance and, still holding the dripping queen, he turns around.

Jacob, blinking at Jeanne, says, "What?"

"I had a vision last night," Jeanne tells us, as if it were the most natural thing in the world. "Michelangelo is here."

"Jeanne," says William. "He's *dead*."

Jeanne smiles. "You don't think Saint Michael, Archangel, is bothered by a little fire, do you?" she replies. "Besides, I think this is his home."

· · ·

William is carrying Blanche of Castile, Queen Mother and former Regent of all France, in his arms like a newborn calf. The sun has risen over the hills in the southeast, and the bay of Mont-Saint-Michel is flooded with the yolky blue of morning. The sea laps at our ankles, the water cold, the foam warm. Plovers run along the sand looking for tiny crabs, and gulls glide and cry overhead.

Jacob walks behind William, his head high, his chest thrust forward. Next to him marches Jeanne, just as determined and resolute. Gwenforte trots alongside them, like the tiny battalion's proud mascot. I follow behind, a silent witness. The causeway has become a sparkling road of stones and white shells, and the quicksand on either side, grim graveyard of nearly a hundred knights, looks as innocent as any beach.

King Louis and Joinville stand at the end of the causeway, afraid to go any farther. I can see, even from a distance, that the king's lank hair is damp with sweat, and his long cheeks are streaked with tears. Joinville's chiseled visage is wan, his eyes haunted.

"I can walk, you know," Blanche snaps, as we approach the king and Joinville. William puts her down. Blanche throws her head back and walks, wobbly and caked with sand, the last few yards to her son. We follow.

Blanche does not greet Louis or Joinville, and when Louis tries to embrace her she holds him off with a small sandy hand. "Yes, yes," she says. "But I'd like to go home now." And she starts walking back up the hill, in the direction of Paris, sand dripping in a trail behind her.

"Are you going to *walk*?" Louis calls after her.

"If I have to," she calls back.

Louis turns to the children. He holds them in his gaze for a long time. No one moves. Finally he kneels and bends his head. Joinville hurries to his knee beside the king. The king is bowing to the children. I am witnessing it with my own eyes. Otherwise, I would not believe it. Not in a thousand years.

"Bless me," Louis says. "Bless me, holy children— oblate, peasant, and Jew. Bless me."

They're all as startled as I am. But no one is more startled than Jacob. "You knew I was Jewish?"

"Always, my little dissembler." Louis smiles, his head rising slightly. "You aren't much of an actor." The king exhales. "Since days of old, God has always worked his miracles through those we least expect. The weakest, the poorest, the youngest. Did not our Lord say, 'the meek shall inherit the earth'? Well, it's yours. The Talmuds, too," Louis adds, staring at the shining shells at the children's feet. "Keep them, and don't let them spread."

But Joinville says, "Louis, they're going to have them copied right here at Mont-Saint-Michel."

"I am going to pretend I didn't hear that," Louis replies. I can see the children smile. The king looks up. He rises to his feet, and Joinville does, too. "I hope," says Louis, "that

I see you again—in that land where I am not a king...and you are not a pain in my royal behind."

Then Louis nods, turns, and follows his mother up the hill.

Joinville bows from the waist and says to the children, "It has been the greatest honor." And then he bends down and rubs Gwenforte's head, before collecting his and the king's horses and hurrying after the royal family.

And just like that, King Louis has lost his war.

CHAPTER 27

The Fourth Part of the Inquisitor's Tale

Marmeluc and Clotho have already disappeared inside the fortress of Mont-Saint-Michel. The abbey is fortified and in its time has been an outpost against the Vikings, the French, the English, and the Bretons. The walls are thick bluish stone, and the only way in is blocked by a huge iron portcullis. But as we approach along the shimmering causeway, a wheel somewhere turns, chains tighten and groan, and the bars lift.

Standing in the center of the cobbled road inside the iron gate is a giant. His nose and cheeks are ruddy, his hair and whiskers unruly, and his red-brown eyes are twinkling. I have never seen him before, but I know, in an instant, that it is Michelangelo di Bologna.

Gwenforte barks, and Jeanne breaks into a run. The little peasant girl, wet and sand-soaked, collides with Michelangelo's huge belly and throws her arms as far around him as they can go. Which is not very far. Gwenforte jumps around them, barking and leaping and spinning in circles.

Jacob and William just stare at Jeanne, embracing the giant red monk.

"I—I don't believe it," William stammers.

Michelangelo looks up. His great red face is split with an enormous smile. "A hug from a child!" he exclaims. "Perhaps God's greatest invention!"

Jacob approaches Michelangelo slowly. He reaches out and touches the monk's fleshy red hand, as if he wants to test his physical existence. "You are Misha-el? God's beloved? The angel?"

Michelangelo's great head goes up and down, slowly, once.

"You don't *look* like an angel," William objects.

"What? You mean clean-shaven and slim?" Michelangelo laughs. "With beautiful flowing locks? I've seen the images you mortals make of me. They're humiliating."

"So, you live here?" Jacob asks. His confusion is so deep it can only be represented with the most banal questions.

"If they named a spot this pretty after you, you'd spend as much time as you could there, too."

"But . . . you're not from Bologna?" William, too, apparently, is suffering from inane question syndrome.

"No, but I do love that town. They call it 'red, fat, and learned.' It's what inspired this form I made for myself." Michelangelo looks down at his own body, as if it were a favorite hat.

"You made for yourself...," William murmurs.

"Sadly, it's all used up now. Half of Paris saw it burn. So I'll need a new one." He reaches out and pinches William's arm. "This one's nice."

William yanks his arm out of reach. "It's taken, thank you!"

Jeanne looks up, her arms still attached to Michelangelo's stomach. "And is that why Gwenforte liked you so much? Because she knew you were an angel?"

Michelangelo gently detaches himself from Jeanne's embrace and kneels down to stroke Gwenforte's head. "We spent some lovely years together, before God sent her back to earth."

We all stand there, marveling at the fat monk, petting the white dog. They are both pilgrims from Heaven. How strange. But, in fact, how very believable. Obvious, almost.

Something, though, is not obvious to Jacob. "Why did God do it?" he demands fiercely. "Why did He send Gwenforte back? And give us these miracles to perform? And put us through ... through *Hell*?" His throat sounds thick and his face is contorted with anger. *"Why?"*

"What do you mean, *why*? To save the Talmuds. To cure the dragon. To find the Holy Nail. To open the eyes of the king and his mother, if only a little bit." Michelangelo's great hand strokes the greyhound's soft white fur. A seagull swoops down out of the dawn-colored sky, lands nearby, and cocks its head at us.

"But why not just ... just *make* it happen? You know"— Jacob snaps his fingers angrily—*"poof!"*

"Because God does not work like *poof!*" Michelangelo says, snapping his fingers back at Jacob. Gwenforte looks at Michelangelo's big fingers curiously and then tries to lick them. He laughs and lets her. "God works through people. Like you."

Jacob mutters, "It's a strange way to run the world."

"Yes," Michelangelo agrees. "Even to me, it is mysterious. Full of wonders—and endlessly maddening."

He looks at me. "Étienne, how nice to see you." I am surprised, for a moment, that he knows me. And then I think, *Of course he knows me. He knows us all.*

"It is an honor," I say, bowing my head.

"Following the children and collecting their story, are we?"

"Yes."

"And threw away our knife?"

"Yes . . . sir . . ." I want to address him. Call him something. But what do you call an angel?

"That's a good boy."

My face turns red. I am pleased and embarrassed all at once. I say, "I saw the error of my ways. Thanks to these children—and Marie the brewster and Jerome the librarian and Aron the butcher and Gerald of Scotland and a little jongleur-thief—oh, and Joinville himself." I don't know why I'm recounting all this. What do you say to an archangel? "And a little nun. She knew a great deal of the story. More than I would have thought possible."

Michelangelo's face falls. "Was she a tiny thing, with silvery hair, shining blue eyes, and an impish smile?"

I say she was.

Michelangelo pulls himself up to his towering height and stares off at the horizon.

"Why?" William says. "Who is she?"

"I didn't see any of those people at the inn," says Jacob. "Aron was there?"

"Yes," I say. "He went to bed. And the nun—" But suddenly I realize that the nun had been inside when the kids arrived in the yard of the inn. But where had she gone? I went out to the stable with them, and when I came back, she wasn't there . . .

Michelangelo's voice sounds like the tolling of a bell. "There are only two beings in Creation that I fear," he said. "One above, and one below. Strangely, when they walk the earth, they both take the same form. Of a little old woman, with silvery hair, sparkling eyes, and a knowing smile." He swallows hard.

And then Michelangelo shrugs. "No matter."

I am not sure if I believe him.

But Jeanne has another concern: "What will happen to us now?" she asks.

"Well, that is up to you."

"It is?"

"Of course."

"But don't you know?" Jeanne insists.

"I do not. You are free to do whatever you like, Jeanne.

Though you might go home. Your parents miss you terribly."

"They do?"

"Of course."

Jacob had begun staring at the paving stones below his feet as soon as the word *parents* was mentioned.

Michelangelo adds, "Jacob, so do yours." Jacob looks up. "Though you will not see them again for some time, I hope."

Jacob exhales, nods, and wipes his eyes with his sleeve.

"For now, though, Yehuda and Miriam would love for you to come to live with them. They would be honored to have you."

William is now looking hard at nothing at all.

Michelangelo has not failed to notice this. "William, there is a place waiting for you at Robert de Sorbonne's college, should you want it." As William hears this news, his back straightens, his neck elongates, and his whole body seems to expand. Which I had really not thought possible. Michelangelo adds, "Between the debates and the fistfights, I think you'll fit right in.

"But," he goes on, "it's up to each of you. You can do whatever you want. Maybe you will want to stay together. Maybe you will want to continue traveling around France, doing God's work."

"Maybe we will," Jeanne says.

I inhale the fresh wind of the sea. It smells, for some reason, like sadness.

"At least," she adds, "until our martyrdom comes."

"Which will be ... when, exactly?" Jacob wants to know. So do we all.

Michelangelo's red hair dances in the sea spray. "William, you should have an answer to that."

"I should?"

"Indeed. What is *martyr* in Latin? Or in Greek, for that matter?"

William says, "My Greek's not so good. In Latin, it means 'witness.'"

"Correct. And have you not already witnessed on behalf of goodness and beauty and justice and God? To Louis and Blanche and dozens of others? Whether you go your separate ways or stay together, you will continue to witness—against ignorance, against cruelty, and on behalf of all that is beautiful about this strange and crooked world. Yes, children, you will be martyrs. Just as you always have been."

He turns to me. "And what will you do?"

I have known the answer since the moment I threw myself, stomach first, into the quicksand. "I will follow these children, wherever they go, and record their works and their miracles," I say. "I will witness their witnessing, so that all the world may share their gifts."

And Michelangelo replies, "Amen."

Jacob reaches out and takes Michelangelo's hand. Jeanne leans in and takes Michelangelo's other hand and wraps it around herself, so that she is enfolded in one of his great warm arms. Gwenforte slithers underneath

Jeanne and wedges her head up between Jacob and Michelangelo. Finally William wraps his arms around them all.

And Michelangelo sighs. "Ah," he says. "Another miracle."

Author's Note:
Where Did This Story Come From?

My interest in the Middle Ages is entirely my wife's fault. We met in college. Even back then she knew that she wanted to be a professor of medieval history. Our first trip together was to Northern England, where we went on a week-long scavenger hunt for missing pieces of medieval stained glass. (We found them!) We continued to take trips to Europe to visit museums, monasteries, castles, churches, libraries, dungeons, ancient forests, and medieval garbage dumps. (In fact, my wife spent a whole week excavating one.) We even lived in Europe for a year. My wife spent all day, every day, in libraries, reading medieval books. I spent all day, every day, cooking, eating, and dreaming up this novel.

So how much of this novel is *real*, and how much is made up?

That's a complicated question.

Many of the characters are real. King Louis, Blanche of Castile, Jean de Joinville, Robert de Sorbonne, Roger

Bacon, Gwenforte the Holy Greyhound (yes, there *was* a Holy Greyhound, though she was a he, and his name was spelled Guinefort).

Some of the events really happened, too. The Holy Nail really was lost (and found). Knights really did sink into the quicksand surrounding Mont-Saint-Michel. And, tragically, some twenty thousand volumes of Talmud really were burned in the center of Paris.

Other events in the book are inspired by legends of the Middle Ages: William's battle with the fiends, the dragon of the deadly farts, Jeanne recognizing the true king.

Below are some notes to help you sort through what is history, what is legend, and what is completely made up in *The Inquisitor's Tale.*

JEANNE's character was very loosely based on Joan of Arc (whose name, in French, is Jeanne). Joan of Arc was a peasant girl, and she, like my character Jeanne, had visions. There is also a legend about her being brought before the King of France and kneeling to one of his courtiers—who turned out to be the real king in disguise. The similarities between Jeanne and Joan of Arc end there, though. Joan lived two hundred years after my story takes place, was a military genius even as a child, led the armies of France against the English, was captured, horribly tortured, and then executed.

My wife and I lived for a time in Rouen, France, right across the street from where some of the worst torture took place. The more I learned about Joan of Arc, the more upset I became. I felt that her fate wouldn't have been nearly so gruesome or so tragic had she not been both a peasant and a girl. To the lords of the Middle Ages, there was no figure more powerless and more exploitable than a peasant girl. I wanted to depict that in my story—but more gently. After all, not every peasant girl was treated as badly as Joan of Arc.

By most counts, PEASANTS accounted for ninety percent of the European population in the High Middle Ages, when *The Inquisitor's Tale* takes place. Just like Jeanne, peasants typically lived in villages near farmland. None of the land they worked or lived on belonged to them, though. It belonged to the "land lord," who was usually either a noble or a religious institution. Each peasant family was given a plot of land to build a house and raise animals on, as well as a furrow of the fields to grow food for themselves. In exchange, they had to work the lord's land, the *demesne*, once a week, and also pay rent or taxes to the lord once a year.

There was a hierarchy of peasants in the Middle Ages. Some were "free peasants," who didn't own any land but could, at least, move to another manor if they wanted. Bonded peasants, or serfs, could only leave if their lord gave them permission. Serfdom wasn't quite slavery (they couldn't be bought or sold, for instance), but it was close. If you want to learn more about peasant life, or about any of the topics I take on in this book, I recommend a variety of sources in the Annotated Bibliography.

The story of GWENFORTE—how she protected an infant from a snake, and how she was killed and then venerated as a saint—comes from the diary of a real inquisitor named Stephen of Bourbon (who inspired my Étienne of Arles). Stephen was sent to a small village in France to stamp out the saintly veneration of a dog. Upon arriving, he learned the incredible story of the greyhound and the snake, and recorded it in his notes. As I said above, the real Gwenforte was called Guinefort, was a male dog, and, sadly, did not come back to life and start an adventure with the child whose life he saved. I made all that up. Interestingly, the story of the "faithful hound" shows up in stories from all over the world. There's a very similar story, for example, from Wales about a dog named Gelert.

WILLIAM was inspired by the legend of Guilhem, or Guillaume d'Orange, a real lord from southern France who became the subject of many tall tales after he died. During his life, he made a name for himself fighting in Spain against the Muslims who had recently conquered that land. But once he was dead, he grew in stature and fame, becoming something like a mix between Paul Bunyan and the Incredible Hulk.

One story told about Guilhem takes place near the end of his life. In it, he commits himself to life as a monk in a monastery to atone for the violent way he's lived. But he is so big, so loud, and so hungry that the miserly abbot conspires to get rid of him by sending him on an errand through a forest known for its murderous brigands. My chapters about William, the golden belt, and the donkey's leg were inspired by that legend. Though I left out the original ending: When Guilhem returns home, he picks up the evil abbot by his feet, swings him around his head, and throws him over the walls of the monastery into a lake, where the abbot drowns.

In creating William, one idea that excited me was turning the historical Guilhem's war against the Muslims of Spain on its head: William's *father* is the crusader, while William is part-Christian, part-Muslim; part-European, part-African.

One reason that I wanted to recast William's background is that I wanted to explore the very different state of RACE RELATIONS in Medieval Europe. Having brown skin in France in the Middle Ages was very different from having brown skin in North America today. The transatlantic slave trade (which is a polite way of saying the mass kidnapping and enslavement of millions of innocent Africans) started about four hundred years ago, in the centuries just *after* the Middle Ages. There was a (comparatively) small amount of slavery in the Middle Ages, and it had nothing to do with the color of your skin; it had to do with whether you'd been conquered in war, or whether your parents or grandparents had been slaves.

Having brown skin in Europe in the Middle Ages was very, very unusual—most medieval French people would go through their whole lives and never see someone with dark skin. But they did not have the kind of hatred based on skin color that we've seen in the last four hundred years. Medieval people hated one another for lots of different reasons: religion, language, culture, geography, politics, and so on. But hatred based exclusively on skin color? That's the modern world's special invention.

Jacob wasn't inspired by a specific historical or legendary character. Rather, I wanted to explore his experience of religion, in contrast to and conflict with those around him. RELIGION was one of the defining facts of life for a medieval person. There was no separation of Church and State in the Middle Ages, as we have today—nor really separation of Church and *anything*. Religion defined the way people lived their lives and saw the world.

You might say that we, today, live in a scientific age. We know all sorts of things—that the moon is round, that the earth is spinning, that microscopic bugs live in our eyebrows—because scientists say so. We don't question these things, even though the vast majority of us have never visited the moon or felt the earth spinning or seen these bugs in our eyebrows. We just believe it, because the scientists say so. The scientists of the Middle Ages were theologians, and what they said about God, pretty much everyone believed. As I tried to show with the great theologian-scientist Roger Bacon (the drunk friar at the inn), religion was science in the Middle Ages.

And for the vast, vast majority of medieval Europeans that religion was Christianity. By the thirteenth century, when this book takes place, Christianity had conquered almost every part of Europe, with the exception of Spain and small pockets in the east and in Scandinavia. Peasants were Christian and kings were Christian—it was the one unifying factor of these highly divided and unequal societies. Christianity was also used to regulate and rule. It provided unity, control, and guidance to all the people of Europe.

Well, *almost* all the people. There were always holdouts, and these people presented a real problem for the rulers of the Christian kingdoms of Europe. One group of non-Christians were pagans. "Pagan" was how Christians referred to people who followed the polytheistic religions that had dominated Europe before the arrival of Christianity, from the pantheons of the Romans or Vikings to the beliefs of the Celts or Slavs. In the thirteenth century, since there were very few pagans left, the word "pagan" came to mean primitive, backward, and un-Christian.

Much more threatening to the Christian hierarchy than pagans were heretics. "Heretics" were Christians who held beliefs that were contrary to the teachings of the church. When *The Inquisitor's Tale* takes place, heresy was rampant—at least, according to the authorities it was.

And it's true that areas of southern France and northern Italy were occupied by the Cathars and the Waldensians, respectively, thus destabilizing the religious and secular authorities. Inquisitors were trained and recruited to take on—and destroy—these groups. It was highly successful—unfortunately for those heretics, who were often killed for their beliefs.

JEWS also presented serious problems for the Christian rulers of medieval Europe. Jews occupied a tenuous position in society. Very few owned land, and they were typically banned from joining the trade guilds that served Christian townspeople. That didn't leave many jobs for them. The poor became ragpickers, restitching and reselling used clothing. The luckier Jews became traders and moneylenders. This made them very important to the kings and lords of Europe. There was a time when no king could wage a war and no lord could build a new manor house without borrowing money from Jewish lenders. Jewish lenders played a similar role to banks today. But when you borrow money from someone, and have to pay it back, it often means you stop liking them. Sometimes it means you start hating them. And that happened, all over Europe.

Jews also presented a problem for the Christian authorities, because, according to the Bible, Jews believed in the same God as Christians did, had witnessed Jesus's life and death, and *still* didn't believe he was God. Popes and bishops and priests saw Jews as a threat to the faith of their followers. Add to that the hatred that grew as Jewish moneylending expanded, and you had a very dangerous situation for Jews.

There were increasingly frequent reports of organized violence against Jewish communities as the Middle Ages went on. Sometimes a group of Christians would descend on a Jewish neighborhood and beat them or set fire to their homes. And sometimes a king would force all the Jews to leave his kingdom—which was a convenient way not to have to pay back his loans from them, and to confiscate all their wealth and property.

The situation of the Jews in France under King Louis IX, the Louis of *The Inquisitor's Tale*, was incredibly complex. The year that my wife and I lived in Europe, we spent most of our time in Paris. One day, we went to the Museum of Jewish Art and History (*Musée d'art et d'histoire du Judaïsme*). As we explored the collection, we came across a small plaque that told the story of twenty thousand volumes of Talmud being burned by the famous and beloved Saint Louis and his mother, Blanche of Castile. For a long time thereafter, the story tormented me. I couldn't put it out of my mind. I knew of the cruelty to Jews across Europe, from Roman times through the Holocaust. I had read books about it; I had been to museums devoted to memorializing it. But this tiny plaque, explaining that the entire collected wisdom of the Jews of France had been burned before their very eyes by the most enlightened king in Europe—the king who had built the beautiful Sainte-Chapelle church, who an American city is named after—I couldn't get over it. I still am not over it. That plaque, more than any of my other experiences in Europe, inspired the story of this book.

We know that Louis hated Jews. He said so, more than once, and he complained of how many Jews lived in Paris (the real number was probably around 4,000 during his reign, but it may well have *felt* like 10,000 to him). And he oversaw the burning of the Talmuds. But he was not all bad. There was only one episode of large scale violence against Jewish people (as opposed to Jewish property) during his reign. Louis condemned this act of violence, and saw to it that the perpetrators were punished—though only with a fine.

Indeed, outside of his treatment of the Jews, Louis seems to have been a wise and kind ruler. One particularly charming example is this: His predecessors used the Wood of Vincennes for their royal hunts. Louis had no interest in hunting. Instead, he went to Vincennes to sit under a tree and invited common folk to gather around him to tell him their problems. He often visited the Grandmontine Abbey there, too, and he did the menial chores the monks did. And when the Holy Nail was lost, he indeed fell to the earth and screamed and wept—at least, according to Jean of Joinville, who wrote Louis's biography after the king's death. In depicting Louis, I tried to show some of these complexities and contradictions, though it would take a book much longer than mine to show him in all his complex glory. There are books that do just that listed in my bibliography.

I could only hope to provide a slender portrait of a very complicated king, and it is possible that I was too kind to him. On the other hand, I may have been too cruel to Blanche of Castile. She was, indeed, a *very* controlling mother. And she really did preside over the burning of the Talmuds. But I have no idea if she would have insulted her dinner companions as I have her do, or been quite so callous toward the knights sinking in the bay. Sometimes our depictions of historical figures have to take on shades of gray, and sometimes they become more black-and-white, as the storytelling demands.

MONT-SAINT-MICHEL, and the bay around it, became a character itself in this book. I first became interested in the site when my wife and I saw the Bayeux Tapestry, in Bayeux, France.

The Bayeux Tapestry isn't actually a tapestry. It's an embroidery, sewed by a small group of nuns in the 1070s, and the best way to describe it is a 230-foot long graphic novel that tells the story of the Norman Conquest. And it's *amazing*. But of all the 236 feet, 6 inches stuck in my mind forever: a knight on a horse is seen drowning in quicksand in front of Mont-Saint-Michel.

My wife and I were so intrigued by this that we hired a guide to take us for a walk in the bay around Mont-Saint-

Michel at low tide. I encourage you to do this—but you *must* have a guide, because there really is quicksand. In fact, the guide showed us how to wade into the quicksand, sink, and then get ourselves out of it. The secret is to lie on your belly and drag yourself out, just as Clotho tells the children to do. We also learned that a person walking on quicksand sinks slowly into it, but a horse, especially a horse with an armored knight, would sink much, much faster, because they are much heavier, and all their weight is concentrated on the horse's four small hooves. Before we went on our walk in the bay, my wife told an elderly friend of hers about our plans. The woman began to *cry*. She *begged* us not to go. She had grown up, it turned out, very near Mont-Saint-Michel, and had owned a horse as a girl. She had ridden the horse out into the bay—straight into quicksand. She managed to get off the horse in time, but the horse completely disappeared into the quicksand, and she never saw it again.

There are many wonderful medieval stories that survive in manuscripts of sermons and chronicles and saints' lives. I stole just a few for this book.

The story that Abbot Hubert tells, about his best friend returning from Hell, is adapted from a tale recorded by William of Malmesbury, a chronicler who lived from 1109 to 1143.

The farting dragon was inspired by a short passage from the "Life of Saint Martha," as told in 1260 by Jacob de Voragine in his book of saints' lives, *The Golden Legend*. He writes that Martha comes to a forest where there is a dragon. "When [the dragon] is pursued he casts out of his belly behind, his ordure, the space of an acre of land on them that follow him, and it is bright as glass, and what it toucheth it burneth as fire." Awesome.

There is a real "Song of Hildebrand," which was written down in 830 or so. It was transcribed in a mixture of Old Bavarian and Old Saxon, and I was lucky enough to hear it sung, in the original language, by a wonderful scholar and performer named Benjamin Bagby. The story basically goes the way I tell it, though my version isn't a translation so much as a retelling. It really does end unresolved, which is just the coolest and most heartbreaking ending to an Old High German battle song ever. I imagine.

I hope, if nothing else, this book has convinced you that the Middle Ages were not "dark" (*never* call them the Dark Ages!), but rather an amazing, vibrant, dynamic period. Universities were invented, the modern financial system was born, kingship as we know it developed—and so did much of the religious strife that currently grips our world.

The High Middle Ages was a time of cultural collaboration and collision. It was, in that way, very much like today. Jews lived among Christians—sometimes happily, often less so. The Crusades, which began in this period, brought Europe into regular (sometimes tragically violent) contact with Muslim kingdoms and Caliphates.

The Muslim conquest of Spain created the Kingdom of Al-Andalus, which was multiethnic and where Muslims, Jews, and Christians all lived and worked together in relative peace and harmony. And the Mongols brought an Asian empire to the very doorstep of Europe.

It was a time when people were redefining how they lived with the "other," with people who were different from them. The parallels between our time and theirs are rich, poignant, and, too often, tragic. As I put the finishing touches on this novel, more than a hundred and forty people were killed in Paris by terrorists. It turns out they planned the attack from apartments in the town of Saint-Denis. The tragic irony of this haunts me. Zealots kill, and the victims retaliate with killing, and the cycle continues, extending forward and backward in history, apparently without end. I can think of nothing sane to say about this except this book.

Annotated Bibliography

While much of the information in this book came from living sources—professors of medieval history and tour guides through ruined monasteries, for example—I also relied on many, many books. Some of these books might be used in a school setting, even though they were written with an adult audience in mind. Others are popular histories and are accessible to adults looking to learn more. And some are fairly dense scholarly works and are best consulted for deep dives into specific topics. I've included just a few of my favorite sources and divided them into those that might be useful to young people and those that are probably best for adults, with a short note on each title.

For Young People and Adults

Bennet, Judith M. *A Medieval Life: Cecilia Penifader of Brigstock, c. 1295–1344.* Boston: McGraw-Hill College, 1999.

This is a wonderful and accessible account of one peasant village in England. It is short, the images are very good, and it provides the reader with a vivid picture of how life was really lived by the peasants of Western Europe. I highly recommend it for classroom use or personal edification.

Coles, Richard. *Lives of the Improbable Saints and Legends of the Improbable Saints.* London: Darton, Longman, and Todd, 2012.
    Saint Denis, who carried his head for miles while it preached a sermon, and Saint Lawrence, who proclaimed "this side's done" while being roasted alive, are just two of the amazing saints described by Coles in these humorous, kid-friendly, illustrated books.

Hozeski, Bruce W. (trans. and ed.). *Hildegard's Healing Plants.* Boston: Beacon Press, 2001.
    This is just a list of plants, collected and written by one of the great geniuses of the Middle Ages—and really, of all time—Hildegard von Bingen. Hildegard was an abbess, a philosopher, a healer, and a composer (her music is still performed today, and it is *beautiful*). Her book of plants is a great source for healing herbs . . . and poisons.

Joynes, Andrew (ed.). *Medieval Ghost Stories: An Anthology of Miracles, Marvels, and Prodigies.* Woodbridge, Suffolk, England: Boydell Press, 2001.

This is one of my favorite collections of medieval primary sources. I mean, how can you beat a collection of genuine medieval ghost stories? Joynes places each one in context, too, which allows you to feel both scholarly and scared at the same time.

Ross, James Bruce, and Mary Martin McLaughlin (eds.). *The Portable Medieval Reader.* New York: Penguin Books, 1977.

A treasure trove of medieval sources. Probably too dense for middle schoolers, but high schoolers (and college students and adults) can use the table of contents to find medieval writings on all sorts of topics, from Italian fashion in the fourteenth century to the founding documents of the University of Paris to how one community of Jews dealt with the Black Death.

Schlitz, Laura Amy. *Good Masters! Sweet Ladies!: Voices from a Medieval Village.* Boston: Candlewick Press, 2007.

While a work of fiction, this Newbery Award–winning collection of monologues is so thoroughly researched and richly imagined that, paired with the Bennet book, you will feel like you really know what it's like to live in a medieval village. Also, it'll make you laugh.

Swan, Charles, and Wynnard Hooper (trans. and eds.). *Gesta Romanorum, or Entertaining Moral Stories*. New York: Dover, 1959.

This book may be my favorite medieval book—and I wouldn't be alone, because it was among the most popular books in the Middle Ages. It is a collection of amusing and supposedly morally edifying stories gathered from the sermons of traveling preachers during the thirteenth or fourteenth centuries. Many of the stories are funny, others are disgusting, and some are amazing. Best of all, they always end in an obscure moral that has *nothing* to do with the story.

White, T. H. (trans. and ed.). *The Book of Beasts: Being a Translation from a Latin Bestiary of the Twelfth Century*. New York: Dover, 1984.

A wonderful bestiary edited and translated by the author of the Arthur saga, *The Once and Future King*. A sample: The Manticora "has a threefold row of teeth meeting alternately: the face of a man, with gleaming, blood-red eyes: a lion's body: a tail like the sting of a scorpion, and a shrill voice which is so sibilant it resembles the notes of flutes. It hankers after human flesh most ravenously."

For Adults

Abelard, Peter. *Yes and No (Sic et Non).* Priscilla Throop (trans.). Charlotte, Vermont: MedievalMS, 2008.

Peter Abelard is one of the most famous and most important theologians of the Middle Ages. While he's likely best known today for his chaste love affair with Héloïse (and the unmentionable thing her father did to Abelard that *made* it chaste), we now tend to ignore what medieval scholars never ignored: Abelard was *brilliant.* This book, independently published, allows someone who isn't well versed in medieval Latin to glimpse Abelard's revolutionary technique. In *Sic et Non,* Abelard asks a series of incredibly difficult questions ("God is the cause and producer of evil . . . or not"; "God does not have free will . . . or He does") and, instead of making arguments one way or another, presents evidence from the Bible and other authorities so that the readers (at the time, students and scholars at the new University of Paris, and elsewhere) could come to their own conclusions.

Baldwin, John W. *Paris, 1200.* Stanford, California: Stanford University Press, 2010.

This is a wonderfully rich scholarly portrait of Paris at the beginning of the thirteenth century. It covers the monarchy under Louis's grandfather

Philip Augustus; the founding of the university in Paris; trades and guilds; the physical growth of the city; personal life in the city; and much more. Just as Judith Bennet's *A Medieval Life* will make you feel like an expert on peasants, this book—perhaps more so—will make you feel like an expert on Paris at a critical juncture in its history.

Chazan, Robert. *The Jews of Medieval Western Christendom 1000–1500.* Cambridge: Cambridge University Press, 2006.
Among the most respected scholarly overviews of various communities and events in the Jewish diaspora during the High and Late Middle Ages.

Ferrante, Joan M. (trans. and ed.). *Guillaume D'Orange: Four Twelfth Century Epics.* New York: Columbia University Press, 1974.
This is the scholarly source for the legends about Guilhem, or Guillaume, D'Orange. The stories are as cool as you think they are.

Gerald of Wales. *The Journey Through Wales / The Description of Wales.* Ed. and trans. Lewis Thorpe. London: Penguin Books, 1978.
My character Gerald of Aberdeen was inspired by this Gerald, who writes a charming account of

traveling through Wales. There may be no better way to understand the cultural assumptions of a different age than to hear a chronicler write about a strange place he's visiting.

Jones, Colin. *Paris: Biography of a City.* London: Penguin Books, 2004.

A fun and readable history of Paris, from its inception to . . . well, who am I kidding? I didn't read past the section on the Middle Ages. But everything through then was entertaining and informative!

Joinville and Villehardouin. *Chronicles of the Crusades.* M.R.B. Shaw (ed.). London: Penguin Books, 1963.

Yes, Jean de Joinville was real, and much of what we know of King Louis comes from the biography/hagiography he wrote soon after Louis's death, when the canonization process had begun. Joinville would be a successful writer even today—he is humorous and quick-witted, and has a wonderful eye for visual detail. In a passage quoted by LeGoff (see below), he comments that when he first met Louis, "the king was wearing a blue satin tunic and an overcoat and a cloak of vermilion satin trimmed with ermine, and on his head a cotton hat that suited him poorly because he was still a young man." (LeGoff, 92)

Jordan, William Chester. *The French Monarchy and the Jews: From Philip Augustus to the Last Capetians.* Philadelphia: University of Pennsylvania Press, 1989.

> Jordan is one of the preeminent experts on France under Saint Louis, and perhaps the preeminent expert on Jewish-royal relations during that period.

LeGoff, Jacques. *Saint Louis.* Gareth Evan Gollrad (trans.). Notre Dame, Indiana: University of Notre Dame Press, 2009.

> This is an 800-page biography of King Louis IX, and it is as well-written, interesting, empathic, and as thoughtful as it is informative. An incredible portrait of a human and his time.

Lipton, Sarah. *Dark Mirror: The Medieval Origins of Anti-Jewish Iconography.* New York: Henry Holt, 2014.

> Lipton tells the story of the "steadily intensifying anti-Judaism of medieval Christianity" as it reveals itself in the art of the period. A guide both to history and to art, the book indeed serves as a dark mirror on our current dark times. Lipton has also written powerfully on our current society, and the way the resurgence of hate speech today echoes the rise of hate imagery in medieval Europe. See her wonderful Op-Ed in the *New York Times*, "The Words That Killed Medieval Jews," Dec. 13, 2015.

Schmitt, Jean-Claude. *The Holy Greyhound: Guinefort, Healer of Children Since the Thirteenth Century.* Cambridge: Cambridge University Press, 1983.

> Schmitt's book is part readable account of the real Saint Guinefort, and part highly scholarly investigation of the tale and its analogues in Western myth.

de Voragine, Jacobus. *The Golden Legend: Readings on the Saints.* William Granger Ryan (trans.). Princeton: Princeton University Press, 1993.

> This is one of the great medieval sources for saints' lives. Enormous, and sometimes slow going, gems will pop out of nowhere, like the detail about Saint Margaret and the farting dragon.

Woolgar, C. M. *The Great Household in Late Medieval England.* New Haven: Yale University Press, 1999.

> A fascinating deep dive into the traditions, practices, and microeconomics of noble households. It was here that I learned a feast often consisted of three courses: boiled meats, roasted meats, and fried meats. And that's just scratching the surface!

Acknowledgments

"When you think about it, each book is a lot of lives. Dozens and dozens of them." William is right, of course. Any book takes a whole battalion of supporters and sources, editors and interlocutors, to complete. This book, because of its subject matter, took an especially large and especially committed battalion.

My director of research was Lauren Mancia, professor of history at Brooklyn College, a specialist in medieval monasticism, and also, thankfully, my wife. Besides curating and procuring my reading list, and acting as my sounding board and first reader, she also connected me with some brilliant medievalists who read the manuscript and kept me from going too far astray, historically speaking: Sara Lipton, professor of history at Stony Brook University and a specialist in medieval religion, Jewish-Christian relations, and anti-Jewish iconography; Karl Steel, professor of English at Brooklyn College and a specialist in animals, race, and the boundaries of humanity in the Middle Ages; Robert

Harris, professor of Bible and Ancient Semitic Languages at The Jewish Theological Seminary and a specialist in medieval Biblical exegesis. A number of conversations guided me to the most amazing sources of the Middle Ages. I want to thank Sarah Novacich, professor of English at Rutgers; Markus Cruse, professor of French at Arizona State University; medieval art historian Elizabeth Monti; and rare book specialist Rabbi Jerry Schwarzbard. I am also deeply grateful to Nancy Wu, Emma Wegner, and the education department of The Met Cloisters for introducing me to Guilhem D'Orange and inviting me to share a very early version of the golden belt chapter at their family day in 2011.

Despite all the advice, and the many corrections, provided by these illustrious scholars, I am certain that I managed to slip a number of mistakes past them, because I am tricky like that; my apologies—those mistakes are my fault entirely.

The brilliant authors Laura Amy Schlitz and Justin Kramon read the earliest version of this manuscript and provided support and guidance that substantially shaped the project. Ryan Downer and Sparkle Sooknanan took a careful look at race and racial dynamics in the text. Carmela Iaria, of Penguin Young Readers Group, gave me important feedback before the final rewrite, and her enthusiasm powered me over that last, high hill. For the last half decade I have relied for spiritual guidance on Rabbi Dan Ain and his wife, Alana Joblin Ain; their wisdom runs throughout this text. M. T. Anderson lent a sympathetic ear and an expert's insight when I was struggling with the technical requirements of the book's conclusion. I want to thank John Pierpont and Raquel Otheguy, and Julia Kelly and Phil Coakley, for exploring the landscapes of this book with me, and listening to me prattle on about the plot incessantly.

One episode in this book comes not from the Middle Ages, but from the twentieth century: The examination of the little boy with the long eyelashes is based on a story told to me by my friend Tony Capra, about his father, Robert Capra.

I am deeply grateful to Hatem Aly for illuminating this manuscript—in every sense of the word.

The team at Penguin Young Readers Group has done an incredible job with my books for years now, and they have gone above and beyond on this one: Melissa Faulner, Rosanne Lauer, Kristin Smith, Natalie Vielkind, Lauren Donovan, Shanta Newlin and her team, Emily Romero and hers, Felicia Frazier and the best sales team in the world; and finally, the one who rules them all, Jen Loja. Also Don Weisberg, whom we still miss.

Sarah Burnes is the most wonderful agent on the planet. I have thanked her again and again for my career, but it never feels like enough.

I could not ask for a smarter, tougher, more critical, or more supportive editor than Julie Strauss-Gabel. This was our most intense and tempestuous editing process yet—and for that, I think it was the deepest and the best. This book is hers, and also Lauren's, as much as it is mine.

Adam Gidwitz is the author of the critically acclaimed, *New York Times* bestselling Grimm trilogy. He spent six years researching *The Inquisitor's Tale*, including a year living in Europe. Adam lives with his family in Brooklyn, NY. Find Adam online at adamgidwitz.com or @AdamGidwitz.

Hatem Aly is an Egyptian-born illustrator whose work has been featured on television and in multiple publications worldwide. He currently lives in New Brunswick, Canada, with his wife, son, and more pets than people. Find him online at metahatem.com.